LIFE'S ATTIC

LIFE'S ATTIC

A Novel

ELIZABETH ELY

BARBAULD PUBLISHING
Victoria, British Columbia

Published by Barbauld Publishing
Victoria, British Columbia
Canada

www.barbauldpublishing.com

Library and Archives Canada Cataloguing in Publication

Ely, Elizabeth, 1967-
Life's attic : a novel / Elizabeth Ely.

ISBN 978-0-9877908-0-4

I. Title.

PS8609.L9L44 2012   C813'.6   C2012-904978-6

Book design by ECE Designs

10 9 8 7 6 5 4 3 2 1

First Edition: September 2012

To those near and far, here and beyond, who have inspired, supported, and encouraged me all along the way. May the journey continue always. With love.

CHAPTER ONE

I T WAS MID-SEPTEMBER and the leaves had begun to turn. A few had already fallen to the ground. Looking up, all thirty-two-year-old Leanne Porter could see was a mosaic of gold, red, and stubborn chlorophyll green. Ever since she had been a little girl, she had loved autumn and welcomed the falling leaves that formed a crunchy carpet through which to shuffle. There was something so restful about meandering along, allowing the best clumps of leaves to be her guide.

But as she grew up, Leanne felt a little guilty for the childhood pleasure she'd kept into adulthood. How was it right to look forward to the end of life for all those leaves? Why did she feel joy after they had died?

Then she realized, it wasn't joy that she felt, but peace. Life was not ending. It was simply carrying on, albeit in mortal cycles.

Since that realization, Leanne had allowed herself to fully enjoy the seasons, trying not to think too hard about what each passing one meant. She may not have been as time limited as a leaf, but each year lived was still another year gone.

She had lost her parents some years earlier, a few years apart. There was nothing like that to drive home the point that all life was too leaf-like.

And while she had been close to them both, Leanne had always been more of a loner. She'd felt isolated from those around her, as if everyone knew some grand secret they were keeping from her.

While she wasn't exactly awkward or ill-equipped to deal with people, doing so never felt the most natural to her. Given the choice, she usually preferred to be by herself. Sometimes that meant the company of books or TV, and other times, a thoughtful shuffle through the leaves as her mind wandered along with her feet.

Understanding her daughter's big need for privacy and solitude, her mother, Maggie, had once suggested Leanne keep a diary. That way, she'd still have an outlet to express her deepest, innermost thoughts. But after a month or so of near-daily entries, the diary was cast aside.

"It's too much like work," Leanne had said at the time. Having to try to remember the high or low points at the end of each day began to feel like a chore. So what if years down the road it might be fun to read what she did or felt in the past? She'd resent writing it down now.

But Leanne definitely liked to analyze all her feelings. That became yet another way she felt disconnected from other people who seemed content to let things lie without so much questioning. Perhaps she was wrong in ascribing that to strangers, but it was how her insides looked to her compared to other people's outsides.

And as for documenting the interior view of herself with that diary? Her inward analysis concluded it was like stopping an enjoyable moment to take a photograph, instead of just living it. She discovered she'd rather remember something than capture it. But in trying to be fair and honest with herself, and always doing a complete analysis whenever possible, she did allow for one contributing factor for her diary distaste—laziness.

And today, that attribute had led Leanne to set aside work for the day. One of the big advantages of working from home was that she could determine her own hours. As long as she got her clients' bookkeeping done, they didn't much care whether she did it at noon or midnight. Leanne liked the balance that seemed to give her. No two days ever had exactly the same schedule, even if the work itself was on the repetitive side.

When she woke that morning, the world outside had beckoned. The first big leaf drop of the year was waiting for her. Unbeknownst to her, that's not all she would find as she strolled through Jonathan Park.

Across town was Jay Hanson, a doctor, who, with some settlement money, had just recently retired to Clementine. The slower pace of his new West Coast locale suited him better than big cities ever had. When circumstances led to his premature retirement, he moved his thirty-six-year-old self to the kind of quaint place he'd always imagined. Although he'd only practised medicine a short while, he was weary and more than ready for a calmer existence.

Jay's mother and father were supportive in their own far-off way, literally. As soon as their only child had gone away to university, they had set off for their own adventures. At eighteen, Jay had lost his family along with his family home, or so he felt.

His parents were in Europe now. Presently in which country? He wasn't sure. The odd letter, or the even rarer phone call, was the only way he knew it was time to update his address book again. But he had happy memories of his childhood. They had been a close family then. So Jay focused on those times when he felt lonesome for his family.

He had some good friends, but most of them had married and started families, or were at least seriously thinking about it. Jay didn't fit into that reality anymore. And so he found himself looking forward to the peace and quiet of Clementine, his new home town. This was his home now.

Wanting to get better acquainted with the little burg, Jay had spent the better part of the day on his bike. The people were friendly enough, offering directions as he explored and periodically got lost or, as he preferred to think of it, when he got a mite confused, to paraphrase Daniel Boone.

Although he appreciated their kindness and the warm welcome he received when they learned he was new to the town, it wasn't the people he most craved. He was in Clementine to more feel like a part of the place itself. It could have been anywhere really, as long as it was filled with trees and mountains, and was near the shore. Yes, it definitely had to be near some water. He'd already spent too much time sequestered in concrete skyscrapers, away from the earth and its oceans.

As Jay rounded the next corner, there was Jonathan Park. It was the perfect blend of wooded trails and wide-open spaces. He could see the Pacific Ocean not far off in the distance. Eager to explore and feel his feet on the ground, he dismounted and locked his bicycle to a nearby tree. He didn't want to be suspicious of his new neighbours, but old city habits died hard.

Setting off down a secluded trail, he was looking all about. His eyes were everywhere except in front of him. That's when it happened. That's when he met her. Well, bumped into, and nearly knocked down, one rather startled Leanne.

"Oh, excuse me. Are you all right?" Jay asked as he steadied her.

"Yeah, I'm OK," Leanne stammered, still a bit stunned by the unexpected impact.

"I wasn't watching where I was going, obviously. Are you sure you're OK?"

"Mm-hmm, it just surprised me." Leanne hadn't been paying attention to her path either, caught up as she was in her leaf shuffling. "This trail is usually pretty deserted. I don't bump into that many people," she said with a laugh.

"Good thing. And just so you know, I don't make it a habit to walk into them. But this park, it's amazing. There is so much to see. I don't know where to look first." But at that moment, he was looking in only one direction—directly at Leanne.

"It is a quite a place, so rustic and unspoiled. I always feel as if I've stepped back in time. I can almost believe I'm the first one to ever explore the place, you know?"

"Yeah, that's a big part of why I moved here," Jay said. "I know it's cliché, but with big-city living you don't get to feel a part of things like this. I want actual earth under my feet, not concrete. Does that make sense?"

"It sure does. I mean, I'm all for modern conveniences, and I probably couldn't live without my VCR now, but I don't think I could live without all this either." Leanne gestured around herself. But even as she did so, her eyes were fixed straight ahead.

"I don't have any plans to move again that's for sure," Jay said with a slight hesitation.

"You know, this may sound kind of crazy, but would you, I mean, if you're not busy, I mean, maybe you're on your way somewhere—"

"Yes—" he blurted out before Leanne spoke again.

"Oh. I'm sorry. I didn't mean to—"

"No," Jay interrupted. "I mean, I'm not on my way, but yes, I'd like to talk more, go someplace with you too, I mean, if that's what you were asking."

Relieved and far happier than she should have been, Leanne said, "It was. It is."

"Good."

They both just stood there for a moment.

"So, where do you want to go?" he asked.

"I don't know. Do you want to just stay here? It's such a gorgeous day."

"I know," he said, grinning at her. "I'm Jay, by the way."

"Leanne."

And so it began, a series of meetings at the park, walking the various trails and occasionally stopping to rest on a fallen-tree makeshift bench that had become their bench. They met up for coffee, and then it was for meals. There were late-night phone calls to share little inconsequential things that happened to occur to them. For some reason they couldn't wait to share every detail. And sometimes, it was only to say good night or good morning.

When they were walking side by side Leanne would brush up against Jay, the back of their hands just barely touching. The first time it seemed to almost go unnoticed, but then Jay turned his hand to meet Leanne's.

This innocent hand holding sort of became their thing. It was kind of nice to go so slowly Leanne thought, enjoying the early stuff rather than rushing ahead, jumping the gun, only to find out there wasn't as much in common as first thought.

In this case, the two definitely had a lot in common, a freakish amount actually. Jay and Leanne certainly did have different pasts and experiences, but as for the big stuff—what they wanted, what they didn't, what they believed, what they didn't—all that was "freaky right," as Leanne put it.

Yet one element was missing. And it was something that didn't make any sense to Leanne. Going slowly was one thing, but it had been weeks with nothing more than holding hands.

The night before, however, there had almost been a kiss good night. Leanne thought he was leaning in, but at the last second he pulled back, almost as if he remembered something that made him stop. It was definitely a conversation stopper and an evening ender. Neither got much sleep that night.

The next morning they met for breakfast at Dufferin's Diner as usual, but both knew something about this meal would not be usual.

"You're awfully quiet this morning," Leanne said finally.

"I couldn't sleep."

"Thoughts of anyone special keeping you awake? I certainly know how that is." She was trying really hard to deny anything was wrong.

"That too, but, Leanne . . . all this, it's been . . . like a dream, a fantasy, almost surreal even."

"I know. It's been amazing. That's a good thing, right?"

"Yes, it is. But, I've let myself shut out reality. I've just wanted, so much . . ."

"Jay?"

"I've wanted to stay in this fantasy."

"This is real too, you know."

"Yes, you are. But me, this, it's not," he said. "It can't be real. It just can't."

"You're married."

"What? No, of course not. But . . ."

"Well, then what, Jay?"

"You'd think being a doctor I'd be better at talking about this. Easier when it's someone else I guess."

"Your specialty was relationships?" she joked nervously.

"No. Immunology."

Leanne said nothing as some pretty scary thoughts whirled through her mind. There had been too much talk of immune stuff in the news the last ten years. Surely he couldn't mean . . .

"There's never a good way to say this, Leanne, but it has never been this hard, not even close." Finally he said it. "I have AIDS."

"Oh, God."

And there was the reason for the innocence of their relationship.

But they both still sat there. Neither got up to leave. Neither even moved. It was as if they were frozen, staring out into space watching all their respective, and indeed mutual, dreams fly off, having been just ripped away by one little phrase.

Seeing that Leanne was still sitting there and hadn't run off at the news, Jay tried to explain. "I never expected, never even imagined I'd meet anyone now. All the years I was HIV positive, ever since I found out, I absolutely knew that side of my life was over. It no longer existed. A mistake with a needle, a punctured glove, and that was it. Going solo was the way it was gonna be from then on. And I accepted it. I had to. There was no choice. Nothing, and I mean nothing, could be worth risking someone else's life."

"Oh, Jay." Leanne's voice cracked. "I'm so sorry. I don't know what to say. You, you just can't be sick."

"Hey, come on now. I'm feeling good these days." Jay tried to be positive. "Life is good. It's still good. The world is still a wonderful place to be, and I'm still here to enjoy it. Not everything, but . . ." He struggled to finish his thought before going on. "Besides, not working anymore has its advantages, you know? It means there's more time for walks in the park . . ." Jay's voice drifted off again. He so wanted to hang on to what they had. "We can still do that, can't we? Still talk?"

"Yeah, of course," she said before hesitating, "I just . . . I want more."

"Even now?" he asked with surprise. "It may be the '90s now, but some people are still pretty scared of even casual contact."

Leanne took his hand. "Jay, you ought to know by now, I'm not like most people. I mean, come on, I'm the one who, sort of, kind of, asked a complete stranger out because I didn't trust fate to give me a second chance."

"And I'm eternally grateful for that, but this isn't helping me let go of that fantasy," he said as he sadly removed his hand from hers.

But Leanne promptly retook it. "That's good, because I'm not ready to let go. I already feel things here that go way beyond talking. Things—"

"You think I don't?" Jay shouted as he shook off her hand this time and stood up, drawing the looks of the other diners. He leaned down and in a very intense whisper said, "Feel like I've never felt before? That I don't want things that I can't have? Well, I do. And there is not a damn thing I can do about any of it. And neither can you!" Prying eyes and ears be damned.

"Sit down. Please, Jay."

He did so with conflicting emotions.

"Oh, I can't believe this day," Leanne said. "I mean, after last night I wondered why you pulled back, but I just, oh, I don't know what I thought, but it wasn't this. Here I am falling in love with this perfect-for-me man—"

"Not perfect now," he interrupted.

"Just listen. I said you're perfect for me. And you haven't changed. The situation has because of some blasted blood, but you're the same as you were. The same man I want."

"Leanne, you know we can't."

"We can't what, Jay? Keep getting to know each other, enjoying whatever this is? Why can't we just see what happens?"

"If down the road, we were to ever . . . something else could happen too, and you could . . . die."

"I won't."

"But you could."

"We all could!" Leanne shouted, completely ignoring the turned heads in the diner. "How many uncertainties in the world do you need to see?"

"Some risks can be prevented, though," Jay insisted.

"At what cost? We give up our happiness, and for what?"

"Your life for one!"

Now everyone in the diner was glaring at them. They were going to be asked to leave if this kept on. But before the waitress could come over, Leanne put a stop to the show for her own reason.

"Look, I can't keep going over this right now. We're saying the same things over and over again. I'm gonna go now." Standing up, she finished quickly, "I'll talk to you later."

"OK." Jay said nothing else.

Part of her felt bad she just left like that, especially after she had been the one to persist that they still give this thing a try. But hearing him go on about what could potentially happen got to be too much. He kept pouring the cold water of reality on her. She needed a break and time to think.

And she needed to do that when she wasn't looking at him, feeling all kinds of things that made the idea of not trying utterly impossible.

Leanne opted to walk the long way home, purposely not cutting through their park. She needed some distance. The thing was, she didn't want distance, not from Jay. And that was the problem. How could he be so willing to be so, well, practical?

Meanwhile, back at Dufferin's, Jay couldn't wait to get out of there too. But he wanted to give Leanne a chance for a head start. He didn't want to appear to be ignoring her wishes by running after her, even though that's what he wanted to do more than anything. Everything he had said was true, not only the part about the dangers, but about his dreams as well.

As the two walked to their respective homes, rivalling thoughts swirled around in their minds.

"What am I thinking?" Leanne asked herself. "The man has AIDS."

"I'm actually considering this. How can I?"

"Why am I even considering this? Trying to convince him we should try. I should forget we ever met."

"What if things worked out? What if I ever gave this to her?"

"If we were ever to have sex and a condom broke or something . . ."

"This is crazy," they both thought at the same time.

"And even if she were OK, would she always be OK with me as I get sicker?"

"We could take extra precautions, but no matter what, I could lose him."

"She'd leave me. No one could blame her. Hell, I'd leave me if I could."

"I can't even bear to say it. I will lose . . ."

"It'll get so ugly. I won't be the person she sees now."

"And what about when he gets really sick? Will I be able to handle that?"

"And how would she feel about some of my choices? I've known all along I won't suffer indefinitely. When the bad outweighs the good . . ."

"What the hell am I even thinking about?"

"This is all too much to throw at someone who can walk away from it."

"The early days of meeting someone, falling for someone, they shouldn't be like this. I shouldn't be having to think about this stuff."

"If only I hadn't stopped that day, if I hadn't let my emotions get the better of me . . ."

"And yet he lives with it every day. What am I complaining for?"

"If I'd only listened to my brain instead."

"Tell you what, though. He should have told me sooner."

"I should have told her sooner. I had no right not to."

"He had no right to let me fall in love with him."

"I was selfish. But can't I have what I want too?"

"No right at all. He should have kept walking that day."

"Just because I have AIDS, my life's supposed to stop?"

"And damn him, now I know him."

"Of course it is you fool, when what you're talking about has the potential to kill her!"

"Why is this happening?"

Again in unison, their minds screamed, "Fuuuuuuck!"

CHAPTER TWO

L EANNE CONSIDERED CALLING one of her friends for advice, or at least a shoulder on which to unload. "Perhaps Becky. She'd understand. Wouldn't she?" They'd known each other since high school. And even though Becky now lived in England, and they didn't talk as often anymore, whenever they did, it felt as if no time had passed. It was almost as if they were having one big conversation that just happened to have a bunch of intermissions scattered throughout.

But not this time. Leanne couldn't explain it, but she didn't want to talk to Becky—or anyone else—about Jay. She only wanted to talk to Jay. Leanne didn't want advice, for she could guess what it would have been. So, screwing up her courage and not knowing what she would hear on the other end, she dialled the number.

"Hello?" a subdued voice answered.

"Jay?"

"Leanne." He let out a breath. She had said she would talk to him later, but he wasn't sure that would happen. For her sake, he'd hoped she wouldn't call. But he couldn't help the joy he felt when he heard her voice.

"I'm scared," Leanne said quietly.

"Me too." Then there was a pause that was less awkward than it should have been. "I wish I could fix things, and we could have everything we want," Jay said.

"Maybe they'll find a cure and just make it all go away. Surely they'll come up with more new medicines or something. I mean, there's AZT, and haven't I read about other antiretrovirals?"

"You know about that?" Jay was surprised she was so up to date on AIDS news. A glimmer of hope that maybe she did know what she'd be getting into flashed through him. "Medicines are better than a few years ago, but—" Jay stopped himself. "Oh, if I could go back and have seen a different patient that day or have had someone hold him more securely. Hell, if he'd not been infected in the first place . . . but I can't, and I . . ."

"I know." Leanne swallowed. "I know." She closed her eyes, and they both absorbed the silence. It was a peaceful moment together amid everything else that was happening. Then Leanne opened her eyes. "Can we meet?"

"The park?" Jay suggested.

Leanne lived a little closer to Jonathan Park than Jay, so she was waiting at their fallen-tree bench when he arrived. But unable to stop pacing back and forth, she had not sat down. Now standing there facing each other, instead of a more normal greeting, they both blurted out what was bubbling inside. "This is my worst nightmare. Meeting someone I can't have."

"Someone that'll leave me," Leanne said.

"Someone that I'll leave," Jay countered. "I guess the universe has a pretty perverse sense of humour."

"But I'm not laughing."

"No, me neither. Look, this is only going to get harder, Leanne. We barely know each other. Look at us already. I think—"

"Don't. Don't you dare."

"We have to. Think about it, we were both happy before. We'll get that back. It'll be easier this way. If we say good-bye now—"

"No, Jay." Her voice was quietly strong. "We may well end up saying good-bye, but not now, not yet."

"Listen to what you're suggesting and what it would mean. I'm doing well now, but I've seen what this disease does. It doesn't get any uglier than AIDS, even if you're lucky. There can be virtually nothing left by the end. I don't know if I can do it. But I don't have a choice. You do. Take it."

"That's right. It's my choice," she said. "I don't know if I can do it either, but I know I can't not try. I can't just say good-bye to you now. I can't walk away and never see you again, knowing you're still here and I'm missing that, that time, time we can have."

Jay took her hands and Leanne welcomed his tacit agreement.

But then he surprised her by holding up their joined hands and shaking them with a sense of futility and grief. "Do you see this? Inside here, inside me! It's never going away, never. You can't want that!"

"I don't!" she yelled back. "But I don't get that choice. I want you, and it comes with you. And yes, it freaks me out to think that inside this hand, this beautiful hand, is something that could kill me. I sit here, and I think back to walking and talking and sitting and just being near you, and I realize how near it's been this whole time, and I haven't known."

"I should have said—"

"Yeah, you should have, Jay. But that's not what I mean. I haven't known, and now I do. And when I think about it, it terrifies me. But when I think about you, I'm not as scared. It disappears almost. It's like you have AIDS, but AIDS doesn't have you? Is that ridiculous and completely crazy?"

"Yeah it is, but I like it," Jay admitted. "What about this hand, this body?"

"Yes," she said, tracing random patterns on the back of his hand, "but see all this lovely skin? Beautiful layers of skin in between, that's enough. We'll be careful."

"How'd I find you?"

"The same way I found you," Leanne said. "Hit and run. Well, bump and stay."

Jay exhaled, letting out a hearty laugh.

Then came that slow-motion, almost time-stopping moment of staring deeply into eyes that will soon close, captivated by feelings felt and reflected back.

Jay leaned in that little bit closer, turning his head slightly asking the silent question. Leanne just smiled before relaxing her mouth completely and leaning up to meet him.

They both looked a moment longer, wanting to imprint their first kiss indelibly in their memories. Not that there was any question of ever forgetting. But they both new the first time was special. There could never be a second first kiss, so that sweet hesitation was savoured.

Then as lips parted, eyes closed. And all the worries, all the fears, felt like they'd been erased, had never even existed. In those tender moments, they were simply two people in love.

Jay relaxed a lot after that. He realized his fear had not only been about what could happen to Leanne physically, but how he could possibly survive if the relationship did not. He'd thought it was safer to put the brakes on before it even started. Of course, he'd been kidding himself, for even though the physical side of their relationship had been chaste, they were both in far too deep emotionally and had been almost from the beginning.

He had never been afraid of commitment and had always kind of liked the sound of the word *relationship*. He'd just never really experienced that degree of feeling before. Prior to that needle stick he'd certainly had relationships in the technical sense, but never what he'd always dreamed could exist. Not that he'd ever voiced his views on the subject, at least not out loud. It wasn't the kind of thing guys were supposed to talk about, though the logic of that escaped him.

But he'd always dreamed there could be another person out there with whom he could actually want to share everything, no holds barred. And with Leanne, anything seemed possible.

Still, there were times when his fears for her safety got the better of him. The rational doctor side of his brain knew how best to keep that one part of himself forever away from Leanne. But in those early weeks, the what-if side of his brain needed the odd talking to.

Walking along the far edge of Jonathan Park, Leanne stared out at the Pacific. "You ever hear the story about the guy with three weeks to live who falls in love?"

"Do I really want to, Leanne?"

"Yeah, you do. It's about a woman."

"Funny sort of man. What was he, a cross-dresser?"

"You are in fine form today." She nudged his side.

"OK, tell me your story, I'll be delirious."

As Leanne glared at him, Jay tried again. "Serious, is that better?"

"No comment." But looking back at the water, she was smiling. "Anyway, it's about this woman who has the option ahead of time of deciding whether or not to meet this amazing man. This man, however, after three wonderful, perfect weeks, will die, just like that. And she has this choice to make. She can choose to have those glorious three weeks with him, along with the unbearable loss and pain after, or she can choose to never even meet him. Miss all of it. Gives new meaning to the saying 'No pain, no gain,' don't you think?"

Jay stared almost blankly at the waves. "What does she choose?"

"I don't know about her, but it's a no-brainer for me. I guess I must be a glutton for punishment." She turned to see him staring off into the distance and took his hand. "I know it's not the same thing here, no physical risks to her in that one, but I think the sentiment's the same."

He turned his head to face her.

"I'd choose to meet you for even a moment," she said.

As Jay squeezed her hand, he pleaded, "Let's hope it's for a lot longer than that."

"Oh, I'll settle for eternity."

Jay leaned down as Leanne stretched up and their foreheads rested together as they breathed in and out.

She then pulled back slightly. "But I need you to know, to put into words, something I've been thinking about more and more lately. And I doubt I'm the only one. There's no easy way to say this. We've hardly even kissed, let alone anything else. For everything we've shared and talked about, there is one thing we have been tiptoeing around for a long time."

He let out the breath he'd unconsciously been holding. "Thus the reason for good ol' inappropriate humour . . . and not."

"Yeah, your cross-dresser comments and stuff. I get it, Jay. I really think I do. But look, we've talked about it. We both know the risks involved and the ways to be safer. I don't have some kind of death wish here, but you know better than anyone how small the risk is with all we'll do. Heck, there'll be so much between us it'll be a wonder if you even feel anything."

"Well, then, sounds like fun. Come on. Let's go," Jay said. "Leanne, I want to, so much. I never thought I'd find myself in this situation, not after I was diagnosed. You know this. But, any risk to you is too great. After all, it's only sex, right? We can do fine without it. Oh, shit, that didn't even fool me. But it is. It is just sex, not life. But it could be death. Not a moment goes by when I don't wish that we . . . could have everything. What I dream each night, and what, when I wake up, isn't. But what we already have is so much more than I ever imagined could actually exist. We should be satisfied, more than satisfied."

"There's a good argument for that, Jay. In the abstract, I'd go for it. But this isn't some hypothetical. The question for me isn't 'How can we?' but 'How can we not?' I know the risks I'm talking about, how absurd it might seem to some, to me, for that matter, before I knew you. But I can't pretend we never met, and that we don't want more. We're into those proverbial three weeks. I couldn't live my life knowing that for fear of something with only the remotest chance of ever happening, that for that fear, we gave up our chance." Leanne took his hands in hers and looked straight into his conflicted eyes. "I love you."

Jay let his heart lead. "I love you, too." But then the what-ifs took over again. "That's why I can't—"

Leanne put her fingers to his lips and stopped him. She kissed him softly but with conviction, even though it was still only lip-to-lip contact. She stroked the side of his face with her right hand. Feeling a hint of moisture there, she pulled back and their eyes locked.

They stood there motionless until Leanne broke the silence. "Living is a risk. Everything is a choice." She caressed his cheek again, rubbing away the tears. "At least we know what we're up against . . . and we can be careful."

"But we're talking about you," he cried out. "If anything ever happened to you because of . . . of what we might do, I couldn't live with that."

"At least you wouldn't have to for long," Leanne said.

Jay let out a raucous laugh, breaking the tension. "That's a good one."

"I learned from the master. Laugh or cry."

"And here I am doing both. That's another one of those choices, huh?" Jay asked.

"Life's full of them it appears. But I like my odds, and I'm taking the bet, eyes wide open." Leaning in, she could feel his breath on her face. "Now, how about . . . you . . . shut yours." Closing the hint of distance remaining, she touched his lips again.

As the tip of her tongue asked for entrance, Jay paused. "Are you sure?"

Glaring sweetly, Leanne rather huskily said, "Don't ever ask me that again."

Jay had no chance to reply.

As fall turned into winter, they continued to learn more about each other. Little childhood details, long since forgotten, were remembered.

There was the story of how a ten-year-old Leanne actually had forgotten how to ride a bicycle, going too long between rides soon after she'd first learned.

And how Jay had never been that good at sports, but not for the more usual reasons. He just could never decide if he should hold the bat, racket, or ball with his left or right hand. Neither felt completely natural, so he ended up switching back and forth, without a great deal of success either way.

There was also the time Jay had taken a first-aid course when he was eleven and learned about embedded objects. A shard of glass or other penetrating fragment was not to be yanked out of a wound but instead supported in place until help arrived. He still remembered how to form the makeshift circular support out of a ripped T-shirt.

The sharing of that particular childhood memory led to Leanne being creeped out by the thought of a piece of glass sticking out of a leg, as Jay had so kindly described in tediously graphic, doctor-like detail.

But after a particularly fluffy snowfall one afternoon in late November, a much less gruesome memory came to Leanne. "You ever make snow ice cream?"

"Like with snow actually in it?" Jay asked, not quite able to picture it.

"Yeah, Jay, with snow." Leanne grinned. "It's great, you take a heavy glass bowl—to help keep it cold—and then you scoop up a bunch of fluffy snow. It can't be the heavy packed-down or icy kind, but like that out there." Leanne looked toward the window.

"Sounds like the dessert version of stone soup if you ask me."

"Not quite," Leanne said. "You see, you don't stop there, you've gotta add some whipping cream, and a little sugar and vanilla. Food colouring too, if you want to make it extra pretty."

"That actually sounds kind of good. But do you have any whipping cream now?"

"That's part of the fun, Jay. It's a good excuse to walk in the snow to the corner store. That way, you feel as if you're making the most of the snowfall by being outside and enjoying it, but you don't have to stay outside so long that you freeze."

"Let's go then." Jay handed Leanne her coat, and they bundled up for their little trek.

That evening they curled up on Leanne's couch watching more snow fall in the dim light. The lights were turned off so they could better see the individual flakes as they floated down. "It's like being inside of a perpetual snow globe," Leanne said.

"And with no periodic shaking required"—Jay's eyes gleamed with childlike wonder—"we're in our own little magical world."

"Mm-hmm. When it's all so quiet and dark like this, it feels as if everyone else must be asleep, and we're the only ones awake." Leanne leaned forward and picked up a cup from the coffee table, finishing the last of her semi-warm tea. "And while we'll be joining them in sleep soon, until then, we're able to witness the tranquillity of a resting world."

She snuggled back against him. Both were sitting almost entirely on one cushion with their legs stretched out side by side on the rest of the couch.

"But by the next morning," Jay said, "all hell will break loose, and those same people will be madly digging out of their driveways. Followed, of course, by them doing all kinds of treacherous things on roads they've been told to stay off of unless it's an absolute emergency."

"That's another perk to being self-employed—no boss to pressure me into coming into work no matter what the weather conditions are. Besides, everyone needs a guilt-free snow day now and then."

"Absolutely." Jay smiled and kissed the back of her head. "Did you know that during the first snowfall of the year, my third-grade teacher pulled the blinds so we couldn't look out the window and get distracted?"

"Oh, that's just cruel." Leanne shook her head. "If your teacher was so concerned about the snow being a distraction, she could have used it as a learning opportunity or something and taught how no two snowflakes are alike, or how snow takes up ten times the space of water. It does, doesn't it?"

"I think so," Jay said. "Of course, I'd know for sure if I'd had the proper snow education back in the third grade."

At that moment, a snowplow drove by clearing their street temporarily. "It's funny, though," Leanne said, "after the snow's been around for a while, and I really am ready to get back to the normal ease of moving about, I still find it kind of sad when I see the snow actually melting."

"I know what you mean, Lee. That sounds like the way I feel when I see falling snow turning into rain instead. It may be easier to get around in, but I still feel a little twinge in my gut when I see snow struggling to be snow."

While Leanne's open window blinds let in the view of the snow, they also let out desired heat. Jay pulled a throw from the back of her couch and wrapped it snugly around them.

They usually alternated between their respective apartments, staying at one and then the other. Lately, it had grown into a few days in a row at each place, reducing the chore of dragging stuff back and forth so often. And while they did spend every night together and slept in the same bed, they were not yet sleeping together.

But things were progressing, and gone were the re-emerging fears. They had been replaced by more of a cautious awareness. There was no deep kissing, for example, if either of them had any mouth irritation. Leanne had not been pleased the time she bit down hard on her cheek when they were watching a movie. She still held a grudge against that offending popcorn kernel.

Now as they continued to watch the snow, so fragile and ephemeral, something occurred to Leanne. "Why is it, Jay, that some people are referred to as dying, called terminal, and others aren't?"

"When we all are, right?"

"Yeah, all because statistics say death is coming sooner for someone who's sick. I mean, we don't call old people terminal just because they're old. But the stats say they have less time left too. I now hate numbers, by the way."

"I never felt venomous toward them before, but you've got a point," Jay said. "I sure wish we didn't measure time. I think we'd all be a lot happier."

"No countdown," Leanne proposed.

"At least not one we'd be aware of, taunting us with what's left."

Shifting to sit on Jay's lap, facing him, she reached her arms around his neck. "And especially considering there are so many better things to do with our time."

"Well, then, time's a-wasting." Jay grinned as he encircled her body, holding her close. His lips found hers without a second's hesitation.

But after a minute or so, coming up for air, he rather breathlessly asked, "You know what I'm thinking?"

Despite panting a bit herself, Leanne put her hands to her temples, as if to channel his thoughts. "Let me see . . ."

Before her psychic routine could go any further, Jay removed Leanne's hands from her forehead. "Uh-uh. I have a better use for those hands." But then he just held them and seemed to retreat into his thoughts.

"Now I do know what you're thinking." She was anticipating feeling his hands all over her.

He hesitated for a moment. "I wish. I mean, that's part of it, always. But I'm realizing how glorious it is not knowing when this stops. I can sit here and imagine I'll live forever, that there really are no limits. There's no set time. I mean, of course there is, but somehow not knowing the exact deadline makes it easier to believe there isn't one."

Despite the seemingly abrupt switch in Jay's train of thought, Leanne gave him a slight smile. "I don't want to know. I don't want a last day with you, knowing that's what it is. I don't want there to be a last night."

"We won't have that then, Lee. It will be a night like any other."

"And when it's time, you'll let me know."

"And I hope I don't know a moment sooner."

"I promise you"—her voice cracked a little—"you won't die alone, not if I have anything to say about it."

"And neither will you, way, way, way in the galactically far future. I'll see to that. I just have to."

Strengthened by their mutual determination, she said, "And so we'll live with the hope of another tomorrow."

"And another after that," Jay added.

They squeezed each other as tightly as they could. But then she felt him hesitate. "What?"

"I really don't want to have to get into this, especially now, but there will never be a good time."

Leaning back, Leanne surprised him with her tone. "You like doing that to me, don't you? Making these big pronouncements. Just say it."

"I'm sorry," he said. "I don't mean to . . . it's . . . it's not easy. There's so much that's not easy sometimes. There are times when I feel I can do this, that I can face death, that

I'll be ready. But then there are other times when that's the last thing I feel."

Challenging him, she asked, "Who says we have to feel all one way anyway? I know I don't. I have absolutely no idea how I'll ever live without you now. How's that for liberated? Me, self-sufficient me."

"Human, love." Jay tried to comfort her as he put his arm around her shoulders. "But there is something you really have to know. It's all been drawn up and is legally secure, but I want—and need—you to know about my plans for later on. I don't ever want to live hooked up to machines or anything remotely like that. You know about DNR?"

"Yeah, it's one of those advance health care directives, right?" As what they were talking about hit her more fully, Leanne inhaled, and then she slowly exhaled. "Do not resuscitate."

"That's right. And my living will states I want no tubes, no wires, no pumps, no noise, no sterile smelling room . . . no hospitals. I mean, short term, if there's any real hope, then yes. I don't see myself completely avoiding hospitals. But I want no heroic measures."

Then he hugged her tightly and whispered, "Let it be just us." Looking directly into her eyes, he almost stoically said, "I don't want to live beyond my death, or die past my life."

"Profound and poetic."

"And true."

"Now it's my turn to ask, Jay. Are you sure?"

Laughing slightly, he said, "To borrow the words of a very wise woman—"

"You're certain. I won't ask you again." Leanne stared deeply into his eyes. "Besides, I'm still holding on to that cure scenario."

"From your mouth to God's ears."

"Does God actually have ears?" she asked.

"Good question. There probably are times when deafness would come in mighty handy, what with all of us asking for stuff all the time," Jay said.

"Oh, sweetie, somehow I think whatever there is, whatever existence or power, however, whoever, whatever it all is ... doesn't mind ... and understands."

CHAPTER THREE

"**T**OMORROW IS DECEMBER 1," Leanne blurted out when they woke the next morning. Her eyes were dancing with delight.

"And today's November 30." Jay played dumb. He knew full well what the first day of December meant to Leanne, but he couldn't resist hearing her describe it to him again.

"As if you don't remember. It's tree day!" Leanne was bubbling over with excitement. "And the official start to the Christmas season. You have go out first thing and look at absolutely a ton of trees, picking your favourite shape for the year. It could be dense and strong to hold the heavier ornaments you can't always use. Or it could the more open and delicate kind for the Charlie Brown years. But whatever the size and type, you've got to smell every one. And shake them all for loose needles. And the final test? Tasting a needle or two to make sure it's nice and piney, really Christmassy." Leanne's face lit up like a child on Christmas morning. And this was from only thinking about it. "The tree's the best part. It feels like Christmas itself gets brought right inside your home, to see, smell, touch—"

"Taste." Jay laughed. "I never thought I'd be looking forward to eating a tree, but you've got me curious. It still seems a little early to me, though. Won't all the needles be on the ground by Christmas?"

"That's why you do the taste test and all the other stuff," Leanne explained. "And you only buy from a lot where you know all the trees are freshly cut. None of that 'cut a month or two before' nonsense." Leanne took Christmas trees very seriously.

"So where do you want to put this magic tree? Your place or mine?"

"I've been thinking about that, Jay, and I think at yours. You have that terrific space opposite the fireplace that would be perfect. And since it'd be nice not going back and forth over the holidays, if we stayed there, it would save you having to pack up a bunch of meds for here."

"I like your thinking. You wouldn't mind not having a tree at home, though?"

"I will be having that," Leanne said as she squeezed his hand. Home was fast becoming wherever they both were.

They had casually tossed around the idea of moving in together, but intellectually it seemed too soon. Maybe they'd do something about it in the new year.

A few days before Christmas, they were at the market to gather what they needed to cook their feast for two. There had been invitations from friends, but this was their first Christmas together, and they wanted it to be just the two of them. That was actually how they usually preferred it. Not that they didn't enjoy hanging out with other people, but they often ended up spending most of that time looking forward to being alone with each other again.

Leanne commented on their rather secluded lifestyle as she pulled out a cart. "Do you think we're too shut off from other people?"

"I don't know. Maybe. Probably. But do you really want to get unsecluded?" Jay asked with a laugh, which was quickly contagious.

And for them, that was the last that needed to be said on the subject of needing more people in the forefront of their lives. They were happy.

As they wandered the grocery aisles, Jay tossed in a package of corn tortillas.

"I still can't believe what we're going to have for our Christmas dinner," she said.

"What's wrong with tacos and beans?" Jay tried to look innocent as he picked out his favourite hot salsa.

"Not a thing. I love 'em. But I've never had them on December 25 before." Leanne had been surprised to learn of the Hanson family tradition of having the cheapest meal they could think of on the day much of the world voted for the most extravagant. "I like it. It's a nice idea. But can we have turkey on the twenty-sixth then?"

"Sort of defeats the purpose." He added some beans to the cart. "How about we do turkey when we get our own place, to sort of christen it."

"Won't we be doing something else to christen that?" Leanne teased.

"Don't know if I can wait that long, Lee," Jay let slip without overthinking it this time.

"Good to know, Jay. Good to know."

While the subject of sex had been broached on a number of occasions, it had always been spoken of as off in the future, not as something imminent, even though they had done just about everything except have intercourse.

Leanne hadn't wanted to push the issue since it was the last step before Jay completely gave away all control. After they went all the way, there would be no going back and undoing it. She would have had sex with someone who had AIDS. Safer sex, but still sex. It was the last vestige of his fear that he would hurt her.

Maybe it was the Christmas season, all the joy and festivity in the air, and the whole sense of rebirth. Whatever the reason, a couple of nights later after Jay put another log on their Christmas Eve fire, they both had this certain look.

The future had become now.

Without saying a word, Leanne went to retrieve something from the bedroom.

They had, of course, used regular condoms for some of their other activities, just to be safe. "Safer," Jay always reminded. But now, for this, there was that new kind of female condom her friend Becky had sent them from across the Atlantic.

Until they were available in North America, Becky had vowed to keep Leanne well supplied. As it turned out, she was at least quasi-supportive of Leanne's relationship with Jay. And since this female variation offered better coverage and protection for her friend, Becky was going to see to it that Leanne had all she needed.

Jay arranged some cushions on the thick braided rug in front of the fireplace. Then he met Leanne halfway between the living room and bedroom. "Hey." His smile was pushing his cheeks so high they were almost squishing his eyes.

She set the little package on the floor as she sat down. "Now for the humorous portion of our evening. I have practised getting this thing in according to the instructions, but I make no guarantee of elegance. I may be a bit of a contortionist the first few times."

"Promises, promises," Jay said, earning a playful flick of Leanne's hand to his side.

They settled down on the rug. The only light was from the fire and their illuminated tree sitting opposite the fireplace. It looked great there as Leanne had predicted. She just hadn't known she would be viewing it horizontally.

"There's nothing like waking up with you," he said. "I can't even imagine what it's going to be like after making love with you, making love to you."

"Well, we're about to find out."

"Lee, I love you, forever."

"I love you too, Jay, forever."

"Why does that always feel so good to say, and hear?"

"Maybe it's like human purring. It resonates in a certain pleasurable way . . . vibrates just right," Leanne seductively suggested as she continued to try to get into the right position to insert the condom.

"Speaking of which—"

"Hang on a sec. This isn't working. I'll be right back."

Leanne soon re-emerged from the bathroom with a look of relieved satisfaction. "Finally. I'm all suited up now. Female condom ready for action."

"Talk about romantic, Lee." Jay laughed as he shook his head and grinned at her.

But things quickly heated up more than ever before. The excitement of each kiss, caress, and hold, the sizzle of every touch was heightened even further because they knew tonight there would be no stopping.

The next morning Jay and Leanne woke up tangled together in a new way. Any shred of hesitation had been shed along with their clothes the night before. They had been lovers in the emotional sense for some time, but now they were lovers in every way. Strange that a biological act designed for reproduction should make such a difference in other ways. It was like sealing that final link. They had now connected in every way possible.

As they stirred, their bodies automatically snuggled closer together. Leanne formed the first word on their first morning after. "Mmmmmm."

Jay was equally eloquent. "Hey."

"Hey, yourself." Leanne turned onto her side so she could smile and stare directly at him.

Mirroring her movements so they were facing each other, their legs still entwined, he began playing with her hands. "Sleep well?"

"What sleeping time there was, you?"

"Exhausted in the most energized way," he said.

"Yeah," Leanne almost purred.

They lay there beaming almost stupidly at each other.

"So, Lee," Jay said with a huge grin, "have any plans for the day?"

"You mean besides the obvious?"

"Besides that, yeah." Their conversation was temporarily suspended for an extended good-morning kiss.

Love was not only blind but apparently missing olfactory senses as well. If there was any morning breath, neither one could tell. Maybe someday that would change, but not today. Or maybe their pheromones would always cover it up. Or maybe it was just part of who they were, smells and all. Perhaps they each now belonged in the other's bizarre private category where personal odours don't offend the way other people's do. After all, they weren't other people to each other anymore, if they ever even had been.

Breaking the kiss to get a full breath of oxygen, Leanne finally got around to answering Jay's question. "Well, if we have any strength left, there is this new trail I've heard about. It winds its way all around and then up Mount Bauldron, if you can call it that. It's more of a big, wooded hill in the middle of nowhere. But it's still the highest spot around Clementine, and there is supposed to be this amazing rest area up there overlooking the ocean. You can see forever they say."

"Sounds great," he said. "I've heard of that place. They have cabins too, don't they?"

"I think so, but pretty rustic from what I hear. Would that be a problem, if you needed something, I mean?" The implication was clear. Sometimes it was nice not having to use specifics. They both knew what she meant.

"Not to worry, doctor in the room remember? The licence may have lapsed, but the knowledge hasn't. And it won't ever if I have anything to say about it." Losing any of his faculties to AIDS was definitely the thing that scared Jay the most. His body was one thing. His mind was nonnegotiable.

"Good point. But you'll tell me if you ever—" Leanne stopped herself and nodded gently. Jay was sure or he wouldn't have said it. And if he had to be sick, at least she had the advantage of having a boyfriend who was a doctor. They might have to have a conversation, though, about another word in that same thought. Boyfriend—or girlfriend, for that matter—seemed like such a radically insufficient description.

"So, let's rent one of those cabins when it's warmer and spend the night, a few even," Jay suggested. "We could even go all the way to the top and sleep outside. I love the way the air smells in the dark, you know?"

"Oh yeah. So fresh, and so vibrant, but like it's resting up for a new day too. And it's all perfectly peaceful, completely at one with, well, everything."

"Like it really is the same sky we're looking at, Lee. The same moon, the same stars, the same everything since it all began."

"And somehow we get to experience it now, to be here," she said.

"Living." Jay smiled without any hint of melancholy. "So that sounds like a plan. A hike for today, bundled up in our ski suits, and a campout later in our birthday suits."

"Oh, you are my funny man." Leanne grinned happily. "In the meantime, however—"

"Ah yes, more latex sex." Jay beamed. "Well, tougher polyurethane in our case."

"Gotta love it."

"And live because of it," he said.

Leanne marvelled at how social mores had changed over time. People spoke so much more easily and openly about sex than they had even a generation before. And condom talk alone had skyrocketed in the last ten years or so, ever since those ubiquitous rubbers had become about not only preventing pregnancy, but death. How ironic it was that condoms helped prevent both the start of life and the end of it.

"Things sure are different from my great-grandparents' day, with some of their homemade birth-control ideas," Leanne said as she reached for another little packet.

Jay remembered hearing similar stories. "To think people tried using a silk handkerchief to stop sperm, as if that could actually work. It is a nice idea, though, and pretty classy, don't you think? Some guy is all dapperly dressed with a handkerchief perfectly folded in his breast pocket, and then he just whips the thing out."

"Yeah, Jay, that's really nice and classy."

"The handkerchief, Lee. I don't know what you could have been thinking of."

Leanne gently tore open the packet as they walked into the bedroom. "Oh, yes you do, Jay. Because you were thinking exactly the same thing, and that's why you said it." She laughed while Jay tried to look innocent.

He then steadied her as she squatted, getting ready to insert the female condom. Leanne found that position the easiest. It was also a good way to make sure everything was properly in place. The process was easier this time since she didn't have to worry about supporting herself. The toilet had steadied her the first time, but this was definitely much nicer.

Together, they were creating their own ways of finding the good side to everything that had to be done. It was like when she helped him with his medicines. He didn't need the help, but it was sure good to have her there, being a part of it, sharing the experience in at least some way. And as best he could, Jay shared in the fine art of female-condom placement.

As they settled into bed, the easy banter continued. Both were great talkers and multitaskers. Jay and Leanne could go from chatting to panting in one continuous motion. "I'm still thinking of all those babies that must have been strained through a hanky," Leanne said while her foot brushed against the bare skin of his calf.

"Condoms aren't foolproof, but they're sure better than cotton." His hands began to wander down her back.

"It's sure a good thing they didn't have to worry about AIDS back then. Other stuff was bad enough."

"I wonder," Jay said, "if when they invented polyurethane and latex they had any idea what we'd end up doing with the stuff."

"Reverse dynamite." Leanne laughed at her own joke. "But this time, there's a good secondary use for an invention. Save instead of kill."

"It's a sure bet, though, whoever first thought to use it for condoms, never imagined the little things would become such a topic of conversation," he said.

"We have sure come," Leanne said, "a long way from Lucy and Ricky sleeping in their separate beds, pun intended."

Jay chuckled and continued his tender ministrations. "I guess Little Ricky must have been your modern-day immaculate conception." Whenever they watched reruns of *I Love Lucy*, it always struck him as so odd when they showed those twin beds, which weren't even pushed up close to each other.

While he realized it was more a sign of 1950s television standards than real-life practices, Jay still couldn't imagine not being able to roll over in the middle of the night to hug Leanne. Of course, having a king-size bed didn't hurt when it came to serious sleeping. They got the best of both worlds that way—the size of twin beds, but with no distance separating them.

"Or how about this," Leanne said, "maybe Little Ricky was the world's actual first test-tube baby, and best-kept secret."

"I wonder if Fred and Ethel knew," Jay quipped as he covered Leanne's mouth with his own. Things were heating up. The time for talking was over.

But then he abruptly stopped, causing Leanne's eyes to widen in surprise. "What?"

"I just remembered something. Merry Christmas, Lee."

Laughing, Leanne turned back to their private festivities. "Oh yeah. It's Christmas today too."

The following week, having had Christmas their way, Jay and Leanne broke out of their comfort zone a little and decided to ring in the New Year with friends. Jay had made a couple of friends since he'd been living in Clementine, but the majority of their guests were originally Leanne's friends, if any portion of the small crowd could be called a majority. That term conjured up a gathering larger than their eight. But it was a nice group, large enough to feel festive, especially in Leanne's small place, but not so big that it was loud and impersonal.

The tree was still up at Jay's apartment. He complained it was a little worse for wear, with more needles on the ground than still on the tree. But neither of them could really bear to take it down. It had been such a wonderful backdrop for the start of what was proving to be a fantastic sex life.

"Let's just leave it up for one more day," Leanne said. "We can't take it down before New Year's. That would be sacrilege."

"Well, we certainly can't have that, can we? But you're picking out all the needles that get stuck in the rug and won't vacuum up."

So as the tree's Christmas season went on, they set up at Leanne's place to watch the ball drop in Times Square.

"I think this works better anyway." Jay hung the last of the streamers. "It's always seemed a little strange to me to see Christmas stuff mixed in with New Year's decorations, as if people can't decide which holiday they're supposed to be celebrating. Have they never heard of scheduling one holiday at a time?"

"We can make it a new tradition. Let's always divide up the two holidays like this."

"And if at some point for some reason," Jay said with a grin, "there's only one place, we can always leave part of it Christmas-free and ready for New Year's."

"I like you're thinking."

As they looked at each other, their smiles grew until they resembled two Cheshire cats.

"And you know what else, Jay? Tomorrow we get to go back to Christmas." Leanne bounced around giddily as she set out the hats and noise makers.

Everyone attending the little party knew about Jay's condition, as it was usually referred to by the others. There had been some initial fear and uncertainty when they'd first been brought into the loop. But the ever-prepared Leanne had actually photocopied a bunch of current literature, which she'd handed out to correct any misinformation that might have persisted.

Jay and Leanne couldn't know for sure if there were any lingering concerns among their friends, but there were easy hugs and kisses on the cheek. And at least most of the time, there was no worrying about whose glass was whose. It was more the occasional second of hesitation wondering if the right drink had been picked up, in a way that wouldn't have existed otherwise.

But it was a fun evening full of celebration, and lots of silly laughs and ridiculous toasts. Raising a glass, Jay's friend Donovan pulled from his Irish heritage. "As you slide down the banisters of life, may the splinters never point the wrong way."

Someone mentioned how if you did happen to slide the wrong way, you could always use something like colloidal silver to prevent any infection from those splinters. Leanne innocently brought up other alternative medicine ideas, and that led to a few awkward moments because her references included one relating to AIDS. Certain words, like *cancer*, and now *AIDS*, triggered guttural reactions that tended to shut down conversations.

But the two hosts didn't want any topic to be off limits. They tried to censor no subject, having grown accustomed to talking about the tough stuff in as easy a way as possible. Doing that made the scary stuff less scary most of the time. For them, it was like shying away from saying "death" or "dying." Covering up the technical words with euphemisms seemed to only make them more powerful. It was admitting something was so bad, the real words couldn't even be used to describe it.

But the looks on their friends' faces reminded them that some things were best left unsaid. Or at least the times chosen to say them could be considered more carefully when other people were around.

Dick Clark saved the party from further silence with his countdown to midnight. But Jay could tell Leanne was angry that one innocuous AIDS reference had disrupted things. He tended to take things more in stride. She wanted to change the world. He guessed he cared less what others thought. Maybe that meant he cared less about the world. But it was certainly a more peaceful way to live. He worried sometimes that Leanne worried too much. "OK, on second thought, maybe we're pretty even on that front after all," he conceded to himself as he tried to stop worrying about her worrying.

Grabbing Leanne up from their couch, Jay whispered, "Forget it. It's just us." They then greeted the New Year with a kiss just steamy enough to deliver a visceral message to their friends.

The cheering and squawking of noise makers both on the television and in Leanne's living room released the last of the tension.

The party ended a little after one in the morning, with the revellers walking home or taking cabs depending on how far they were going. "This has got to be the biggest benefit of hosting—already being at home. We can fall right into bed after everyone leaves," Leanne muttered tiredly. She fell asleep while Jay was still turning off the lights.

Crawling into bed, he was tired as well, but not like the champagne-filled Leanne who had no drug interaction issues to consider. "I guess that makes me the designated driver for life, except for one thing, we don't have a car. Hmm, what does that make me then, and for how long? Oh man, it's way too late for that kind of existential puzzle now," he told his tangent-driven self and closed his eyes.

As much as Jay and Leanne had enjoyed the anticipation and the holiday season itself, it was kind of nice to get back to normal life. The regular routine was welcome after being suspended for those few weeks, suspended for a good reason, but put on hold nonetheless.

But Leanne did make one change to the normal routine. She cut back on her bookkeeping business. She kept her steady clients whom she really enjoyed helping, but was grateful she could afford to work less. Years of saving without really spending, along with the flexibility of working from home, had come in particularly handy since meeting Jay. Having the most time together overshadowed making the most money. But practicality dictated she did still need to work, just not as much as she once thought she did.

Jay, on the other hand, was enjoying his forced retirement, or forced but voluntary retirement as he chose to think of it. After all, it had brought him to Clementine and, most importantly, to Leanne.

He could have kept on practising with informed consent and no invasive procedures, among other things. But what clinched it for him, the part of the *forcing* that made retirement *voluntary* in his mind, was that he knew he couldn't keep dealing with the immune problems of his patients all day, and his own all night. Weekends and holidays too. There was never a break.

So, as much as Jay cared for his patients, he had decided to walk away before the toll became too great. He figured he was entitled to be a little selfish.

He didn't want his whole life to be defined by any one thing, least of all AIDS. He took some comfort knowing he wouldn't end up suffering the agonies he'd seen too many others endure. Jay wondered a few times if maybe he would change his mind. That's why he hadn't yet brought up the subject with Leanne. Every time he was about to, part of him seemed to waver a bit.

"Maybe I should just stick it out," his mind would tell him. Or was it his heart speaking? But the longer he and Leanne were together, the more he began to understand his conflicting emotions. It wasn't that he was any more prepared to stick around until AIDS finally took him than he had been before meeting her. He wasn't, he was sure of that. He would not die that way. But it was the idea of not being alive that seemed so much more unbearable now, than it had pre-Leanne. It was unimaginable. And it was so totally unacceptable that they wouldn't grow old together. They wouldn't be two crazy old codgers on that clichéd front porch someday.

No matter how much they were trying to live for today, some planning for tomorrow was needed. One of those tomorrows would become a *last* today. "There's something I want you to read," Jay said, handing her a well-worn but fairly new-looking book.

"*Final Exit*? What's it about?" she asked before seeing his face. "Wait a minute, it's not—"

"You knew from the beginning how I felt."

"And you knew how I felt. How I feel," Leanne said.

"Before you say anything else, please, just read it. And think about it from my side."

"DNR stuff is one thing. What you're asking me—"

"No, I'm not asking you. And you won't have to do anything. I'll decide. I'll do it, while I'm still able. You won't have to—"

"Yes I will!" she cried out. "I may not have to actively do it—"

"Say the words! Please say the words, Leanne."

"But this is different from other words. You're asking me to be OK with you killing yourself! And losing you even sooner than I have to. I want every second I can get with you."

"Oh, Lee, so do I. But there is going to come a time when enough is going to have to be enough. Not enough of loving you. It could never be enough, never. But of living in a body worn out, just not quite dead."

"No, no." It was difficult to tell if Leanne was agreeing that that was no way to live, or if she was still protesting his early exit.

"We don't ask animals to suffer past their time. Put to sleep. That sounds so peaceful, doesn't it?"

"But it's not. It's still death," Leanne said. "Maybe not a violent, loud end, but still the end."

"Who's to say? How do we know? Maybe what makes you you, and me me, what makes us us, maybe that part goes on," Jay said. "I mean, why can't it? Souls can't need much space or anything. I'm not talking heavenly harps or angelic clouds here, but still an existence, some way to be that's beyond our understanding, our understanding so far anyway."

"I want to believe that, but isn't it too good to be true? That sounds too much like what I want," Leanne moaned.

"Hey, come on now, who's the one that convinced me from the beginning to take a chance, to believe anything was possible?"

"But at least we had some control over that, Jay. This, whatever comes next, if there even is anything, that's beyond me."

"Exactly." He nodded.

"I hope you're right."

"Well, one day, we'll know. Some of us sooner than others," he said with a laugh.

"Don't joke."

"Why? Why not find the humour? Is not talking about it, not using the real words, for that matter, is any of that going to make this go away? I am going to die. We all will. Remember that old rhyme with the doctor and the sick child? 'Doctor, Doctor, will I die? Yes, my child, and so will I.' You said it yourself—we're all terminal."

"It just hurts. We're talking about you. I hate thinking about it. It kills me to," Leanne tried to joke. "And at the same time, I can't not think about it."

"I'm not saying I'm always able to deal with it either," Jay admitted. "Don't think I am. I can't count the number of times I've pretty much freaked out about it, knowing there is absolutely no way I can do this, this dying thing. I mean, I've never done it before. Do you just stop? Does it hurt? Do you see it happening? What? What is being dead like? Is it anything?"

After his raft of questions, Jay paused. Then he said, "Maybe it's because I've had more time to deal with this, or maybe when it's happening to you something else happens too to ease the transition. I don't know. What I do know is, as time goes on, besides being scared out of my mind sometimes, there are more moments of calm, acceptance, peace almost. Oh, I don't know," he said again. "But I sure know what I want that to mean."

"Oh, me too, let's let it mean that," Leanne implored the universe. "There has to be something next, something more than we can really imagine. Maybe that's why it's so hard to even conceive of now."

"So you understand," Jay said, "why I have to do this, and why I've made preparations for it. I have to be ready to put myself to sleep."

"Now who's the one using euphemisms, Jay?"

"Good point."

"I hate this," Leanne said, stating the obvious. "More than anything, it just sucks."

"But not in a good way."

"Gotta love language." She shrugged.

"Here's to double entendres then." Jay raised his arm, toasting with an imaginary glass. "Long may they reign. But, all joking aside, when it's time, I need to be the one to do it, so nothing can be pinned on you. Everything's legally documented. It will clearly have all been me."

"But I will, you know, if you . . . can't, I will." Leanne couldn't begin to imagine how she ever could, but she knew she would want her wishes respected, and help if she needed it. People bandied about the expression "It's a matter of life and death" when they were talking about trivialities. This really was a matter of life and death.

"Thank you," Jay said. "I don't know what else to say, Lee. I know what I'm asking you to accept, and I'm not sure I could do it if it were you . . ."

"Just be OK, huh?"

"Come here." Jay gathered her up in his arms as they leaned back against the couch and stared out the window.

CHAPTER FOUR

IT WAS A PERFECT day to be outdoors—shorts-weather warm but not too warm for exercise. And the sky was overcast so the sun wouldn't be in their eyes. They needed all the help they could get when it came to anything sports related.

Jay was a better athlete than Leanne, but that wasn't saying a whole lot. "At least I wasn't the last kid picked for teams, I was the next to last." He laughed as they shared childhood sporting stories, or horror stories as far as Leanne was concerned.

"I actually got picked once for the school volleyball team," Leanne began proudly. "I was so excited when I was given a team uniform and everything. It felt great to be part of the cool group for once, even if we didn't have anything in common."

"You had volleyball," Jay pointed out.

"Well, yes and no," Leanne said. "The first game? Oh, boy. I didn't hit one shot right. In fact, I even missed the ball completely most of the time. But you know, the only thing that surprised me was that I hit all those successful shots in the first place. The day I tried out I was setting stuff up at the net, hitting those painful bump shots left and right, and making a bunch of great serves. None of that had ever happened before. Hasn't happened since either. It turned out to be my volleyball debut and swan song all rolled into one." She could laugh about the experience now.

"Or volleyed into one," Jay said.

"Touché." Leanne laughed as she double-checked that she had everything in her sports bag.

"Are we switching to fencing now?"

"If you keep up the puns we might." She stuck out her racket pretending to score a fencing hit on her partner.

The playful banter continued as they made their way to the community badminton courts. They liked to go there in the middle of the week, on either side of lunch when it was quieter. Leanne tended to squeal when she made a shot and sort of growl when she missed. And usually there were a lot more growls. For his part, Jay sounded like he may as well have been playing tennis, the way he grunted every time he hit the birdie. They were used to each other's noises, but they saw no reason to subject unsuspecting strangers to them unnecessarily.

Later, as they were packing up their stuff after another lively growl-and-grunt match, Jay said, "That was quite a game today."

"I don't think we've ever played better."

"What was it? Twenty-seven?"

"I think so. Twenty-seven successful returns," Leanne said with pride.

Jay tried to be more objective. "I don't, however, think that's quite how they intended badminton to be played."

"No, probably not, but they are entitled to be wrong aren't they?" Leanne grinned at him.

"Yeah, and it's much more fun our way trying to actually get the birdie back to the other player," Jay said, picking up their bags.

"Instead of all that keep-it-away stuff."

"Much less antagonistic." Jay slung his free arm around Leanne's shoulders as they sauntered back home. "And considering how poorly we play, it means there's a whole lot less bending down to pick the darn birdie up all the time too."

"Or constantly retrieving it from those trees. Trees, I might add, that don't even come close to being far enough away from the courts." Leanne laughed as she leaned into him, wrapping her left arm around his waist.

"At least we don't have to trespass to do reconnaissance like when we play in my apartment's backyard and overshoot the fence," Jay said, shifting the bags to his shoulder.

"True, but it's kind of like our own little treasure hunt that way." She squeezed his side as they walked. "Hey, did you catch my little under-the-net shot?"

"I sure did. Most impressive." He reached for her free hand, absentmindedly stroking it. "I'd like to see you do that one again, though."

"Well, you see, that's the problem with those trick shots, they're tricks, apparently even to me."

They laughed at both their badminton ineptitude and their silliness.

Walking along, they fell into a peaceful silence. Jay was unconsciously rubbing Leanne's right hand when he suddenly stopped and began staring at it in awe. In silent communication, she seemed transfixed as well. It was one of those moments where it felt as if they were looking at something for the first time, but simultaneously had never taken their eyes off of it.

As they continued to stare, they saw more than their joined hands. They began seeing right through each other, experiencing the formless beings inside.

"You've got the most beautiful hands," Jay finally said. Speaking out loud broke the spell.

What had just happened didn't fully register on either of them as their physical communication carried on.

"Pardon me if I beg to differ, but I prefer these." Her fingers traced a path all around the back of his left hand.

"I guess you are entitled, like those badminton guys, to be . . . wrong."

"And so are you." Leanne smiled at him.

"I can tell neither one of us is going to win this," he said, grinning broadly.

"Nope."

The inane conversation of blind love continued.

One warm evening, they were wandering through town after dinner. Neither was much for desserts. Leanne had more of a starch tooth. For Jay, it was salt. And hot buttered bread satisfied them both. But the best after-meal treat was going for a leisurely walk around Clementine, breathing in the great evening air.

With their arms around each other, they ambled past the shops that lined the idyllic burg's main street. They avoided the other side of town where the impersonal big-box stores were starting to sprout up.

Passing by a jewellery store, Jay had one of those light-bulb moments. For the life of him, he couldn't figure out why he hadn't thought of it sooner. He just didn't know if in this case, what he had always hoped for would also be what Leanne wanted. This wasn't a subject they'd discussed yet. It had never come up. Could it be that they both felt the same way, and that's why neither had mentioned it?

Until now.

"Did you ever want to get married, Lee?"

"I used to, as a kid, doll babies and all that. It seemed to be what everyone did. But then I started to really think about it." Leanne paused, wondering why he was asking her this now. Having seen him glance at that jewellery store wasn't helping her nerves any, but she had to forge ahead regardless of what she feared he might be thinking. "You know, I used to seriously worry how on earth I was going to find someone who felt the same way I did. What a combination, I mean, someone who wanted commit-ment—the forever kind—but minus the legal stuff, and all the pomp and circumstance."

Jay grinned in delight. "Just us. Just the two-people-forever kinda thing."

"Exactly. To be together because we keep choosing to be, not because there's some document saying so. But I figured, and this may sound kind of crazy—"

"Impossible," Jay interrupted. "You?" He gently nudged Leanne's side as they kept walking.

"Ha-ha, but I had actually resigned myself to the fact that, in order to find the kind of commitment I wanted, I'd probably have to give up my ideal and end up getting married after all. How's that for twisted?"

"Perfect," he said.

"Do you mean perfect as in perfect the right idea, or perfectly twisted?"

"Both." Jay grinned broadly as he stopped and turned to Leanne. Taking her hands, his expression grew serious as he looked into her eyes with utter amazement. "You found him, by the way."

Leanne couldn't speak. She just looked up at him with equal wonder. She should have known.

"Lee, will you not marry me?"

"I will not." She squeezed his hands.

"Will you love me only until death?"

"I will not."

"Will you spend eternity with me?"

"I will," Leanne said, drawing out the last word, and completing their vows.

"Then I now pronounce us man and woman," Jay said conspiratorially.

"Two people living in sin," she whispered.

"Always, my love." A happy tear rolled down his cheek.

With no official permission, and no witnesses or corresponding need for propriety, the deep kiss that followed their simple vows seemed to last forever.

As Jay and Leanne walked the rest of the way home in giddy silence, they were glad they were living at Leanne's that week since it was closer. She was also the one with an old phonograph—perfect for an old-fashioned romantic dance to cap off their little ceremony.

The record player had been a gift from her grandfather many years before when he was clearing out old things he no longer used. While CDs were the current format of choice, Leanne preferred the old LPs. There was something intangibly appealing about the vintage vinyl discs with their random scratches and flaws. Plus, there was no note-perfect digital editing on those old recordings. What came out of the speakers was exactly what the performers had played.

Not only did that feel more real, but Leanne had an easier time getting her head around the idea of a needle running along the grooves to make the sound. Binary code was fine for computers, but seemed an odd concept to her for music. Zeros and ones seemed so far removed from how the original sounds had been produced.

Leanne conceded that she'd probably end up getting a home PC one of these days. The prices were certainly better than they used to be, and it might be fun to see what the fuss was about. But the whole idea of the information superhighway escaped her. If she wanted to look something up, she reasoned, she already had a perfectly good set of encyclopedias.

But Jay already had a home computer and was excited by the prospect of what the Internet could be. He hoped it would become a great research tool and a way to keep up to date on the latest AIDS information. Currently, however, he used his computer more as a glorified word processor for storing all his medical records and notes, as well as checking out a few games, of course.

Not surprisingly, Leanne preferred the clickety-clack of the old manual typewriter she'd found secondhand. If it weren't for her need to be living at the same time as Jay, she'd have sworn she was born into the wrong century.

Most definitely sharing the same time, not to mention the same train of thought, the two walked through the door anxious to take their non-marriage celebration to the bedroom. But they also wanted to extend the moments of anticipation. Not that their declaration of eternal commitment was anything more than an affirmation of what they were already living, but there was something special about putting it out there verbally.

Jay went over to Leanne's collection of old records and pulled out his favourite.

As the first notes of old Louis filled the apartment, Jay held out his arms in invitation. "Dance with me."

They just folded into each other's arms. Falling right into an easy rhythm, they swayed back and forth to Louis Armstrong's inimitable "What a Wonderful World."

"God, you feel so good, Jay." Leanne squeezed him more tightly, imprinting him on her. "There is nothing like being in your arms."

If ever there were a time for ham, or for being cheesy, it was now. Yet somehow it felt like only what it was—heartbreakingly sincere. "Yes, there is," he said, "having you in my arms."

Nuzzling her head under his chin, she inhaled deeply. "Mmmm. You smell so good too. So you. I could breathe you in forever and never have enough."

"Eau de Jay, huh?"

"We could make a fortune. But I'm not that generous. This scent is all mine." She sniffed again.

"You got that right." Jay then exaggeratedly sniffed her. "Well, eau de Leanne'll do too. If you've got nothing better, I suppose."

She playfully swatted his arm and they both stopped moving. As they stood there embracing, they were nearly overwhelmed by the headiness of everything they were feeling.

"Seriously, Lee, I hope I get to remember all of you— every single detail—for eternity. Experience it forever."

"Well, then, I think we'd better imprint it that much harder." Leanne pressed into him even more. There was absolutely no space between them.

Soon, however, Jay was breaking them out of the tender moment. "Oh, wow, if you keep that up . . . too late."

"Nice sword in your pocket, by the way." She couldn't resist the cliché. "Very nice."

"The record player can shut itself off," Jay said as they hurried to the bedroom. "It really is, you know, like this song . . . a wonderful world."

As they tumbled onto the bed, Leanne tried her best to imitate Louis Armstrong, inflection and all. "Oh . . . yeah."

CHAPTER FIVE

UNMEASURED TIME CONTINUED to pass, and with it came reminders that Jay wouldn't live forever. Not that anyone would, but instead of life often being two steps forward and one step back, his was more the other way around. But by trying to avert their gaze and not looking forward or backward, the changes and challenges had a better chance of going unnoticed, or at least of resembling something closer to blissful ignorance.

But today was actual bliss. It was moving day.

The ordinary moving headaches were almost relished. Dealing with packing, the resulting clutter, and the general uprooted disarray for a little while were experiences to be welcomed. They all signified that this was one ordinary dream they got to live out. Jay and Leanne were moving into their new home, their first place together.

They'd never been particularly concerned with where they lay their heads each night, as long as they were side by side.

While it would have been practical and financially smart to have let one apartment go already, that hadn't been high on their list of priorities. Money wasn't a huge issue for them given Jay's settlement. And it saved having to do something far worse than packing—sorting out their respective accumulations of stuff. Just where was George Carlin before all the acquisitions?

In some ways, going back and forth between apartments had given them the feeling of having one bigger place. It just so happened that the rooms were in two different neighbourhoods.

That arrangement gave them the added benefit of having two kitchens to perfectly accommodate their different cooking and cleaning habits. Leanne liked to clean as she cooked, keeping everything nice and tidy so there was no big mess to clean up later. While Jay appreciated the logic behind her approach, when he cooked, it never quite worked out so neatly.

He usually managed to put the ingredients he was finished with back where they belonged, but as for the used dishes and utensils? They rarely found their way to the sink until after he was finished cooking. By then, a nice semi-dried coating of whatever he was making tended to remain on them. The countertops shared the same fate.

Jay just didn't notice those things as he worked. He was too caught up in the creating to think about the cleaning. Of course, he paid the price later when he had those dishes and counters to tackle. But he did have some terrific company while he did so.

But now there would be only one kitchen, one set of rooms, one home. Out for an evening walk near the beach, discovering streets they'd never had reason to travel, Jay and Leanne had happened across an old Victorian cottage with a big wraparound porch.

It was for sale, but not for long.

They may have had very different kitchen etiquette, but they were definitely on the same page when it came to making big decisions quickly. While they had casually looked at the outsides of a few other houses, they had only gone inside this one.

"It's either right or it isn't," Jay had later said to his friend, Donovan, when they told him about their quick house purchase.

And the place on Montrose Avenue was right. They knew the first time they saw it. Much of the Victorian character of the house had been maintained, but there had been some changes.

The front of the old house still had the original multi-paned glass. The back, however, now had large picture windows. The view into the very private and intentionally overgrown backyard was unobstructed. It felt wild and cared for all at the same time.

Inside, the wood trim and mouldings were exactly as they had been when the house was built a century earlier. "Jay, they haven't been painted!" Leanne exclaimed when she saw the unspoiled wood. "No paint to strip."

"Yeah, just paint to get off of us," Jay said, looking at the salmon-pink living room, "after we most definitely re-paint these walls."

"You think so?" Leanne feigned surprise. "Well, if you really want to, I guess I could give up these fish walls. But, oh, look at these floors. Look at the old fir boards." Leanne knelt to feel the smooth wooden planks. They had clearly been refinished recently, but they still held the history of thousands of footsteps.

"And what a great spot there by the fireplace for the braided rug," Jay said. "Lots more room to stretch out too."

While they did spend a fair amount of time actually using the furniture they had, often they chose to sit on the floor. It felt more primitive, more like the naturally easy way kids crawled about, sitting wherever they happened to end up. And with a few throw cushions here and there, along with an arm or two to prop up on, the floor became a great lounging area.

Ever since their first Christmas together, they also occasionally liked to fall asleep on that rustic rug. Nestled close to the fire, it seemed like the perfect spot to doze off whether they had just made love, or had simply been talking or watching a movie. There was a definite appeal to being able to close their eyes and fall asleep exactly where they already were without having to get up to go to bed.

However, that could leave the odd kink or two to deal with the next morning. But more often than not, they avoided them by waking up in the middle of the night and sleepily dragging themselves to the bedroom. It was kind of like a mini campout.

"Plus," Jay pointed out, "we're sort of getting two nights in one." Waking up and still seeing darkness outside, and then changing sleeping locations, meant they got to fall asleep and wake up all over again the same night. That doubled the good parts of the sleeping process as far as they were concerned, since there was no awareness anyway of the actual sleeping time in between.

They might have felt differently if either had trouble sleeping, but as it was, a short stumble later to their bed and they were comfortably falling asleep again.

"I can see us curled up in front of this thing," Leanne said as she admired the old wood-burning fireplace. "And look, there's a little built-in cabinet thing to store the logs, so no stacking them on the side anymore."

As Leanne was admiring the built-in, Jay was looking up. He had an idea. "Since this front part of the house juts out from the rest, do you think we could put in a skylight?"

"Oh yeah!" Leanne squealed as she pictured them falling asleep in the living room under the stars, all cozy and warm. "We absolutely have to check that out."

They proceeded to explore the rest of the house and were greeted with surprise after surprise.

The kitchen stove was new, but thankfully it was a replica of the vintage wood-burning ones. Except for having gas burners in place of the original lift-out iron lids, it looked as if it were as old as the house. But the modern features of the white-enamelled gas stove were very welcome. Wood was great for the fireplace, but when it came to cooking, quick and easy won out.

Everywhere they looked there was something else that drew them to the house. Whether it was the claw-foot tub, the old but clean tilework, or the small stained-glass windows scattered about, character and history oozed out of the place.

Coming up from the basement they thought they had seen everything. But then the realtor reached up and lowered a hidden drop-down staircase from the hall ceiling. Not realizing how thrilled his clients would be with this last feature—one he'd almost forgotten even existed—the realtor casually threw in, "Oh, and there's this attic space up here for storage, if you want."

Covered with cobwebs and the dust accumulation of many years, the attic had become their favourite part of the house—not for what it was, but for what they saw it could be.

Ideas started bubbling forth. They imagined windows, skylights, and wood all around—on the floors and on the sloping ceiling.

They saw a dormer, too, on the south side of the house, with a cluster of windows overlooking the backyard. They wanted light up there, and lots of it.

Despite the charm of the disappearing steps, a proper staircase was definitely in order. Maybe one with a nice landing and sturdy banisters on both sides. That part of the plan was not so much for the aesthetic value as the practical when, down the road, climbing stairs might pose a challenge.

"This space needs to be lived in," Jay said as he looked at the exposed rafters in the near-empty attic. There were a few dusty boxes stacked up in one corner, abandoned and long forgotten, possibly never looked at again after they were packed away.

"Let's sort before we move," Leanne suggested.

And that's what they did, despite the temptation to do otherwise when they were face to face with closets and drawers of stuff they didn't even remember.

"Am I ever glad we bit the bullet and didn't throw everything into boxes," Leanne said as she flopped down on the couch.

"It was definitely worth it. It felt good getting rid of stuff that just sat there, other than the stuff that's supposed to do that." Jay laughed a little tiredly.

He hadn't been able to help much with the heavy lifting during the move. It hadn't exactly sat well with him either, but he'd had a releasing rant or two, and a few well-deserved poor-me moments that Leanne understood and quietly listened to.

When he was done, she'd pick up another box of stuff to unpack. And taking out the first thing she saw in the cardboard carton, she'd hold it up and ask him, "Where do want this to go?" Normal, everyday questions provided a comfort and distraction all their own.

Jay and Leanne were determined not to live with unpacked boxes for weeks on end, so instead of their walks and mini hikes, much of their relaxation time was spent putting the remaining things away. It seemed the lesser of evils compared to feeling imprisoned by stuff. "George Carlin sure got it right," he said when they were finally done. "And let's not go on vacation and 'buy more stuff' just to fill every place in a hotel room, OK?"

"You got it, Jay. Besides, I don't feel any need to travel anywhere. In fact, let's go sit on the front porch and look at all the free nature stuff right here."

They had found a great old glider the week before at their favourite antique store. And while the seat was wide enough for three, it fit the two of them perfectly since Leanne liked to pull her legs up and lean into Jay's side as they glided back and forth.

Shortly after they'd settled into a nice gliding rhythm, Jay's pal Donovan wandered by. "I figured you two would have had a couple of old rocking chairs on your porch," Donovan remarked. But as soon as the words were out of his mouth he stopped. He hadn't thought how that might sound. Sitting in rockers on a front porch was something old people were supposed to do together. And Leanne and Jay wouldn't be doing that.

But they rescued him from feeling as if he had to pull his foot from his mouth. "Hey, Van, it's not like we haven't thought of that," Jay said. "Why do you think we've got this big old glider here instead?"

"I don't get it. If you guys have thought of it, and you want that rockin' routine . . . I mean, you bought a house with a big front porch just begging for those things, then why not have rockers?" He hesitated for a second. "Why not get them and . . . shit, man, enjoy them while you can?" He really didn't know how they could talk so freely about everything.

"We do want that, Donovan," Leanne said, "but in our own way. If we got rocking chairs it would be as if we were trying to squeeze everything in. It would be saying what we have right now isn't good enough, and that we have to skip ahead and grab something from the future."

"We don't want to have to pretend what it would be like to be two old birds rocking away, reminiscing on a front porch, waxing poetic over the last fifty years to-gether," Jay explained. "Don't you see? Trying to re-create that experience, or I guess pre-create it, that all presup-poses we won't ever really have it."

"But seriously, Jay," Donovan said, "I mean, that really doesn't fit with how you guys always talk. I know you never mention time frames and stuff, but fifty years? I wish, man, but—"

"He's not talking literally, or at least not corporeally, Donovan," Leanne interjected. "Who knows what the future is? It isn't anything yet. So right now, we're here on our porch, side by side, a couple of young birds on a glider."

Two birds who were building their nest.

They were already used to living in a bit of upheaval from both the packing and unpacking stages of moving, so it seemed easier to renovate right away and get the rest of the commotion over with all at once.

Besides, putting things off was not how they liked to live. Having no guarantees in life imparted a greater sense of urgency when that life was expected to be shorter.

But before any construction could begin on their attic master bedroom, they had to clear out the existing boxes that someone had stored away. From their cursory look at the contents so far, they could tell the boxes didn't belong to the previous owners who had been in the house for decades.

Despite their curiosity, they couldn't help but feel as if they were invading some long-ago person's privacy. It felt a little like an archaeological dig, rummaging around through part of the history and remains of someone's life. Feeling rather nostalgic in the old house, they let their minds wander off, making up stories and life histories for the items they found.

"Memorabilia boxes." Leanne lifted out another handful of papers. "That's what these must be."

A matchbook fell from the stack in her hand. It was from an old restaurant she had only heard about as a child. And wrapped up in a yellowed newspaper was a half-burnt candle, with wax drippings forever frozen on its sides.

"I bet whoever these people were, they had a special dinner and this candle burned, on this day," Leanne said, pointing to the paper's date.

"I wonder what ever happened to them. Did they both live here? Did they share many more dinners?" Jay hoped they did.

"Whatever happened, somebody sure remembered it." Leanne looked toward the sentimental bits and pieces.

"Hey, what's this thing?" He picked up an old leather-covered book. Flipping through the pages he realized it was a journal. Handwritten "Dear Diary" entries proved the book was a collection of someone's private thoughts. "Should we be reading this?"

"Judging by the dates in here, I don't think anyone's still around to mind, but I know what you mean," she said. "It says 'Dear Diary' not 'Dear World.'"

"Hardly what the person this belonged to had in mind, I bet. You know, Lee, it kind of reminds me of this new Internet thing. Once something's out there, it's out there for good, floating around. You never know who's going to find it. Just like this diary. I can see why you stopped writing one after—what was it—a month?" Jay remembered Leanne telling him about her failed diary-keeping efforts. "Live it don't write it, right?"

"Yep." She smiled at him. "I mean, it would be cool to have it to read now, but if I can't remember something on my own—without that written trigger—how important could it have been? And even if it were, and I would want to be reminded of it, the written memory wouldn't be complete anyway. I don't want to be defined by whatever I thought worthy of notating about my life and feelings in the past. That would only be a partial snapshot of those moments. It might be interesting, but it wouldn't be me. Not me now, and not even me fully back then. And if there's no way to tell all of me from something like that"—Leanne eyed the mysterious journal—"then better none at all."

"I love you, Lee, my ever-analyzing Lee." Jay couldn't help himself, seeing her sitting cross-legged in the nest of old papers and trinkets, with cobwebs dusting her hair, thinking, always thinking. "Don't change a thing."

"I don't think I could if I wanted to." Leanne laughed as Jay set down the journal. She scooted over next to him. "I love you, too. And so much more than that little word says."

"Well, then, we'll just have to be stuck with the complete inadequacy of language," he said before adding suggestively, "the verbal one anyway."

Their trip down someone else's memory lane was put aside as they headed downstairs. They had more of their own memories to create and, most importantly, to live in the first place.

They hired a great renovation team that, while not thoroughly agreeing with all of Jay and Leanne's choices, worked hard to accommodate them.

Out of a sense of respect, and a feeling that they were now the custodians of the attic memorabilia, they made a rather odd request of the carpenter and his crew. They were to enclose all the old boxes behind the attic walls. Another person's memories had been upstairs for so long, safe and alone, it seemed unfair to make them move now.

And what else would Jay and Leanne have done with them? Although it was their house now, it felt wrong to simply chuck the stuff as if it didn't mean anything. It had all meant something very dear to someone. "Even though that person did end up abandoning these things," Jay said.

"Yeah, that's true, but who knows why? And it was special enough to have been saved in the first place. These boxes feel like part of the house, part of its history. Like us now."

As the renovation proceeded, everything they'd originally envisioned for their attic sanctuary fell into place. The results were stunning as far as they were concerned, even though that view was not completely shared by the carpenter.

The biggest bone of contention had been the massive expanses of bare wood Jay and Leanne had insisted upon. Most notable was the unfinished-pine ceiling that sloped from the steeply pitched roof down to the short stub walls.

"You'll regret not getting that pine treated," their carpenter had said. "It's going to dry out and crack or warp. There are some great new chemical products that'll protect the wood—"

"No thanks," Jay had interrupted, cutting the carpenter off politely but firmly. The two homeowners had then shared a look and a knowing smile. Why should their wood want what they did not? While Jay did have to ingest a certain amount of chemicals himself, he tried to avoid optional chemical contact. And they were going for a more rustic, rough-hewn look up there anyway.

The floors were oak, but they'd chosen the lowest grade. Again, thanks to Jay's settlement, money was not the issue.

They simply preferred the wilder, more barn-like appearance of the cheaper oak and its character-rich knotholes. Every piece of wood was like a piece of art with unique swirls and lines. They were the wood's fingerprints.

Pragmatism and laziness both factored into the decision of not only their new solid staircase, but the addition of a roomy bathroom upstairs. Down the road, easier access might be a necessity. And for now and later, nothing could beat the coziness of going from bubbling bath to beckoning bed in a few short steps.

"After all, who wants to be stumbling downstairs in the dark? I might be tempted to use an old mason jar instead, but that could be a bit trickier for you, Lee."

With everything pointing in its favour, a bright new bathroom now stood in one corner of the attic. And there was still a mason jar, but it rested on the windowsill, full of flowering weeds brought in from the garden.

They chose the largest windows available, despite recommendations to go smaller so the sills wouldn't be unusually low. "But this way, we can see out even if we're sitting on the floor," Jay had tried to explain. Judging by the look on the carpenter's face, he couldn't see why that would be a concern, or even something that adults would want to do. But it was still to code, so big low windows went in.

Along with a large skylight for the living room downstairs, there were eight smaller ones dotting the peaked roof—four on each sloping side—opening the attic up to the sky as much as building integrity would allow.

The higher up in the house they went, the more natural light there was. Even though they were physically going away from the doors en route to the attic, there was a feeling of being closer to life outside.

The little nook formed from the addition of the dormer was a mini version of the larger room. With windows on all three sides of the alcove, sunlight flooded in.

Theirs was the tallest house in the neighbourhood, so sunrises and sunsets and everything in between became slow-moving pictures, privately delivered all day long.

A padded bench seat was built in beneath the wider south-facing window of the dormer, with plenty of extra cushions resting at either end.

The storage area under the bench was their version of a memorabilia box. As such, it was not to contain remnants of old memories, but things to make new ones, items that meant something to them now. They were to be used and looked at actively, not stored away waiting to collect dust.

There were already things in the box they wanted to share with the other, including a couple of funny newspaper cartoons, an interesting article Jay had read, various games and toys, and a takeout menu from a new pizza place Leanne wanted to try. Favourite records, CDs, videotapes, and DVDs lived in harmony there too. They didn't belong on the shelves downstairs with all the ordinary discs and tapes.

And some things were purely practical in nature. There was a small food stash—though larger than they'd had in their apartment bedrooms—that included popcorn, raw nuts, and dried fruit to satisfy their more healthy cravings. And every once in a while, a bag of potato chips or cheese puffs found its way in.

Not only was the food convenient for their impromptu middle-of-the-night parties in bed, but sometimes it also made them feel as if they were on a little vacation. They could pretend they were staying in a motel, eating road-trip food, watching an old barely-even-colour television.

But afterward, all they had to do to be home was turn off their imagination along with the lights. And they could go to sleep on their own sheets, in their own bed.

For the full effect, though, the food needed to include pizza. Specifically, it had to be delivery from somewhere new, further simulating the whole motel-staying experience. Leanne had turned Jay on to that trick.

There was something intrinsically entertaining about eating delivery food while lounging on top of the covers. But it was even better at home, since they didn't have to worry about who, or what, had previously been on the bedspread.

Their friends couldn't see why they didn't actually go on a road trip and stay in a real motel if that's what they wanted. Excuses of not having a car or of having to rent one didn't seem to wash.

"You should just go, get away. Have a change of scenery," Donovan had said to Jay.

"We like it right here, Van. Why bother with the hassles of travelling when we're already where we want to be? We just have fun with the travel food sometimes."

And delivery pizza was now on its way to help them celebrate the completion of the attic bedroom. It seemed a fitting tribute to their renovation journey, marking their arrival at the little sanctuary they had imagined the first time they saw the barren space.

This bedspread meal also had a practical purpose. They were both way too tired to cook. The construction had been completed a few days earlier, but Jay and Leanne had chosen to paint the interior themselves.

As she climbed down from the ladder Jay was steadying, Leanne reconsidered the wisdom of that choice. Her body had been strained and contorted in a number of unintended ways as she reached for the nearly impossible bits above windows, over the stairs, and wherever drywall met ceiling wood.

But the last of the butter yellow was on the walls and the doorbell was ringing. Dinner was served.

Life was good.

CHAPTER SIX

T HERE WAS SOMETHING different about the talks they shared after making love. The afterglow, and the moments after that, seemed to have an added mellowness. Communication then was as close to talking without any conscious thought as they could get.

Not that they were guarded at other times, but talking of the larger worries was somehow easier when they were lying safely in their bed, tucked away from the worries of the day.

It was almost as if they were talking about the bad stuff in the abstract. In their satiated state, they could process things that were still too scary anywhere else. In bed, it felt more hypothetical.

As they lay there tranquilly, Leanne asked, "Do you want a funeral?"

"I don't know for sure," he said. "Part of me wonders why I should even care since I likely won't be there. But that's the thing, what if I am? If we are right, that this isn't it, and life in the broader sense doesn't end with death, if all that's true, would I really want to see a bunch of sad people gathered around my used-up body?"

"It does seem like a strange idea when you put it that way," Leanne said. "And no matter what, everyone would be there saying good-bye to a form that wouldn't be you anymore. It's sort of like the whole God idea. If God, or you someday, has no form and is everywhere, then what's the point of going to one set place, whether it's a church or a funeral to see you?"

"Thanks for putting me in such revered company, Lee." Jay nudged her side affectionately. "I guess it's more the symbolism of it, and a tangible way to deal with grief and maybe find comfort. I mean, at least it's something that can be done, that can be controlled when you feel out of control. And it's a way to show respect for a life well lived and all that, to honour yours truly, the dearly departed."

"Sometimes I think funerals should happen later than they do. And I don't mean delaying the whole dying part, Jay, because that goes without saying, but the actual cere-mony. If it's a time to grieve, isn't it too soon when you're still in shock and disbelief, feeling as if the whole thing can't really be happening, let alone that it has happened?"

Leanne rolled onto her side to face him. "And if the purpose is to remember, isn't it too soon for that too, with everything so new? Emotions have to be way too raw to be much good for smiling about happy times yet."

"So have the funeral on what, the first anniversary of the death?"

"That rather smacks of time measurement," she said.

"You're right, scratch that. So if not then, when?"

"I'm not sure . . . I just can't wrap my head around the whole idea of your funeral, or ever having to coordinate such a thing."

"They do have funeral directors you know. It's not as if you would have to cater the thing yourself." Jay stated the obvious in a way that he hoped would cause Leanne to smile.

"But even then . . ." She barely reacted to his comment. Her mind was drifting backward, travelling to another time. "You know, I still remember being asked what I wanted my parents' obituaries to say in the newspaper. As if those blurbs were really on my priority list then. But it sure adds to the argument for prearranging your own after-party if you want one."

"And so here we are, planning, or planning not to plan maybe." He shrugged with a slight smile.

"As long as I know what you want—and what you don't want—after."

"I want . . . I think I want the beach. I want the waves washing the shore, renewing the sand with every cycle." Jay closed his eyes. "I want the water lapping back and forth, on and on. That'll be my music. And you, living, permanently safe from my cells, going on and on like the waves. That'll be my memorial service. And see? No time constraints. It'll just keep going."

"So you're putting all that on me, huh?" Leanne gently teased. "You're making me promise to go on living. What if I don't want to?"

"Don't promise me. Promise yourself. Vow to breathe the air and live it all. For better or worse, it won't be forever. Dying will come soon enough, even if it's a hundred years from now."

"I just can't see myself living without you." Leanne reflexively grabbed hold of his arm. "I can't imagine it."

Stroking her cheek, he said, "And I can't imagine being dead without you. But we'll do it. We'll find a way."

"Somehow."

So there was a plan of sorts, however vague and uncertain. And while there would be other conversations to follow on such matters, even the sensation of having figured something out was comforting. And it was a good send-off to sleep. As they shifted into their sleeping positions, her right arm remained locked securely around his left.

When Jay woke up the next morning, Leanne was lying on her back looking up at the ceiling. If not for her open eyes, he would have sworn that she was still asleep. She was so still.

Usually they woke up completely entwined, their legs and arms tangled together randomly. Sometimes they'd get that way during the night, and other times it wouldn't be until after one of them began to stir. But their bodies always gravitated to one another once sleep had provided some initial rest.

But not now.

He propped up to face her side. "Lee? What is it?"

Leanne kept staring at the ceiling. It wasn't as though she were looking to it for any answers, as much as she was almost looking through it. As if by not focusing on anything, she would somehow feel better. She could get out of her thoughts—ones she'd been having since she woke up an hour earlier. "I feel . . . I just feel . . . icky."

"Are you sick? Do you need—"

"No," she interrupted quickly. "Nothing like that. I feel blah, but for no reason. No, that's not true. I know why."

Jay started to speak but stopped himself when Leanne moved to face him. She was still staring off into the distance, but that changed when she spoke. Gazing into his eyes, she said, "I want to freeze time."

"Ah, Lee." Jay shifted them both so that she was half lying on him with her head tucked under his chin. He gently stroked her hair. That's when the sobs came.

There had been tears before at different times. Some were brought on by their conversations and wishes, and others were triggered by inane little things they saw or thought, reminding them of the one part of their relationship they wished they could change.

But this time, the floodgates really gave way.

Their talk the night before had unleashed something new. And while Leanne was dreaming, her brain took her in a scary direction. There was a new image she couldn't shake. "I saw you." She nearly choked as she tried to catch her breath.

"After I was dead, my body," Jay finished. "It's OK, Lee. I'm here. I'm feeling good—"

She cut him off. "No, not your body, at least not like that. They, they handed me . . . you . . . you were in this little box," she cried out. "Your name was on this cardboard box. And your ashes . . ."

There was little Jay could do, and even less he could say. He held her as tightly as he could, pressing his body up against hers so she could feel his presence through as many nerve endings as possible.

Her body clung desperately to his.

He hoped their shared surface contact would help to counteract her nightmare, reminding her body at least that he was still there. His hands moved back and forth slightly, caressing her where they held her.

The two lovers stayed like that for a long time, each needing to feel the other's solid warmth.

Gradually, Leanne's head sank into Jay's chest, relaxing. Her breathing returned to normal as the moisture on her tear-stained face began to dry. She was exhausted.

And she wasn't alone. Jay had his own inner demons pounding at him. Although they did a pretty good job of living in the moment and carrying on as normally as possible, the fact remained that Leanne was going through this hell now because Jay was sick. There was no shortage of resurgent guilt on his part. Some of his earlier fears were coming true. It really would have been easier if they had just said good-bye in the beginning.

"I'm so sorry, Lee. This is all my fault."

"No, it's not. Don't say that. Don't blame my sweet Jay for this. I just wish . . . oh, you know what I wish, love." Leanne pressed her nose against his bare chest and inhaled deeply, closing her tired eyes.

They'd been connected all along, and there was no way either one could have turned down this time together. Jay knew that. But that didn't stop his mind from circling around trying to find an answer that didn't exist, one that could somehow spare Leanne all pain always.

"There won't be a box then." It was the best he could do.

She just nodded.

They both felt pretty drained the rest of the day. If they'd had their druthers they would have bailed on their evening plans. But Becky was visiting from London since her family still lived in Clementine. And that night, there was a welcome-back party at Becky's parents' place.

Her family had wanted to arrange a welcome-home celebration, but Leanne had convinced them that while Becky would always come back to visit, she was home before she left England. Some things were easier to hear one person removed.

At the party, gesturing toward the "Welcome Back" banner, Becky whispered, "Thanks for that," as she gave Leanne a hug.

Although they were tired and not normally big party people under the best of circumstances, Jay and Leanne were glad they had come, even though there were a few times when they definitely felt like sneaking off to one of the bedrooms.

"We sure are a couple of wild party animals," Leanne remarked when Jay began fantasizing about the big bed that held everyone's coats. However, it was no exhibitionist fantasy, only one of sleep and recovery.

Still, overall, they had really enjoyed seeing everybody and spending time in such a festive environment for a while. It was such a sharp contrast from the way their day had begun.

But they both felt the most themselves, and the happiest give or take the odd emotional trauma, when they were alone together. All the awe-filled moments of their lives—when everything felt absolutely right—happened when it was just the two of them.

Becky was going to be in town for a few weeks so there would be plenty of time for more catching up in person. Even though they had only been at the party for an hour,

Jay and Leanne called a cab and said their good-nights and talk-to-you-laters.

It felt a little strange being inside a car. Clementine was small enough, and they liked walking enough, they simply took a cab on the rare occasions when they needed a car. That was another thing on a long list of things they instinctively just got about each other, but that their friends accepted more than understood.

"We should have kept our drinks," Leanne said as she settled back against the cracked vinyl seat. "We could pretend this was some fancy limo."

"Excuse me, driver." Jay leaned forward. "Could you please take the long way home."

"Huh?" grunted the unamused cabbie.

"He means, could you please drive us around for a little while before you go to the address we gave you," Leanne explained to the nonplussed man up front. He most certainly did not get these two, who were taking such delight in his rather musty old taxi.

"It's too bad there's no privacy divider in this fine limousine," Jay said as they shifted closer together in the big backseat. "We really should enquire about that next time. This is so terribly déclassé."

"Well, since our driver already thinks we're crazy, let's give him more reason." Leanne started to climb onto Jay's lap, but settled for draping one leg across when she heard the cabbie cough rather loudly. Pretending to pout, she whispered into Jay's ear, "Just wait till we get home, then."

"Driver, speed it up!"

While they had only had a drink and a half between them—with Jay the half—they both got the giggles. As the cab wound its way to their home, they started laughing like two overly tired, silly people whose exhaustion was finally catching up with them.

After a few days, they once again broached the subject of that dreaded box. "You know, I've been thinking," Jay said. "There's no reason why you have to be given my remains." He coughed. "God, that sounds weird. But you don't. If nothing else, don't ever pick them up."

"I can't just leave you there."

"You won't be. Come on, Lee, that won't be me. I'll be long out of there and hanging out with you." He squeezed her right forearm with his left hand to reassure her—and himself—that his words would be proven true.

"You better be right here until I'm right there," she said.

There was still the matter, however, of what to do with what was physically left over. Simply never picking up his ashes would put the people at the funeral home in a very awkward position. Maybe sometimes they had to make phone calls or send reminder letters, but Jay and Leanne kind of doubted that. It was hardly like dry cleaning that someone might honestly forget to pick up.

"Do you want me to take care of it when I make the prearrangements?" Jay asked.

Wishing she could say yes, Leanne instead said what she'd want to hear if the shoe were on the other foot, or the coffin around the other body. "No, you shouldn't have to do that alone."

Perverse though it sounded, Jay and Leanne decided to try to make a day out of it—a little field trip to the funeral home. They also decided to set things up for each of them. That approach felt more like regular long-range planning, and not something specific to Jay.

But it was also a reminder that no one got out of this life alive.

United in their task, they began asking the funeral director a multitude of questions. He wished he hadn't been called into work on his day off once he heard what they wanted. His job, of course, was to accommodate them as much as possible, but part of him wondered if this was some kind of practical joke. "You want what?" he finally asked after their last request, or rather, their latest request.

"A funeral tray," Jay repeated as if it were the most normal thing in the world. "You know, like they had in that new Strickland play. What was it, Lee?"

"*A Guide to Mourning*. Have you seen it?" she asked the puzzled funeral director.

"No. I tend to avoid funeral-related entertainment." He hadn't meant to snap or be impertinent, but his patience was wearing thin from the string of unorthodox questions. Fortunately, his remark did nothing to upset them.

In fact, they just laughed. "Get enough of that at work, do you?" Jay asked.

"Especially today, I imagine," Leanne said. She was actually beginning to feel a little sorry for the guy. He probably didn't get too many clients like them. "But really, sir, what we're looking for is the cheapest, greenest way to go. Literally." Leanne then laughed a lot more than her pun really warranted.

Despite appearances, there was still some discomfort with where they were, and with what they were doing. They weren't usually quite so giddy. Not in public, anyway.

Jay soldiered on. "While admittedly a bit unusual, we do really like the idea of having a funeral tray, you know, like a door or flat panel of some kind, something instead of an entire coffin, especially since it's going to be burned up anyway."

The funeral director now really wished he hadn't answered his boss's phone call and was at home right then. "Look, I don't think we can help you. I'm not even sure if this request is for real. I mean, what you're asking—" He suddenly stopped himself when he looked at their expressions. This was no joke. Despite their oddness, they were totally sincere. "But, what we can do," he said, changing his tone, "is the most basic pine box, no lining or anything. Would that work for you?"

"Well, it's no funeral tray," Jay said before Leanne nudged him in the side. The guy was trying to help now.

"That could work," she said, much to the relief of the man on the other side of the desk.

"Then let me show you both what it looks like."

As they quietly followed the mortician into the display area, Jay gave Leanne's hand an extra squeeze as he tipped and nodded his head, giving her a muted smile.

Other decisions were also made that day. But the main thing was that there would be no small box handed over to Leanne.

CHAPTER SEVEN

LIFE ROLLED ALONG pretty smoothly until one day the phone rang, reminding them of what could so easily be forgotten when problems stayed away long enough.

Leanne had been reading in the living room, so Jay had picked up their bedroom extension. "Who was on the phone?" she asked when Jay came back downstairs. There was no answer. "Jay? Who was—" Then she saw his face.

"Ben." Jay sat down next to her on the couch.

"And?" Leanne was anxious. He only knew one Ben— Dr. Benjamin Barnes.

"Guess that's one of the perks of the medical profession, more friends who are doctors. Friends who don't make you go to the office to hear bad test results."

"Shit. So you haven't just been extra tired lately."

"No. Apparently not."

Leanne tried to sound positive even though her heart was racing. "Well, this has happened before. What do they want to try this time, different antiretrovirals?"

"No. I don't know. My T-cell count is in the proverbial toilet, sewer actually, never been this low. Don't even ask about my viral load now. Ben said he didn't know how I was doing as well as I am. I'm supposed to be in far worse shape apparently, given everything I've got. And I thought Kaposi's was bad."

Leanne was trying to ignore her fear, which was only exacerbated by his Kaposi's sarcoma reference. Jay almost never referred to his AIDS-related complications specifically by name. He only did so when he was scared. Being vague made them all seem more minor, so it was easier to feel upbeat. It was similar to how as a kid, he immediately felt sicker when a doctor told him he had acute viral rhinopharyngitis instead of just calling it a common cold.

Seeing Jay so incredibly despondent now, Leanne tried to compensate. "That shows what little they know. Look at how much better you're doing than those tests showed. That must mean what you're doing is working, and it just hasn't shown up yet on the labs. And I know how much you hate some of the treatments, but maybe there's still something else to add to the regimen."

"We're already doing everything, Leanne. There's nothing else." Jay sounded defeated.

"But we're not going to accept that, are we? We can't stop now. We'll keep thinking, keep trying. There's gotta be something else we can look into."

Jay's voice was different when he finally replied. "Yeah, but, I need to face it too. We both do. We need to start dealing with this, not treating it like it's in the future and planning ahead as best we can. I think I need to . . . I need to really live with the idea it's in the present now, not the future anymore."

"Isn't that what we've always done?" she asked. "We've talked about it, dealt with it, and cried about it. Hated it. We've lived with it."

"But not like this. It feels as if it's some kind of anti-race now, the kind you don't want to win, ever. From HIV status to my early AIDS days through to now, it's been this progression downward, each stage worse, one step closer to that checkered flag."

"But you've gone on. You've been OK," Leanne said. "What's so different now?"

"Remember what I said about knowing my body and listening to it? I can't explain it. I don't just feel tired, I feel as if I'm getting ready, that I can't fight anymore."

"Now stop that!" she shouted. "You're reacting to some shitty test results. That's all. And you're reading more into them right now."

"Maybe. But I want to get off this roller coaster now, Leanne," he practically moaned. "I'm so tired of it. I'm so tired." He hung his head down, feeling as if he didn't have the strength to hold it up anymore.

Leanne stroked his back. "I know you are, sweetie. I know. But please give yourself time to consider all this, to take it in. And remember what you told me, about how you felt when you were first diagnosed? It makes sense to me that these latest numbers—more damn measurements, which, by the way, I thought we agreed to hate—are just that next stage you were talking about. But you have no way of knowing how many more stages are left. You don't need to race to the finish line now any more than before."

Jay looked up slightly. "Oh, you mean to tell me I have more of these lovely little surprises to look forward to?"

"Some people have all the luck. I know what you're say-ing, how in tune you are with your body, and much as I want to"—Leanne's voice cracked—"I can't guarantee . . . well . . . anything. But I also know you sometimes have these knee-jerk reactions to things. All I ask is that you listen to what your body really tells you, and not to some stupid test results."

"I just . . . hearing those results . . . and knowing what they mean . . ." His voice drifted off. "It kind of makes me wonder why I even go in for those tests anymore."

"Well, it keeps the doctors happy, makes them feel as if they're able to do something. And all this time they have been. And they will continue to," Leanne insisted, for both their sakes.

"Thank you . . . for reminding me. I felt as if I actually sank right through the floor when I heard those numbers."

"No more thinking about numbers, OK? No test num-bers, no clocks, no calendars, none of it. Screw 'em all."

"Screw 'em all," Jay agreed desperately.

"Why couldn't we be on a merry-go-round instead of a roller coaster?" Leanne sighed.

"But we'd be going around in circles then."

"Good point, but merrily nonetheless."

"Yes," Jay conceded before adding, "but without the roller-coaster lows, there'd have been no roller-coaster meet-a-certain-someone-in-the-park highs."

"Now how am I supposed to argue with that?" Leanne glared at him as she resisted a smile. "But still, why can't we change the laws of gravity and simply eliminate all the lows?"

Jay sat there grinning and shaking his head.

"What?" She laughed. "You actually expected me not to try to argue the point?"

"Ah, Lee, thanks for the further distraction there." He felt life returning to normal again, their beautiful normal.

It took a while for Jay's body to catch up to his mind in the feeling-better department. But as before, thanks to medicine both ancient and modern, it did. Every time he returned from a scare, Jay found himself feeling as if he'd been granted a little reprieve, reminding him of how grateful he was for his life.

It was funny how after all that fear, and all the doom and gloom, they could end up feeling deliriously happy. Regular life could simply resume, and before they knew it, they were thrilled to again be able to say "Nothing" when asked "What's new?"

Sometimes the status quo was absolute bliss.

Purposely having no calendar anywhere in the house meant no conscious celebration of one day above any other. They were all equally special and uncounted. In some ways, minutes and hours took on the same importance as days and weeks, or months and years. Jay and Leanne owned watches and did use them on occasion when a specific time needed to be known, but mostly the little devices lay stored away in a drawer.

Generally, when the old inbred habit of wanting to know the time crept in, they preferred the vagueness of looking at where the sun happened to be. They joked that it was a good thing neither of them was particularly adept at reading the sun's position, or else it would've defeated the purpose of their desired imprecision in the first place.

Donovan commented more than once that he thought their obsessive preoccupation—as he called it—with avoiding all things time related was rather ridiculous. It seemed to him that it would be easier to acknowledge the hour or date, rather than obsess about not doing so.

For Donovan, that might have been true. But it was now second nature for Jay and Leanne to carry on moment by moment, truly unaware of precisely where each moment fit into their timeline.

It was kind of like approaching a red light when driving. Some people just automatically stopped giving the vehicle gas when a light was red up ahead, wasting no energy or thought doing so. It happened almost instinctively.

But for others, thinking about that pedal movement in advance was a real chore. It felt like an added burden to have to look that far up the road and plan a response, all based on the colour of the light, a light that hadn't yet been reached. For them, it was better to think about it when they got there, or at least were a lot closer to it.

Jay used the traffic-light analogy on the last occasion he'd tried to talk to Donovan about their different attitudes toward time. Jay started the story envisioning himself as the driver who automatically reacts, who doesn't need to think about what to do with his foot rather far in advance of the light. Easing off the gas well before braking had always happened naturally when he'd had a car. No conscious thought or planning had been required so that approach felt more carefree to him.

But an interesting thing happened as Jay went through his little analogy. He began seeing things another way. Maybe the driver who reacts only when he gets to the light was him after all. Wasn't that person living more in the moment?

But as soon as he confused himself with that possibility, he was back to seeing his original view. Surely it was better to react almost subconsciously, instinctively sensing what was up ahead and rolling smoothly on, rather than having to consciously keep track of what had to be done later. It didn't matter if that was having to stop, or die.

On the other hand, there were times when planning was unavoidable.

Sitting at their kitchen table over breakfast the next morning, Jay was reading the paper while Leanne was focusing on her glass of orange juice. "Jay?"

"Hmm?"

"It'll go in the juice, right?"

"What will?" Even though he'd set down the newspaper, Jay's mind still hadn't made the shift.

"Your pills. Your way to let go when uh—"

"Ah. That. Yeah. In the juice. You've been reading?" While Jay had given his well-loved copy of *Final Exit* to Leanne, he had noticed other books and pamphlets lying around the house too. But it was a sensitive area, and one that he, after initially bringing up the subject, wanted Leanne to get to independently.

She had said she'd be there for him, but that didn't remove the need for a deeper understanding of all that would be involved, all that went into the decision, and all that was required in actually carrying it out. It was asking the profound and perhaps ultimate favour of her to share his death, so he would not be forced to die alone because of his choice to time it himself.

"I have been reading, as you know." Leanne glanced in the direction of the book-laden coffee table. "I think I never considered the process. No, I know I didn't. I mean, you know how scared of death I was as a kid, of losing loved ones—"

"I hate the term *losing*. It sounds so wrong," Jay said. "I'm sorry to interrupt. You were saying? But, man, I just hate that word."

"It's OK. I'm not so keen on it myself," Leanne said before continuing. "As scared as I've been, I never really thought about what if the dying part itself went badly. I was more focused on the dead-and-not-being-here part. Now I'm realizing how much I was ignoring how it would happen. It's so damn scary. There are so many bad ways for it to go."

"And no sign-up sheet that I know of"—he signed his name in the air—"for going to sleep one night and simply not waking up again."

"And that's why you're making your own. Can I sign up for it too?"

"I don't know, Lee. It's not right for everybody. My gut tells me you won't need to. I sure hope you won't have to help things along. But you'll know. You will, for you. As I know, for me—"

"It'll be in the orange juice." She was the one to interrupt this time.

Jay smiled at her. "Yeah."

Their conversation then turned to the specifics that would be involved. They talked about the required pills Jay had accumulated before he retired as a doctor, the cool dry place where they were stored, and the potency-degradation concerns as the pills aged. They discussed the potential legal consequences if Jay waited too long and wasn't able to do it all himself. They even came up with an alternative plan in case he was no longer able to swallow or keep powdered pills down. And they spoke of all the legal documents and letters confirming his wishes.

To reduce the chance of required police involvement or investigation into his death, Jay planned to visit his doctor, Dr. Barnes, at least every two weeks. That way, the doctor could sign the death certificate legally without an autopsy, even if he wasn't present at the death. Even though they considered him a friend, they didn't want anyone else there. Jay and Leanne wanted it to be just the two of them.

By making the appointments part of their regular routine, they wouldn't have to worry about scheduling a specific last visit to the doctor. That would mean too much advance notice. Jay and Leanne would have to know for almost two whole weeks that that was all that was left. Regular appointments ensured he would be ready to go when it was time, but without marking time to dwell on last days.

As the various details were checked off, their conversation turned from the personal to the more general. How sad it was that books like *Final Exit* had to be written in the first place, that help for humans wasn't available the way it was for other animals on their last legs, and that while suicide was legal, assisted suicide was not. "How can helping someone do something legal be illegal?" Leanne was completely perplexed.

That led to talk of religion, fear, politics, and slippery slopes. Advances in modern medicine had raised so many questions that the law hadn't seemed able to adequately answer yet. Talking about that bigger picture helped to carry them away from the smaller one they lived. The issues could almost become the seemingly remote ones that were talked about in the millions of homes where death still felt more theoretical than real.

CHAPTER EIGHT

THE CABIN WAS SMALL. It was just a room with a bed. Or perhaps it was more a bed with a room around it. The walls were made from rough-hewn logs, and there was an old wood stove in the corner that completed the quaint atmosphere of having stepped back in time. "This reminds me of what I used to build with my Lincoln Logs." Leanne admired the interlocking log corners, envisioning the cabin as one of her childhood constructions.

"I hope the roof on this thing is more solid than the little green wooden strips that went in the grooves of those logs. Or, I should say, 'logettes.' But this sure is something, much better than the main lodge building where we got the keys. That place felt way too modern. I mean, I think it even had indoor plumbing."

"Well, we might wish for that building in the middle of the night," Leanne said as she admired the old-fashioned quilt and cushions that adorned the place. They provided the only vibrant colour in the naturally log-brown cabin. Even the rag rug was an earthy, faded brown.

"Glad I'm a guy," Jay said ever so helpfully, grinning.

"Just call me Iron Bladder from now on. No way am I using leaves unless I absolutely have to. And I don't plan on walking half a kilometre in the the dark to get to the lodge either. We would have to choose the cabin farthest from civilization." Leanne laughed as she crossed her legs in anticipation.

"We did want rustic. And we got it. All the other cabins sounded too fancy, too new." Jay proceeded to unpack, which consisted of little more than unzipping the larger backpack and removing their clothes for the next day. He also took out his medicines for that night and the next morning, setting them by the bed.

Leanne checked out the small stove to see if she still remembered how to use wood burners from the time she spent at her grandparents' cabin as a child. It was too early to need to light the stove, but a good supply of wood lay next to it, ready to cast a flickering glow on those Lincoln Log walls later that evening.

"Whaddya say we start exploring them thar hills before dinner, Jay?"

"Got a hankerin' to get a feel fer yer land, do ya?" he replied in kind. It did feel as if they were staking claim to their own piece of undiscovered territory.

They set off for a short hike around their cabin and down to the nearby creek. Sitting on a large rock at the stream's edge, they soaked in the view of their temporary plot of land.

While they had hiked some of the lower trails around the base before, a number of springs had somehow come and gone since they'd first talked of camping overnight on the mountain.

And more recently, there was an aborted attempt to get there. A couple of months earlier a routine exam—as much as any appointment was routine for Jay—had turned up something disturbing. While not completely unexpected, it was scary all the same each time AIDS decided to rear its ugly head and show itself in a new way.

But Jay continued to take everything in stride the best he could, doing what was medically necessary, employing both conventional and alternative approaches. "I may as well hedge my bets." It also made him feel more proactive to do things besides just popping pills.

They made a point of trying to talk quickly about the details of tests and procedures, getting those conversations over with as much as possible. Sometimes, though, total resolution didn't come immediately, and they knew they would still have to talk about it more later. But until then, the subject was put on a figurative shelf.

They found this was a good working solution for getting back to normal life. Once something was put on the thought shelf for the day, it couldn't be brought down again until the next day, at the earliest. It was a little built-in forced break-and-relief system.

While Jay recovered from his latest foray into the vagaries of AIDS, he knew he was closer to dying. All his medical training told him AIDS was still too new a disease to expect a cure, or even great management in time to help him.

But in some ways, it was easier to deal with the dying part than the sick part. He could almost successfully pretend that he was some ancient guy who was dying of natural causes. Because either way, his body was wearing out, so ultimately what was the difference? What was the point of dwelling on the brutal specifics of the reason?

And on days when letting go was harder to do, there was always that shelf.

Now that Jay was feeling better once more, their camping trip was on again. Tomorrow they would hike up to the mountain's peak. Finally.

Once they got there, they planned to sleep under the stars in their cozy two-person sleeping bag. "Time to properly christen it," Jay had said when he packed it.

But already, fertile imaginations had been able to work wonders at home. That big sleeping bag had already seen many nights under the stars. It had just always been through the skylight in their living room. And a fireplace could make a fine substitute for a campfire in a pinch. But tomorrow night would be the real thing.

Jay and Leanne woke up feeling rather giddy and anxious to start their climb. They were the first ones in the lodge for breakfast. And after finishing quickly, they picked up the food they had ordered for their campout. "I still feel a little funny not getting all this stuff ready ourselves," Leanne said on their way out of the building. "It's as if we're cheating somehow."

"Given how last minute this trip was, there really wasn't time. And remember last time? We had all that camp food sitting at home while I was in the hospital. This way is better—just pick up and go. We can trick the damn disease into thinking we don't have any plans."

"So we're covertly sneaking off, huh? I like it." Leanne slung the heavier of their two packs onto her back.

It was automatic and accepted that Leanne was the muscle in the relationship now. "It's my turn, don't you think? We share everything we can," she had said to him a while back, when Jay's face first dropped upon seeing her do the manual tasks that he had always been the one to do. Putting her hands on his visibly withered shoulders, Leanne had added, "This is all just stuff. You will always be you."

The kiss that had followed was anything but withered. "Good thing my lips are still strong, Lee."

And now, after Jay put on his lightweight pack—with only his meds and their down-filled sleeping bag inside—they set off for the top of gently sloping Mount Bauldron.

They chose the winding, gentler trail for obvious reasons. But it was also the most scenic. Around every curve in the path was another little wildflower they'd never seen before, a miniature waterfall trickling over a few rocks, or some sun-dappled fern or bush. There was always something special to see. That also had the added benefit of giving them built-in rest breaks, which, while necessary, felt more like mere stops to enjoy the scenery.

They took a longer break for food when they were about two-thirds of the way up, according to the trusty little markers surreptitiously tucked away on stumps of old fallen trees. Unzipping their sleeping bag for use as a makeshift blanket, they had a picnic among the trees.

It was idyllic. And the significance of being up there together was not lost on either of them. They were lucky to have gotten there and they both knew it. But their conversation showed no signs of melancholy. Jay and Leanne had become masters of the moment.

As they resumed their trek up the mountain, there were times when they couldn't stop talking. Sometimes they chatted about what they were seeing or smelling, and other times it was more about what they were feeling. Joy was bubbling out of them.

But there were also moments when the joy was more internal and no words were spoken. And all the while they meandered along, there was a mix of touches, with arms linked, or hands held, or bodies just tucked in close together.

Although the mountain was not steep, their pace still slowed some as the day went on. Jay assured Leanne he was fine. It was the truth. He felt great. He was a little tired, and a bit sweaty and hot, but they were hiking after all, or at least their version of it.

And then they rounded the next bend and they were at the top. Off to the side of the lookout point was a flat, grassy area where they set up camp. They had opted for no tent. The forecast for warm dry weather, and part of the reason for wanting to be up there in the wild was to be in the open air. "And that means open all around," Jay had said when the people at the lodge learned of their plans.

As the sun set golden orange in the sky, there was a slight chill in the air. But it disappeared with the campfire Jay built with sticks and Boy Scout ingenuity, and the help of a match.

Dinner was the usual campout cuisine, save one exception. Instead of the traditional roasted wieners on a stick, they were having pizza. Neither were big fans of hot dogs, but pizza was another matter. So their perfect campfire food was going to be a simple veggie pizza with a thin crust, which cooked beautifully over their little fire. And the slightly burnt crust only added to its perfection somehow. "I think I've found a new use for our Hibachi back home," Leanne said, eating her last bite.

Jay was still chewing. "Mm-hmm."

It may have been their time in the wilderness, but they did bring one particular item from modern civilization, something that allowed them to be together in every way. While they didn't shy away from using the real words for things, they had come up with their preferred name for those female condoms. It seemed only fair there should be a slang term for them, as there was for the male version.

They'd toyed with calling their female rubbers "polys," since they were made out of polyurethane, but settled instead on "packages." The word could be variously interpreted so nicely. A package might be a gift, a protective enclosure, a wrapper, a little treat. "I'd call sex a rather big treat," Jay had said.

"Colossal I would say. And to continue with the slang theme, they are packages for my package to enjoy with your package."

Now, having finished dinner on the mountain, and with a package securely in place, they gave themselves their own gift. They made love under the stars. But this time there was no skylight barrier.

As they lay basking in the afterglow, Leanne said what she had said many times before after the post-coital warmth rushed over her. "Ahhhh, that surprises me every time. I can't describe it. It's like this amazing bonus—that's not even the word. There are no words. I feel as if I'm still swooning over a mind-blowing orgasm and then, right when I'm coming down from that, there's this little 'wow' moment out of nowhere, this feeling of such bliss, such peace, such awe. Oh, I can't explain it right."

"It sure sounds pretty good like that. You feel so, so everything, so you, so me, so us, so all," he tried to explain too. "You know, I think the right words simply don't exist to describe what I want to describe."

"I know what you mean, Jay, with or without words," Leanne mumbled as she grew drowsy. Not that it mattered. They both understood.

As the early morning dew began settling on the ground, the cool dampness caused them to stir. Sleeping outside, completely open to the elements, heightened their awareness of their surroundings. "And I thought sticking my head out the window before I closed it at night was something." Leanne inhaled the 4:00 a.m. air of the mountain. "But this, waking up like this, and the way it smells ... so sweet and green, a million more times of everything, as if free of all responsibility. With nearly everyone asleep and out of the way, the universe can quietly go about its business, recharging, letting all this freshness out in the process. At least it feels like that."

"And the light too, all dark except for that hint of a beginning sunrise over there." Jay pointed eastward to the wakening horizon. "It makes me feel as if we're witnessing the first dawn ever. It's that new."

"And yet it's gonna happen again tomorrow and again after that." Leanne marvelled at everything around her. "It is an amazing world."

"You got that right," Jay quietly echoed.

They then settled back into their warm sleeping bag and dozed off and on. It was difficult to tell when they were asleep and when they were half awake. Their hands seemed to keep on moving, touching, regardless of their state of consciousness.

There was something very special about being able to watch another person sleep. In between one of her dozes, Leanne watched Jay so completely at peace. His face, his hands, his whole body was totally relaxed. Leanne wished he could look that way all the time when he was awake.

Generally, he remained amazingly upbeat and strong. But there were still times when it definitely got to be too much for him, for both of them. There would be tears and rants and rages against the universe and its unfairness—everything from the obvious dying part to the added injustice brought on by AIDS.

What other disease tried so hard to take away one of life's most primitive and fundamental desires? An orgasm meant moments of freedom, a break during which reality was suspended. AIDS tried to deny people that. When comfort, closeness, and connection were needed more than ever, one was told to forever look at being alone in that most intimate physical way.

While Jay and Leanne had found ways to be safer—ways that had happily become just a normal part of their lovemaking—not everyone was so lucky to find someone willing to assume the risk. No matter how small, there was always a risk.

"But who completely knows anyway, Becky?" Leanne had asked when her friend began seeing someone new in London. "This guy, Brian, could have been exposed since his last test and not even know himself. But Jay and I do know, and we're always careful. Maybe in a weird way that's even safer."

Becky had not been too thrilled with that notion. It was a lot nicer to pretend scary stuff didn't exist. Leanne and Jay were too strong a reminder that it did.

On their mountain, as he crossed back into the world of the awake, Jay murmured, "Hey, you."

Leanne's thoughts were still on sleep, but sleep of a different kind. She kicked herself for making an unwanted connection to something Jay had once said. He had been talking about not wanting to suffer past his time. "Put to sleep" was how he had put it. Leanne tried to brush away the terrifying thought that it could come to that.

Now was not the time for such concerns. They belonged on that shelf instead. Their mountain was waiting. They were hiking down today.

"Hey, yourself," Leanne said, mustering the best smile she could. Her eyes gave her away.

Jay didn't have to know the specifics of what she wasn't saying to know the general direction her mind was trying to take her. Sometimes a hug, smile, or hand squeeze, or just getting moving and doing something, anything that distracted, was the quickest way back to the present. When no words were enough, using any almost seemed to prolong the agony.

"We better get a move on," Jay said as he unzipped the sleeping bag.

After eating, they gathered up all their belongings to leave the place unspoiled for some new campers to explore. Neither was too anxious to head back down the mountain.

There were still so many other trails and quasi trails left unexplored. And the vibrant smells seemed even stronger and more abundant with their lungs completely clear of non-mountain air. Not that tiny Clementine had any real air-pollution issues, industrial or otherwise, but up on the mountain the only industry at all came from industrious birds and squirrels.

Despite the very energizing nature of their current surroundings, Jay knew he still had to at least moderate his activity, especially given his increased exertion over the last couple of days.

With their adventure on Mount Bauldron nearing an end, their steps down the mountain were a little slower than the ones up had been. But it helped to know they would still have another night at their rustic cabin before they left the mountain altogether.

One of the things they saw no point in talking about was whether or not they'd ever return. No comments were made one way or the other. To have spoken of a "next time" would have felt disingenuous deep down. To say it was the "last time" would have felt too certain, and been damned depressing.

Instead, they talked about and celebrated every simple thing they saw as they wove their way around the uppermost trails before finally heading down.

They were making memories without any labels of time—no lasts, no firsts, no noting when they were there, just that they were there.

But about halfway down to the base, Jay started having a really hard time breathing. "Lee." He struggled to speak. "Gotta stop."

It wasn't the first time he'd had breathing troubles, but it was the first time when they were more or less cut off from civilization.

Pneumonia was one of the big concerns. They refused to use the full "*Pneumocystis carinii* pneumonia" name that was so connected with AIDS patients. When they didn't reduce the term to an impotent "it," they just used the more generic "pneumonia," preferring not to be so specific.

It wasn't so much because PCP was more heavily associated with AIDS than other types of pneumonia, as what the former infection meant for the bigger picture. His recovery from PCP was less likely and therefore it conjured up more dire consequences. But deep down, they both knew that any and every opportunistic infection that found its way into Jay was another sign his body couldn't go on forever.

"Is it like before?" Leanne thought back to what he'd been through at the hospital last time.

"Don't know. Don't think so. Not sure," Jay said in short bursts, grabbing for Leanne's hand.

Leanne helped him sit down on the ground since there was no nearby stump or rock. Trying to keep her own breathing in check, Leanne rubbed his back in an effort to help him relax to see if he could catch his breath. "It's OK. I'm right here."

Grabbing her right hand and clutching it, he held on as he forced himself to try to relax. Under different circumstances he would have laughed at the irony of trying to force relaxation.

"Close your eyes, Jay. Don't think about breathing, just focus on all the smells. Find the scent of pine warmed by the sun, and those blue wildflowers we can never re-member the name of, and the hint of skunk in the air. You smell that?"

Giving an almost imperceptible nod of his head, Jay started to loosen his grip on Leanne's hand. There were a few more scattered gasps as he tried to inhale, and then more when he exhaled, but they were starting to become less frequent.

"That's it, just keep smelling." Leanne continued to gently rub his back as she felt him relax into her.

After what was way too long by her nonnumerical count, Jay's breathing began to return to near normal.

"Rather prosaic, don't you think?" He finally spoke. "Dying after climbing to the top of a mountain."

"Doesn't count. This may be called Mount Bauldron, but this is no mountain. It's a hill. And it doesn't count then. You get no trite farewell on a hill, Jay. That's not allowed."

"It could be a really good way to go, though. Out here, where it's so fresh and alive. Because I don't feel so fresh and alive sometimes."

"Yeah, but think of all the mess you'd leave me with." Leanne wasn't about to let him get down now, especially since the immediate scare appeared to be over. "I'd have to hike down the rest of your mountain—my hill—all by myself. And I'd have to bring help back here to get your body. And there'd be all these questions about why we went up here in the first place if you were sick. It'd be a really big mess. You wouldn't want to leave me with all that now, would you?"

"Not when you put it like that. But this place—"

"I get it, Jay, I get it. And I agree with you. It would be a good way, relatively speaking . . . but not now. OK?" Leanne fought to keep her voice from shaking.

Jay felt awash with relief as he was finally able to exhale fully on his next breath. "Not now."

CHAPTER NINE

As it turned out, Jay had simply been out of breath from overexertion, just like any ordinary winded person. True, it took less for him to get that way, but it was still a relief. It was also a reminder how much the mind could overwhelm and create fear where none needed to be.

It may not have been the smartest thing to climb a mountain—even low-lying Mount Bauldron—and even less smart to sleep outside risking a chill, but no permanent harm had been done. And even if it had been, Jay knew he still wouldn't have changed a thing. He wouldn't have missed sharing the mountain escapade with Leanne for anything.

However, had he not known that she felt the same way, there would have been a measure of guilt to try to ignore. "I could have gotten permanently refreshed along with the night air," he joked later, "right into oblivion."

But some risks were worth taking, and none more so than the adventure begun a few years earlier in a park and continuing everywhere, with as few nods to its brevity as possible.

Sometimes that led them to sleep late into the day, and other times to be awake far into the night. They listened to their own variable internal rhythms, sleeping whenever they were tired and waking when they were not. Being awake in the middle of the night, or asleep during the day, had the added benefit of blurring the line between the two.

It became harder to keep track of the days, even if they had wanted to. And since they didn't want to, their changeable sleep patterns made it even easier to honestly have no idea how much time was passing. A cool day could be a typical fall or early spring day, a warm winter one, or a cold summer one. The mystery of exactly which was kept alive and well.

There was, however, one notable exception to consider. Christmas. The sentiment, decorations, music, and overall festive feel were too much to resist. It was such a giving time, and so peaceful when the quiet side of the holiday was allowed to seep through.

While they both considered themselves spiritual people, neither had chosen to follow any particular religion. It was with no disrespect that they chose to follow the secular traditions of the Christmas season and not the religious. They tried to be good and to live kind lives. And they hoped, to the point of belief, that there was indeed a force beyond their comprehension.

Loving Christmas, however, did have one downside. Even as relatively blissful children they had experienced the inevitable letdown every twenty-sixth of December. Although Jay's family hadn't spent as much time building up to Christmas as Leanne's had, he'd still felt that odd, unwanted feeling of having something you had so looked forward to suddenly being over. They knew that sense would be magnified a thousand times at least if they counted Christmases now.

Trying to ignore the holiday was ruled out. It would have meant not venturing out of the house for several weeks, perhaps even longer given the growing commercial hype of Christmas.

It was too noticeable an event not to be counted, despite their best intentions. Besides, neither of them could really bear to give it up anyway. Christmas was simply too special, and too much fun. They had shared traditions to keep alive now—like snow ice cream, and tacos for Christmas dinner.

"What if, instead, we have a whole bunch of extra Christmases?" Jay had a twinkle in his eye that would've made Santa Claus himself proud. "Whenever we want, just do Christmas. It'd be a beautiful mess to try to figure out how many we get that way."

"But we have to allow enough lead-up time to enjoy all the delicious anticipation," she said.

And so began another tradition for Jay and Leanne. If either of them started feeling particularly Christmassy, they'd pick a day for tacos and tree lights.

If their impromptu holiday happened to come when it was cold outside—but not officially Christmastime—a big evergreen branch from the backyard filled their house with scent, and was home to a few miniature lights and special decorations. Fresh boughs were also strewn about to make the house smell just right. The attic received special attention.

Their degree of decoration varied each time.

Sometimes going minimal was nice, especially when it came to taking the stuff down.

Other times, the attic looked like a forest had moved in. And strands of twinkly lights draped gently all around, supported by small hooks in the pine ceiling. Looking up at the illuminated dots and through the skylights beyond, it was almost as if they'd created another layer of stars.

If their Christmas came when it was warm outside, regular ice cream stood in for the snow variety, while a big houseplant made a valiant Christmas-tree substitute. One of their favourite plants to decorate was a big palm tree in the living room. Its sweeping leaves evoked the broad evergreen branches and held their lighter decorations perfectly.

It also seemed rather appropriate to go on the tropical side when they celebrated Christmas in warm weather. "After all, for places like Australia, Christmas is officially in the summer," Leanne said, adjusting her sunglasses while hanging the last string of coloured lights in their private backyard.

Even they weren't so crazy as to decorate the front of the house in the off-season. There was no need to encourage odd glances or unwanted questions.

As they lay in bed one night, Jay and Leanne had never felt more alive. After making love in every inventive way possible, a collection of used condoms was secured in the trash. But the trail of benign empty packets still lay strewn about. "Think we're keeping the condom companies in business, Lee?"

"Yeah, for both kinds of them too." She chuckled. "We could teach a class on condom management."

"Yes. 'Class, use the female kind if you do X,' well, XX literally." Jay earned a good-natured nudge in the gut.

"And use the male kind for one of my favourite oral activities," Leanne said. "You know it's funny, though, it never was a favourite before you. I must just have a taste for latex."

"Ouch." Jay feigned hurt feelings as they snuggled even closer together.

In those warm and perfect moments, wrapped up in each other, they felt nearly invincible, that nothing could threaten their bond. Their shared energy could sustain them forever.

On some occasions they lay in silence, absorbed by the surprising waves of sensations and emotions they felt wash over them. Other times, the mellow security of their bed led to more of those difficult conversations.

It was hard for Leanne to talk about her parents, not because of anything that happened, but because of what didn't. Her family had never talked about the important stuff, as far as she was concerned. "No life-and-death talk that's for sure," she told Jay. "If there's anything to that turning-over-in-a-grave bit, then they've both probably spun around so many times since we met that they've drilled right through their coffins by now."

"Nice graphic there, Lee." Jay said. But his expression remained serious. He could see from her face this joke was a delaying tactic. He knew how much not talking about something scary could make it even scarier. That was a big reason why he promised himself long ago to at least try to boldly face things he didn't want to. "Minimize the damage that way," he remembered out loud.

"Hmm?"

"Sorry, that brought back some memories. It can be tough to talk about some things, can't it?"

"It can be near impossible sometimes, Jay. The one time, well OK, it happened a bunch of times, but it was still the same one thing over and over." Leanne was starting to ramble as the difficult memory tried to ooze out.

Jay said nothing to interrupt the process as Leanne continued to try to explain. "I don't know how old I was exactly, probably six or seven judging by where we were living at the time. My childhood memories are pretty vague and sporadic since nothing traumatic happened or anything. So it's hard to remember what I actually remember myself, and not just what I remember being told happened, you know?"

Jay nodded.

"But I sure do remember lying in bed waiting for my parents to come in and say good night. All I could think of was how scared I was something was going to happen to them. But whenever I tried to talk about it, the subject was quickly redirected to happier things. I guess we found some sort of unspoken compromise. I just made them promise, every single night for I don't know how long, that they would not die that night. I mean, deep down, I knew they couldn't really make that promise, but it was enough reassurance that I could at least get to sleep then.

"It's funny, Jay, for all the not talking my family did about death, our one spoken thing said a lot. I never made them promise not to die at all, just not that night. And they never offered a longer guarantee either. I guess we all knew there was absolutely no way any of us could promise that, so best not to ask for it."

"So how did you possibly end up with me? Talk about a cruel twist of fate."

"You're telling me." Leanne almost laughed. But then, half asking, half demanding, she cried out, "Hold me!"

Sometimes it was all too real.

And then sleep, especially in those arms, allowed her to be able to face the world and their reality again.

Finding fun wherever they were or whatever they were doing created among other things, an unwritten mission that gradually developed, a silly ritual that resulted in many wonderful moments, and a lot of good food. Pizza. More specifically, making pizza in every way and place they could think of.

There would always be room for the odd delivery pizza when they felt the stationary travel bug in their attic "motel" room. But they were getting a kick out of playing with the preparation process themselves. And each pizza they made was different and yet deliciously familiar all at the same time.

Jay and Leanne had already cooked campfire pizza on Mount Bauldron. And while that may not have been particularly original, some of their later barbecued versions bordered on the more bizarre.

They turned one of the empty paint buckets from their attic renovation into a hibachi-inspired makeshift grill. Once all signs of paint had been removed, the metal container made a really great holder for charcoal, crumpled newspaper, and dry sticks from the backyard. A cooling rack fit nicely on top, even creating classic grill lines.

Sometimes they would cook frozen mini pizzas on their paint can, but more often than not, they'd try some homemade variation. But the toppings were oddly predictable. Once they had their favourites, it could be hard to give them up. So usually they went with plain cheese, or green peppers and onions. Occasionally they topped one with fresh basil for their version of pizza Margherita.

But the sauce and crust were always fair game. The tomato sauce could be full of different spices, or kept simple with just a bit of garlic. The crust could be made using a bit of leftover bread dough, or by following an actual pizza crust recipe. And other times the crust was whatever they had around—a piece of toasted bread, a pita pocket, or a tortilla.

Pizza-specific cookbooks made up half of their recipe collection and were great for inspiration when they grew bored with their own ideas.

Another old paint can nobly served as an ice bucket for something sparkling. Whether the fruit juice was fermented or not, the bubbles still delightfully tickled their throats. The two adults enjoyed the sensation every time with childlike abandon.

Pizza making moved indoors when the temperature dropped. True to form, Jay and Leanne avoided speaking in terms of seasons. Where once Leanne had relished the fall and found peace in seeing the cyclical change of the seasons, it would now have been too hard to see them ticked off in a poignant countdown. Noting the change of one season into the next felt as if they were rushing the tally.

The fact they'd been living without calendars made it all the easier to be oblivious to the seasons. It wasn't that they could force themselves to forget them exactly, but they could not try to remember.

So when it was too cold to cook outdoors—whenever that happened to be—the two-person pizza party moved indoors where there were different delights. They loved their old house, and the kitchen was no exception.

They especially loved the old farmhouse-style wooden table in the main part of the room. They'd found it abandoned in the basement. Cuts and wear marks were evident from many decades of use. But the wood was also worn smooth in places from the many hands that had touched it.

The kitchen counters were marble and not so prone to wear. Their beautiful stone veins and swirls were almost like drifting clouds that seemed to transform into different images with every glance. Using one of those marble tops, Jay and Leanne were having a rip-roaring time with their latest pizza.

To the accompaniment of some vintage jukebox hits, they were taking turns slapping a ball of dough onto the stone surface. Kneading it a bit each time, the dough was becoming stretchy and smooth. Whether it was to Bill Haley and his "Shake, Rattle and Roll" or Fats Domino's "I'm Walkin'," the dough hit the counter in rhythm.

Parts of their little dough dance saw the crust-to-be bouncing back and forth between them in time to the music. For other steps, one danced on the spot or bopped around the table, while the other transformed the ball into a disc.

As they let the dough rest, Jay and Leanne danced around the kitchen as if they were at a classic sock hop.

"I definitely got born at the wrong time," she said as Tommy Edwards' "It's All in the Game" track came on.

They fell into a swaying slow dance. "I love 'em all, a century ago when this house was built, the fifties when this song came out, and especially," he whispered in her ear, "right now."

"Oh yeah, but it's still too bad we missed out on the whole rock 'n' roll era." Leanne rested her head on his shoulder. "I'd have looked great in chiffon."

"That would've been like crazy, baby," Jay said with a silly grin. "And can you see me with one of those hip ducktails?"

"I can dig it, man. You'd have been one cool cat."

The nostalgic trip down memory lane for a time they never knew continued until the song ended. The return to upbeat pizza-throwing music saw them finishing the dough preparation and then applying the toppings.

As the last of the grated mozzarella was being placed, "That'll Be The Day" came on. Jay and Leanne finished bopping around the kitchen, joining Buddy Holly as he sang "'Cause that'll be the daaay when I die."

Both hearing and singing that last word had a strangely positive effect. It took out the remaining sting the word still sometimes held for them, turning it into just another word of a song—one that rolled off the tongue even more easily thanks to the music.

CHAPTER TEN

ECKY WAS PREGNANT—with that guy she'd met in London. Jay could hear Leanne's squeal of delight from the other room when Becky called to tell her the news.

An hour later, and with a sore ear, Leanne emerged from the downstairs bedroom to tell Jay she was going to be an honorary aunt. Jay already had a bottle of sparkling apple juice and two champagne glasses set out on the coffee table.

"I guess you heard." Leanne laughed as she joined him on the couch.

"I think the whole neighbourhood heard, Lee. When is she due?"

"In about seven months. They're both just thrilled. They weren't exactly trying, but they weren't exactly not trying either," Leanne said.

"That's just great. I'm really happy for them. They getting married?"

"Yeah, but they decided to elope. I guess our private version rubbed off on them a little bit, at least as far as size goes."

"Our non-wedding, yes." Jay smiled at her. "But they're making it legal, huh? Good for them. I can see it."

"Me too. She was so excited about not only becoming a mother, but a wife now too. Her childhood dream is coming true all at once, white gown and all. It's what every little girl is supposed to want. You can see why I felt so out of place, Jay."

"Until I ran into you, literally. No 'till death do us part' for us."

"It still amazes me." Leanne shook her head in wonder.

"What?" He could guess, but it was nice to hear, to savour how lucky they'd been in the most important way.

"That you exist, that I do. That we exist at the same time. And that we found each other," she said.

Jay and Leanne toasted with their fake champagne.

They no longer drank any alcohol. Jay figured if there was even a chance it could interfere with any of his meds, it wasn't worth the risk. Fizzy bubbles were fizzy bubbles. "Besides, this way, Lee, we can guzzle the stuff if we want and still find our way to the bedroom."

They toasted again. This time it was to the two people—soon to be three—on the other side of the Atlantic.

Later, during their evening stroll, the subject of babies came up again. It was a topic that could have been touched on many times before. A perfect opportunity to broach the subject presented itself every time they saw a baby or toddler in the park, at the beach, in the grocery, or any number of other places.

They had made quiet comments on observed behaviour, good and bad. They shared the belief that both were largely thanks to the parents.

Sometimes they'd notice how much seemed to be going on behind a little one's eyes. "Talk about taking it all in," Jay often remarked with wonder.

For a couple of reasons probably, they'd never talked of babies in the personal sense, never of their babies, of the ones that wouldn't be. But they'd come close. Sometimes after safely disposing of a used and ironically then dangerous condom, there were postcoital murmurings, and brief yet longing looks as potential seed was just tossed away.

Perhaps they were being overly cautious. Science was indeed advancing all the time, so maybe a workaround could be found. But the soothing afterglow never seemed to be the right time to discuss it. That was for either pillow talk or harsh-inevitability talk, not for adding more potential things to be sad about.

And when fully awake, Jay's overriding instinct for Leanne's preservation above all else, coupled with her understanding of that, kept them silent on the subject. Faraway looks of a previous night's melancholy were forgotten, overridden by the "nearaway" looks of a new day.

Now with a real live baby on the way—one who would be part of their small inner circle—baby talk took on another feel. Some people got babies, some found true love, some settled, some got companionship, some were alone, but no one got everything they wanted.

And whether actually true or not, Jay and Leanne felt as if they were the luckiest people ever, each having said to the other, "No one else has you." Big picture, they'd gotten far more than their share of the good stuff. That tempered the cheated feeling they also felt when they saw things like babies, or rocking chairs on a front porch.

As they walked along, the cool night air mixing with the last remnants of the day's heat, Leanne couldn't resist saying again, "That really is something about Becky and Brian." The news kept spinning around in her head and was viscerally more intense because it was happening to someone she loved.

"It sure is. I wonder what they're feeling right now. I mean, I can imagine," he said as his own head did some spinning. "Imagine if it were us . . ." Jay swung their joined hands as they walked along. It was almost as if they were parents swinging their child between them.

Swinging their arms higher, Leanne asked a question she was afraid would break both their hearts to hear spoken out loud. "Jay, you want a child, don't you?"

"I want a lot of things, Lee. Most of all to keep on having you. But yeah, I do. Or I should say, I always did," he corrected himself.

"There are other ways to have children. Don't eliminate the possibility completely."

"No." Jay slowly shook his head. "Don't think I'm trying to be some kind of martyr here, but I couldn't knowingly ask a child to grow up without a father. Forget not seeing him graduate from high school, we're likely talking me being lucky to make it to preschool."

"Don't talk like that, Jay. That sounds way too much like time counting." Knowing in the semi-abstract that their time was limited was one thing, seeing it thrown in front of her took it to a whole other level.

"Well, there are times, much as we may hate it, when it's pretty hard to be completely oblivious to time. But before you go thinking I'm a counting convert, that's not the only reason I said I did want children, past tense. Speaking selfishly, I don't think I could handle taking care of a child as well as taking care of myself now. I know that must sound bad. It does sound bad, but—"

"No, it doesn't. It sounds sad." Leanne hesitated before saying, "And true. Maybe I'll regret it someday, but when it comes down to it, I'm selfish too. I wouldn't want to take time away from being with you, not for anything else. For no one else," Leanne added guiltily.

"Maybe we just know our limits, Lee." Jay gave their hands another swing. "And besides, if I weren't sick, I know something else too. We would not be having this conversation. We'd be picking out paint colours and baby booties."

They continued to gently swing their joined hands as they walked along.

Before they went to bed, they occasionally watched television reruns their way—by candlelight. "We've got the best of both worlds," Jay said one night as he set down the remote, "newfangled TV and old-fashioned candles." Maybe it was their mutual love of the simpler approach to life—which they perceived the past to be—but it was easy to forget the hardships and struggles to survive of those who actually lived the life portrayed on shows like *Little House on the Prairie*.

The romantic notions of a bygone era overshadowed the harsh realities of those earlier times. But one thing that could not be disputed about life a century or more before, was that lives were usually lived much closer to birthplaces. And if a person did venture forth—as Jay had when he came to Clementine—the new landing spot was likely to be permanent. Distances were more daunting when travelled by horse instead of horsepower. For Jay, his destination wasn't by default but by pure choice.

Leanne, however, had been born in Clementine and moved away as a young adult. First it was for university and then for work, but most important of all, going away told her she wanted to come back. Living in other places gave her the confidence to return to Clementine, knowing it was not out of fear or a need for the familiar, but a genuine desire to be there.

And neither of them wanted to be anywhere else, even temporarily.

Friends would sometimes talk of their travels abroad, but they never directly brought up the subject of why Jay and Leanne did not travel. It wasn't because they understood, but because they thought they already did. They automatically assumed that Jay's condition prevented it, not realizing the two had different reasons. Even Becky and Donovan refrained from bringing up the matter, out of a combination of their own discomfort and the belief there was nothing to be gained.

From Jay and Leanne's vantage point, it was just another thing that set them apart from the rest of the world. But there was no resentment, no desire to try to make their friends see their side of things. Instead, it only increased the feeling of gratitude for having found someone who did understand.

Maybe it wasn't always the healthiest way to live, being so exclusionary and introverted toward everyone except each other, but they couldn't help it. For all their dismissals of time counting, there was always a subtle awareness of the frailty and briefness of life. If they most wanted to just be with each other, why should they give up any moment of it?

They only had one reservation. What would Leanne do when Jay died?

And there was no denying that Jay's health was deteriorating more quickly now. They didn't need test results and numbers to tell them that. But rather than focusing on what complications Jay did develop, they tried to focus more on what he did not. Most significantly, his mind had been unaffected. For Jay, AIDS-related dementia was the scariest of all the possibilities. Not only for the obvious reasons, but because it would also make deciding when to exit all the more difficult, if not completely impossible.

Having a living will and durable power of attorney for health care at least stated his clear intentions, confirming what he did and did not want done, but neither could cover active euthanasia, only the passive withholding of treatment. Still, it was the best that could be done.

The irony did not escape them that despite all their distaste for measuring time, Jay getting the timing right with that one decision was beyond crucial. It was life and death altering.

Jay also wrote an official suicide note, as he unfortunately knew it would be named were it ever needed as evidence. But he preferred to call it what it really was—a self-euthanasia note.

Suicide was defined as "killing oneself," and as far as he was concerned, that implied giving up on life, as if death were somehow avoidable in the near future. And it also tended to be an act done secretly and without the support of loved ones.

Euthanasia, on the other hand, quite literally meant "good death." Why society had such a problem with the idea was lost on Jay. Though he did have to admit that during his so-called invincible days, the idea of choosing to check out early would have never seemed "good" to him. It was amazing how perspective could change when something left the abstract and became personal.

While only Leanne knew every little detail, Dr. Barnes did have some idea from conversations with his patient. Preliminary discussions on the subject had been part of the first medical meeting Jay had had with his then prospective doctor. Although they shared similar views, no one would overstep the law. And Jay's appointments every other week—for medical and legal reasons—had indeed become routine.

The long-distance calls with his parents were largely spent exchanging updates back and forth on everything but health. There would, of course, be the opening how-are-you interrogatives, but "fine" always seemed the best approach if Jay wanted the conversation to continue at all comfortably. And outliving their son was about as far away from comfortable as they could get. But despite all that wasn't said, Jay understood what was behind their more forceful "good" than a reply of "fine" ordinarily warranted. Once Jay said that four-letter F-word, he could hear the relieved exhale a continent away.

Aside from Donovan, Becky, and by extension her family, Jay and Leanne had few close friends. But even the more casual ones had heard Jay say, "That's not going to happen to me" or "That won't be me." However, those statements could be interpreted in different ways. It was easier for them to believe he was just trying to be optimistic and thinking positively about his health. But on some level, they knew too, given their responses, or lack of them.

While Jay had clearly felt better in the past, he was still enjoying life. As his condition changed, so did their lives, but Jay and Leanne were still together and wanted to relish that. Although not always successful, they tried to take another lesson from the supposed lower animals. Not only was euthanasia commonplace for animals ailing beyond a certain point, but they also embodied the ability to accept whatever is, instead of begrudging what was.

So now, while old rock 'n' roll songs played, Jay instead sat and swayed to the music, tapped his foot, or on his more energetic days, waved his arms in the air like a bit of a madman. He tried to let go of the fact he used to do a full-on pizza-making dance in the kitchen. He was still with Leanne, still in their kitchen, and still being transported by Fats Domino and Tommy Edwards.

Infections came and went and came again. It seemed at times that no part of his body was to be spared. For a while, Jay had been able to block out most of the pain from all facets of the disease and treatment. "It's only my brain telling me it's received certain neural messages," he rationalized. "It's up to me what I do with those signals. I choose to ignore them. Fine, body of mine, you've notified me, but there's nothing I can do about it, so shut up and quit reminding me." He fought his growing impatience. "Stop sending me those damn messages! I hear you, and now I'm going to ignore you."

But that intellectual approach didn't always work, even with the help of pain pills. Sometimes the agony got to be too much, too constant and unabating to bear. And medically knowing what was to come only added to the bleakness of the situation. "Why did I have go to medical school anyway?" he muttered in his weaker moments when he yearned for ignorance.

Jay had made it as far as the couch. Aside from frequent trips to the bathroom, he had remained there all day.

When he was first diagnosed with cryptosporidiosis he had tried to joke about the parasitic infection. "That seems like a good name for it, since it could send me to my crypt."

Dr. Barnes had tried to appreciate the humour, but he wanted to focus his patient on the course of treatment. It was vitally important Jay get rehydrated and correct his electrolyte imbalance, and that he stay that way. All that could really be done for the pain was to try to manage it. It didn't help that swallowing was becoming difficult at times. If it wasn't one problem, it was a bunch of others.

Leanne had learned to read his planes of pain, as they called them, and she could judge his stamina and mood pretty well. She knew how hard to push and when to just hold him, or leave him alone.

After she gave him his latest round of fluids, he was starting to feel a little better, at least physically. His mood was another thing entirely. Even the positive and proactive Jay had his bad days.

"Come on," Leanne said as she set his jacket beside him. "Put on your coat. We're getting out of here."

"Wait." Jay didn't move. "I can't."

"No, we have to. We've got to get out of this place for a while. We've been cooped up in here for way too long. If I can't take it anymore, there's no way you can. I can see the tension in your whole body, Jay. You might as well have stayed in the hospital this time. I thought the deal was only brief stays and then back to living. Come on, we're not going far, but as my grandpa used to say, 'Let's get the stink blow'd off.' So get dressed, and let's go breathe some fresh air, feel some life."

Their walk was more of a shuffle. They only went as far as their front porch, but it was doing the trick. He gradually relaxed into the glider as Leanne moved it gently back and forth. Once more, Jay was brought back to himself despite his body.

Finally he spoke. "I hear the wind in the trees. That little bird's really chirping away. And the neighbour kids are out playing and laughing."

"And smell—"

"Oh yeah, Lee, the smells, the fresh-cut grass, and the hint of salt air and seaweed."

"And don't forget the best part."

"The smell of french-fry grease." Jay inhaled as deeply as he could. "Never."

Even though they rarely indulged in such fare anymore, the deep-fry smell from the nearby beach concession stand still triggered nostalgic taste buds. Focusing on that simple thing was making the day better. His stomach and throat were calm now, allowing him to enjoy the present smell, as well as the many memories associated with it from when he felt better.

There were other good days after that. Occasionally, they even walked the short block to an old wooden bench that overlooked the beach. It may not have been Jonathan Park's fallen-tree seat, but at least it was wood and not the concrete kind that seemed to be popping up everywhere.

Jay and Leanne reminisced some, but mostly they were still trying to make new memories.

One warm afternoon, sitting on that bench, Jay took Leanne's hand in his left. Slowly raising their joined hands to his lips, he began fragilely kissing her palm with all the passion and love he felt inside. All eyes were closed. "I'm making love to you right now," he whispered.

"I can feel it," Leanne whispered back. Time didn't freeze, but it at least cooled down in that moment.

Becky was coming for a visit to introduce both her husband, Brian, and their new daughter, Lissa, to Becky's family in Clementine. It had been a long time since her welcome-back party, which came in the midst of Jay and Leanne's box-of-remains discussion. Phone calls made it feel as if everyone already knew each other, but now they could all see each other face to face.

Day to day, the changes in Jay weren't usually too noticeable, but jumping big chunks of time accentuated how much things had really progressed. Becky's motherly reassurance skills were put to the test when they came over to see Jay and Leanne. But this time, it wasn't Lissa waking from a nightmare whom she was telling, "Everything will be all right," it was herself.

Becky wasn't prepared for the lesions she saw all over Jay's skin, especially those on his once flawless face. His withered frame made him look as if he'd been "through the wars" as they used to say, which Becky guessed, he really had been. If Jay hadn't been there leaning on Leanne, Becky really didn't think she'd have known who he was.

Miraculously, it didn't seem to Becky that Leanne had noticed the changes. She was still looking at him with the same adoring and joyful eyes Becky had witnessed years before. "I don't know how she does it," Becky said quietly to Brian.

"He's so—" Brian started to say before Leanne came within earshot. They wouldn't dream of consciously hurting their friends' feelings, but the shock was still evident.

As the evening wore on, though, their discomfort lessened. They started to hear the familiar Jay more than see the unfamiliar sight. It wasn't quite like before, as certain thoughts kept creeping back in, but it was a good visit overall.

Phone calls, letters, and the odd email were great, but there was something special for Leanne and Becky about being in the same room again.

And best of all, Jay and Leanne had now met Lissa, who was every bit the wonder they'd heard all about.

Later that evening as they were lying in bed, they were talking about the visit. "I don't think Becky and Brian quite knew what to make of me." Jay wasn't upset so much as sad about the whole situation.

"You are so beautiful," Leanne said sincerely, and Jay accepted the same way. "But I guess I should have described things better." She gently stroked his face. "It's just that I don't think about that when we're talking about you. We get going about all the good stuff, and I don't think about describing this lesion or that infection, or that you're on your way to being half the man you used to be." It was easier for them to joke than focus on the reasons for his pronounced weight loss. "It's kind of like you with your parents, a 'fine' suffices for the icky stuff, and then Becky and I move on to other things."

"You know," Jay said, thinking of his mother and father, "that'd be really hard if I didn't know I could say and share all the icky things with you, Lee. Maybe it's crazy, but being together makes what goes on in the outside world not matter in the same way. Not really. I mean, I care, but, it doesn't get to me the way it did before."

"Forget AD or BC."

"Yeah. How about AU or BU?" Jay proposed. "After us or before us." Momentarily the more familiar meaning of AU flashed through Jay's mind—alternate universe, and maybe one that went on forever.

"But, God"—she caught the irony of her word choice—"that sounds arrogant to hear, doesn't it? Before or after us, just who are we?"

"Just that," Jay said. "We're just us. Two people who found each other and are lucky beyond belief."

His words had become quieter and were growing more laboured. Before turning off the light, Leanne removed her gloves and safely discarded them. It may have been overkill—another of their moment lighteners—but they always erred on the side of caution when touching any open sores. And sometimes, it was just nice to be gloved so Leanne knew she was free to touch him wherever she wanted, without having to think about it at all.

CHAPTER ELEVEN

THE BOTTOM OF THEIR figurative roller coaster seemed to grow lower, and last longer, with each descent. The latest valley was bad. Not just physically, but the way Jay reacted to the latest complication.

He couldn't explain it. He felt really mad at the world, and more like the hateful, screaming, pissed-off person he was when first diagnosed with HIV many years before. He'd been mercilessly and tearfully angry at the needle that had slipped and punctured his skin, at himself for letting it happen, at the patient who had infected him, and just plain angry at the whole damn disease.

But that's not where he was anymore. And he hadn't been for a long time, which only added to his angry irritation now.

He was also mad that he was mad.

But instead of shouts or tears as he revisited thoughts and feelings he'd thought were long past, Jay got himself into a real pout. It was perfectly understandable, but no less discouraging.

Since meeting Jay, Leanne had read a lot about dying and what it felt like on both sides of the drama. In a perverse way, she sometimes wondered if they were living a sort of cruel experiment to see what happens when two people—destined for each other—were thrown together only to be torn apart. And just who was watching this unfold? Who was getting some sort of twisted kick out of it?

Neither of them actually believed a sadistic joke was intentionally being played on them by some omnipotent overseer, but sometimes it felt as if there simply had to be someone to blame.

Leanne knew Jay better than she'd ever known anyone else. Sometimes she even felt she knew him better than she knew herself. There were situations where her own reaction surprised her more than Jay's. So it was no surprise to her that he was in his current funk over the latest medical time-out.

What was a little surprising to Leanne, however, was her own terming of his life-and-death angry mood of late, as a funk. But then again, minimizing the significance of certain bad things made them more manageable. Blissful ignorance was still sometimes an admirable goal.

Jay had not left the attic since he'd gotten home from his latest hospital stopover. Other than the few requisite trips to the bathroom, he hadn't even left their bed. And those brief forays into movement had been more staggers than walks.

It was due not only to physical weakness, but a rebellious desire to complete the poor-me picture. Even if no one else was in the room to see it, a little part of him felt better for having asserted himself, even if it was in this self-pitying way. It was a little "so there, I told you I was sick" statement.

Leanne was attending to her bookkeeping work in her office downstairs when the intercom alerted her to movement in the attic.

It wasn't actually an intercom system, but a renamed baby monitor. It was a way for her not to worry that she would miss hearing him if he needed something and, at the same time, he wouldn't have to feel as if she were hovering. "I won't be able to really rest or sleep if I know you're watching me, waiting for my every breath. Now go and play with those numbers," Jay had said after they got the radio setup, nudging her not to become his ever-present caregiver.

As Leanne came upstairs upon hearing him stir, she gently asked, "How'd you sleep?" She set down a basket with his meds, some food that was easy to eat, and something else she'd show him later.

Despite his voice being stronger than it had been, Jay snapped, "Lousy, thanks. And all those medicines you've got there suck. What good do they do? Still have AIDS, don't I?"

"Well, you do look better anyway," Leanne calmly said, "even if you don't particularly sound like it."

Silence. No reply.

It didn't surprise Leanne. She understood where this, and earlier outbursts in the week, had come from. But Jay wasn't doing himself any good by wallowing in self-pity.

"So," she carried on, "I had an idea earlier, and I know it's rather juvenile, but silly fun always has its place, don't you think?"

"Whatever," Jay grunted. "I'm in no position to argue."

"Well, you are in a rather submissive position."

"If that was your idea, Lee, you can forget it. I'm in no condition to—"

"Give me a little credit, Jay. Besides, since when is sex a child's activity? And this"—Leanne reached into the basket she'd put on the floor—"is." She presented him with one of their latex gloves blown up and tied off to make a five-fingered balloon.

"Leanne," Jay groaned.

"Don't Leanne me. Stupid fun is exactly what the doctor . . . well . . . what I order for the doctor. Besides, aren't you the one always saying to see the humour in things, to laugh, not cry?"

"But it's a waste of a perfectly good glove. We might need it."

"See? You must be feeling better. You're planning for the future," Leanne said with a sense of victory.

Jay glared at her, feeling both annoyed and grateful.

Before he could react any further, Leanne tossed the inflated glove to him. He halfheartedly tossed it back to her. In silence, they kept casually patting the thing back and forth.

"How'd you blow this up anyway? The opening is so big," Jay said finally.

"It wasn't easy I tell you. Just be glad I didn't do as I first considered and fill it with water."

"Of course, now that I think about it, you do like things big, Lee."

"Ah, that's my Jay."

"So, water, huh? Maybe we can try these glove balloons that way in the summer."

"My Jay is back."

"That is, if I'm still—"

"Fine," Leanne acquiesced, letting him hold on to some of his remaining pout. "If. But for now, would you care for the more adult version?"

As she reached down into the basket again, Jay was getting curious. "Just what have you got there?"

Upon seeing this particular balloon, his body erupted in a relative burst of laughter, releasing a wealth of pent-up emotions. It felt so good to them both. And it was all thanks to one inflated condom.

"I've never seen a condom stretched that big," Jay said when he got his laughing and breathing under control. "I must apologize for that, sweetie," he joked.

But Leanne took the opportunity to be serious instead. It was hard to tell whether it was out of a desire to make it clear in words—and not just through actions—something that was beyond blatantly obvious, or if it was more a symptom of the swirling mix of emotions in her head. For all her focus on lightening his mood, perhaps in this instance, she missed the humour herself.

She was so tied up in knots as she felt time running out. "Don't you dare apologize, not ever. That's something you've never had to worry about. I said it long ago, way before I even saw, well, before we ever had any need for these things." Leanne glanced at the cylindrical balloon. "You've always been perfect for me."

Switching gears as well, Jay grew serious too, and ridiculously obvious as far as he was concerned. "You're the one who's perfect."

"No, I'm not," she said. "But how about we settle on we're perfect for us?"

"Deal." Jay kissed the back of her right hand, closing his eyes just as if it had been a kiss fully on the mouth. The sentiment was the same.

"Oh, Jay." Leanne closed her eyes for another reason. She was willing time to stop.

When it didn't, she leaned over and kissed him gently on the lips. Circumstances meant there was no longer the deep kissing there once was. But their lips were locked, holding still. The almost innocent pressing together of their tender skin sent waves of love and deep-seated passion through them both.

When they gingerly broke apart, he tried to express his gratitude for her bringing him back to himself once more. "Thank you for . . . well . . . everything. Words . . . not enough . . ."

"I know, love, I know," Leanne said. "And hey, that's what partners are for. Team Us. Besides, we can all use a helping hand now and then."

While the depression may have lifted, pain and tiredness was descending again on Jay. Leanne had another idea—one they would both enjoy. "Speaking of hands . . ." She reached under the covers to touch him. He startled slightly at the unexpected contact. While not an unusual activity, the suddenness of her movement was, given his exhausted condition.

"Lee—"

"No need to worry. No cuts on my hand. Consider this a new form of organic pain management."

Getting more on board with her idea by the second, Jay said, "Don't you mean orgasmic pain management?"

"If I do it well anyway," she teased.

"And that's not something you've ever had to worry about. You've always . . ." Jay lost his train of thought. "Uhh . . . ohhh . . . your touch . . . God . . . your . . . can't talk . . . so good . . . just . . . more . . ."

Then, before nearly long enough, there was that smell again. Familiar but always unwelcome, the scent of disinfectant mixed with sickness filled the air. Jay was back in the hospital.

Despite being so ill, he had fought sleep upon hearing the latest news from Dr. Barnes. But his body had other ideas, and at last he was sleeping.

Leanne moved from his bedside to look out the room's small window. Gripping the sill, she stared blankly ahead. She soon allowed her head to fall and hit the glass, keeping it pressed against the cool surface.

Still expressionless, she finally looked up, and whether from her own exhaustion or a vain attempt to forestall the truth of her words, she spoke with almost no sound. "It's going to happen. It's actually going to happen."

After taking another moment emptily gazing out the window, Leanne moved back toward the bed. Sitting on the edge of it, she just looked at him, seemingly so peaceful at rest. Long-fought sleep was his temporary escape.

She slowly lay down with him. Her arms encircled his shrinking frame, and she let her tears fall as she closed her eyes.

Until she joined him in sleep, Leanne kept murmuring in his ear, reminding herself he was still alive. Talking would surely keep him there. One way conversation or not, she knew their communication continued.

Their sleep brought a duet of dreams that echoed their thoughts of a day that seemed so long ago, when relationship doubts and fears had filled their heads as they each made a solitary trip home from Dufferin's Diner.

Now, as they slept, Leanne's mind agonized. "How am I going to do this?"

For Jay, "I feared this from the beginning."

"He's been sick before, but never like this. There was really something different about him this time."

"Is this really the proverbial beginning of that proverbial end? Is this what it's gonna be?"

"How can I ever go back to the life I had before, before we met those years ago? I was happy then, complete in myself. Why does it feel so empty now to think of that?"

"We knew this was going to happen. I'd get sick beyond the point of recovery. I'd leave her just as I said I would those years ago."

"I can't do this. But I have to. I promised. Oh, can I please run off screaming now?"

"She'll be OK. She has to be. She promised."

"Seeing him like this, and knowing what's ahead so soon, it all staring me so viciously in the face, this vile disease . . ."

"I want to be there for her, help her deal with this, help her through it. But how can I now?"

"We've gotten through so much together. I feel so separated from him right now. I don't understand. I hate this. I really can't do this. This can't be the end."

"Why can't I be with her? I feel fine right now. In fact, I haven't felt this good in years. Why is that? It's so weird. I don't understand. Why can't we walk away from all this together? Why can't we have more time? Please. Why do I feel as if I'm drifting away somehow?"

Jay woke first. It was a shock. Not that he woke up, but the way he felt as he did. For the first few moments he couldn't understand where he was. And then when he figured that out, he wondered what he was doing in a hospital bed. Was he sick? He'd been feeling great, walking and running around like . . . like he used to. It all started coming back. He'd been dreaming.

Leanne stirred as soon as Jay's breathing changed from sleep mode. She was still surrounding him from behind.

Jay held on to her hands, which were clasped tightly in front of his chest. He struggled to speak. "Lee? Take me home." Then came a slow, laboured breath. "I wanna go home."

"Yeah." It was all Leanne could say as she buried her face in the back of his neck.

"Thank you."

Even with Donovan's help, it had been a bit of a challenge to get Jay up to bed. It would have been far more practical to switch over to the downstairs bedroom. But that was not their bedroom, and there, in the attic, was the only place Jay wanted to be.

Donovan had been treated to Jay's still-intact macabre wit when he'd repeated the downstairs suggestion. "You gonna deny a dying man his final request there, Van?"

Leanne stood quietly by as the two friends had one of their last conversations. This was Jay's battle—his stand against the disease. It may have been only a room assignment, but it was his choice to make. She was very grateful that despite all the ravages of the disease, at least his mind had indeed been spared. "Please don't let that change," she pleaded silently.

Later that day, with a grand flourish, Leanne pulled a bag of cheese puffs out of their memorabilia box beneath the bench seat. "I thought in honour of the occasion of you being back where you belong—"

"Don't know if I can—"

"Already thought of that," Leanne interrupted. "That's why it's puffs not chips. There's no irritating chewing required since they're almost all air anyway. And you used to joke about them practically dissolving in your mouth. Well, let's take advantage of that now."

Leanne crawled into bed beside Jay. Being propped up on brightly coloured cushions made it feel more like a lounge seat than a sick bed. Trying for further normalcy, she reached for the TV remote.

Wheel of Fortune was on, and the familiar clicking of the spinning wheel allowed them both to sort of zone out. The puzzle solving taxed their brains just enough to keep them from thinking about other things for a bit.

They sat in unusual silence. Normally, whenever they watched the show, they called out crazy guesses. It was fun to see what silly phrases they could come up with that still fit whatever was showing of the puzzles. Other times, they actually tried to get the right answer. Once, Jay had guessed a "Thing" puzzle with three letters, three letters, and four letters. "Ham and eggs," Jay had called out the second the blank puzzle popped up. He was only being silly. Yet a number of spins and letters later, there was his answer on the little screen.

But tonight, the only sounds were coming from the TV. It was as if everything were now so delicate, so precarious, that even speaking would somehow shatter it. Hanging on to every moment, they half sat, half lay there, pressed tightly together.

Gaining strength from the other's presence and the gentle escapism of the show, they began to relax some and sank more deeply into the pillows.

"Let me try one of those puffs," Jay finally said, breaking the silence.

Not much was left of his taste buds. But there was a subtle hint of something cheesy that managed to get through as Jay held the puff in his sore mouth. He savoured being able to savour something still.

CHAPTER TWELVE

THEY WEREN'T GOING to do the "lasts" thing. There would be no conscious "this is the last time we do this, or see that, or go there, or come here." They weren't so naive as to think such thoughts wouldn't cross their minds, but why make it feel more final by ruling out all hope by speaking of last times?

But that didn't stop them from wordlessly deciding to do things that were special to them both. It wasn't that they went out of their way to be sure certain things got done as much as they tried not to stop doing them in the first place. However, sometimes the line got a little blurry. When did something go from "it's been a while" to "we've stopped doing that"?

Going to Jonathan Park was one of those things. Leaning on Leanne, Jay steadied himself as he sat down on the closest bench. Their visits to the park had been set aside for some time. But because it happened so gradually, it wasn't such a shock when they realized they didn't go there anymore. Hikes had been the first to go, followed by walks to their fallen-tree seat, and then finally just getting as far as the bench nearest the park's entrance was history.

They hadn't been there since well before Jay's latest hospital stay. Sometimes, when he had been asleep amid the disinfectant, Leanne had found herself wandering toward the park, but she could never bring herself to go past its perimeter without him.

"It's good to be here," Jay said after he'd recovered some from the immense exertion of getting to Jonathan Park. He let go of Leanne's right hand and reached up to caress her cheek. The movement took real effort. "If it weren't for this park . . ."

"Our park." Leanne smiled. "It was a good idea to come." Intruding thoughts of the uncertain future were quickly banished, if only temporarily. They sat totally in the joyful present, side by side, breathing the same air.

But time mixed together cruelly. And brought into the present was the embodiment of a conversation from the past when Jay said that they would not have a last night. It would be a night like any other when he knew it was finally time.

As it turned out, it hadn't been a night at all when he knew. Falling asleep the previous night had felt more or less like the night before, and the ones before that. It was harder to notice the decline inching along between the more noticeable ups and downs, most notably his sojourns between hospital and home. A couple of those times he had even feared, or more wondered, if he should break out those pills, but that feeling was fleeting.

Waking up today, though, something was different. It felt like it was a day he could die that he could actually live with, a day when dying would be all right. He was still strong enough to physically do it, but weak enough so he wouldn't feel completely cheated. Sure the disease was depriving him of being alive as long as he felt entitled, and he was being cheated in that sense, but those angry it's-not-fair moments were largely behind him.

Acceptance was it? Maybe it was just tiredness. Tired in every sense. He'd reached that point where he didn't even want more. He just wanted to let go. He wanted to feel and thoroughly live those last moments of being alive, and then silently thank his body for sustaining him, and let go.

Jay really hadn't expected to change his mind about wanting to doing any "last" things. But that morning he couldn't get the idea of Jonathan Park out of his head.

He knew he probably sounded a little hypocritical, not to mention trite, when he'd told Leanne that he needed to go to the park today. It all seemed a little too full circle. But there they were.

"Lee, we've been through so much together . . . I . . . I just . . . I don't know how much, how much longer . . ."

She nodded sadly. Part of her already knew why he insisted they come here today.

"I'm not ready to leave you, but this body is." Jay's left hand fell from her face to rest again on his lap.

Leanne clasped both his hands. "I know." Her voice cracked and their eyes locked.

Their foreheads then gently fell together and rested there quietly.

Looking up, Leanne spoke again. "I'm not saying good-bye."

"I know." Jay smiled weakly, repeating her words from the moment before.

Even though they had taken a cab the short distance to the park, the trip was exhausting for Jay in the extreme. But it had been worth it, clichéd or not. He'd needed to go back to where they met, where the universe had brought them together.

Surely that same universe wouldn't tear them apart.

Jay conked out almost as soon as he was back in bed. The cabbie had helped Leanne get him up to the attic. It was actually the same cab driver who'd been less than amused years earlier when, after Becky's welcome-back party, the pair had acted as if his cab were some sort of limo. But he had developed a soft spot for them. With their walks reduced in range, he'd increasingly driven the two whenever they went much farther than their own yard. He was not only used to some of their antics but was secretly amused now. "You sure got a funny way of saying and doing some things, the both of you, but you're OK," he had said on one of his more emotionally demonstrative days.

While Jay slept, Leanne did as he had asked her right after the cabbie left. She removed something from their memorabilia box. Having it in there with everything else spoke to their conviction that death should be dealt with right alongside life.

Buried at the bottom of the box was a tray that Jay had prepared for this day. A small envelope sat on the tray, happily faded yellow from years of not being needed. He had ground up the pills, adding an extra one for every ten since he'd hoped they would end up being old and likely to have lost some of their strength. "I know how they feel," he had joked back then, looking at the weakening pills.

Leanne set the wooden tray down next to the glass of juice she'd brought upstairs. Both items now lay on the slide-over top of his modified nightstand. Then she just had to lie down herself. Settling in beside him, she lay there motionless except for the rising and falling of her chest as she tried to breath slowly and deeply. She focused on enjoying the energy of his presence and feeling the radiating warmth on her left side.

On this afternoon, Jay's sleep didn't last long. It was as if his body knew it had something else to do. And he absolutely wanted to be the one to do it, not only for legal reasons, but because he didn't want his decision to rest any more heavily on Leanne than his death already would. They had discussed it many times. Jay had written and said the words needed for legal clarity, but now it was just them. Words of how it was technically going to happen were unnecessary, and unwanted.

Leanne helped him prop up slightly so he could be in a better position to swallow. "I know I'm going to say it, Jay, just so you know. And there's nothing you can do to stop me." Even now, three special little words would not be said as a good-bye, but simply because they were true and felt so good. They smiled at each other. Both sets of lips rolled inward and pressed together tightly, holding back tears. They wanted to see smiles.

She stood beside him waiting to help if he needed it, as she said she would. That would certainly complicate matters and could get Leanne into serious trouble given current laws. But her priority was in that bed, and he didn't deserve to suffer because of other people's concerns about precedents and slippery slopes.

Jay struggled to reach the packet on the nightstand. After clasping it in his hands he looked at it for a moment. Then he tore the envelope open, and without any struggle he poured the powdery contents into the juice.

"Come here," Jay said weakly but with an inner determination, motioning her with his eyes to sit on the bed. Jay put his left hand on her right. With the other, he picked up the glass of juice. He squeezed her hand almost imperceptibly as he drank the liquid. Then he put the empty glass back down. "There."

They'd said it all before, not as final good-byes or last "I love yous," but as part of their everyday living. It truly felt as if nothing had been left unsaid, and for that they were eternally grateful. But Leanne still felt the need to say something one more time. "I'm going to be OK, you know. Don't you worry. The way you've lived, we've lived, you've shown me, your love . . . I . . . I can't do this." What started out as reassurance for Jay morphed into her own need of it.

This need was met with a relative burst of strength. "You can, Lee. You have to. Remember everything we've said, everything we've talked about. Everything. It . . . it'll help. I need it to help."

Nearly lying on top of him, sharing body heat and heartbeats, Leanne wrapped her arms around him. They stayed perfectly close, holding on to each other, sharing the moment. The moment before he will die, and she will not.

Jay shifted and Leanne rose up a little so they could better see one another. He spoke very quietly. "Maybe we'll . . . maybe there is . . . just as we hope." And then, as if it were the most natural thing in the world, Jay closed his eyes.

"Please that," Leanne pleaded. "I love you . . . always and forever."

His voice was now barely a whisper. "I love you . . . always . . . and for . . ."

Then his hold on her loosened and she knew. Leanne squeezed him even more tightly as she cried out. It was a sound that came from the deepest reaches of her being— a guttural, crying moan that filled the air. It seemed to echo around the attic until it was swallowed up by the silence and stillness of the room.

Leanne lay there sobbing, pressed against him. But it wasn't him anymore, and she felt it. She heartbreakingly felt it.

Her hold on his body loosened as her mind began going blank. Then suddenly she looked up and over toward the tray. "Jay?" Her eyes landed on the glass. "What?" she asked the air as if it were an utterly common thing to do. Then she repeated the answer she received. "We were right . . . we were . . . we're right."

Instantly, Leanne knew what was happening.

For some reason that she could not understand now, they had never talked about trying to get word to one another. They didn't have any kind of clue set up. There was no prearranged message from the beyond. That was part of what made this communication so special, and so believable. She had never thought she'd hear his voice again. And while it wasn't a voice exactly—not one she heard with her ears—and there was no accompanying image or form, it was definitely Jay.

And Jay was telling her, "We were right." It was better than any message she could have ever imagined. After being alive, there was indeed something.

Tears Leanne didn't even know she was still shedding continued to stream down her face, in a strange mix of grief and solace.

CHAPTER THIRTEEN

THE FOLLOWING MOMENTS went by in a real blur. Despite all the advance planning Jay had done, one thing could not be done ahead of time. And that was the phone call to Dr. Barnes letting him know his patient had died. "It's me, Leanne." She didn't need to say anything else.

Fortunately, that one call set everything else in motion. At Jay's request, besides signing the death certificate, Dr. Barnes was to take care of details like transportation of the body and collection of his remains. No box of ashes for Leanne. They were instead going to go to Jay's parents who actually wanted those tangible leftovers of his life.

Dr. Barnes was also to call Donovan who, in turn, was to call Becky. From there, everyone else was to be contacted, including Jay's parents. When Jay and Leanne had first discussed the prospect of her passing that presumed duty over to Becky, Leanne had fought the urge to feel guilty.

But Jay had raised a good point. "Isn't it kind of like sending flowers after someone dies when you haven't sent flowers when they were alive? Don't get me wrong, I want them to be notified. But I don't think you should have to do it, not when we hardly ever talk to them as it is. I know they'll be sad, but for them I think there will also be some relief. It'll finally be over. They won't have to wonder when it will happen. That's something they've struggled with since they found out they'd outlive me. Part of me died to them a long time ago."

Any lingering guilt twinges or not, Leanne realized she had to look after herself, and that obligatory phone call was not something she could face.

Donovan took care of the practical concerns, such as seeing to it that Leanne had food, and company if she wanted it.

And although she was thousands of kilometres away in London, Becky was on the other end of the phone almost constantly for the first few days. But few words were actually exchanged. It was more of an open line in case Leanne felt like saying or hearing something.

Just as Jay had wanted, there was no funeral service or formal memorial. There had been some initial objection from his parents when he'd first told them of his wishes. It was hard for them to get past forgoing such an established tradition. But as Jay had explained to them then, his wish not to have any formal ceremony on his behalf did not preclude them from remembering him however they wished. If they wanted to have a memorial, that was fine, but it needed to be for their sakes and not his.

He had only one stipulation. It was not to involve guilting anyone else into attending. "You think of me or not in whatever way feels right each day I'm alive. So do the same when I'm dead and let everyone else choose as well. Just don't go giving me flowers I can't smell."

Jay hadn't meant to be abrupt or dismissive of their feelings. He wasn't even sure if he'd been all that insensitive. It was second nature for him to blurt out whatever thought happened to come to him. And he was momentarily a little resentful that here he was the one dying, and yet he was also the one expected to do the comforting. His life was the one being cut short after all.

But on the other hand, he would also be the one freed from the sadness first. Leanne, his parents, his friends, they would have to live with their sadness long after his was over.

With that thought in mind, he tried to lighten the mood of the conversation with his parents. They all seemed to try to focus more on the earlier family years when everyone lived under one roof, and they were a stronger presence in each other's lives. Not normally a big one for reliving old memories, Jay actually had a good time being reminded of his childhood antics and the innocent security those years had brought.

For his part, Donovan had wanted to have a gathering of friends all together in one place at one time, sharing memories and laughter, and a few beers. Jay had not objected, understanding that he might feel the same way if the roles were reversed. "Just don't go making it the only time you mention me from then on, Van," Jay had said.

"Don't worry about that. You've given us more than enough material for ribbing you long after—" Donovan stopped himself. He was trying to talk how he knew Jay wanted—openly and freely about death—but it did not come naturally. He really didn't know how Jay did it, or Leanne either, for that matter.

It made Donovan feel terribly depressed whenever he let himself think about what was going to happen. And it reminded him it was going to happen to everyone one day. He just didn't see why they would want to be reminded of death any sooner than they had to. "So," Donovan said, composing himself, "moving on—"

"Enough said." Jay rescued his friend. "Now tell me, what's going on with you?"

More easy conversation followed, and after Donovan left, it occurred to Jay that he was beginning to have something he vowed he wouldn't, at least never with Leanne. Lasts. Not absolute-for-certain lasts, but maybe lasts.

He tried to dismiss the thought of which conversations would one day be looked back upon and dissected as "the last time we talked . . ." Why couldn't they all be of equal importance? "That's one more big fine reason to never stop talking with Leanne, to never let the conversation die," he said to himself then.

But now there was silence.

Every day since his death, Leanne had made the short journey to the beach—the site of Jay's self-proclaimed funeral ceremony. No one else knew the full extent of her reason for going there every day. It was one more thing that was just for the two of them.

As Leanne stood at the water's edge, she heard nothing. At least, nothing registered that meant anything to her. The waves kept rolling in and washing the shore—as Jay had pictured—but their music fell silent upon her ears.

Sitting on their beach bench, she would stare out, and up. It was as if she were looking for him, waiting, desperately needing to sense his presence again.

But it didn't happen. And she didn't ask why. With his absence, she had too much anger brewing inside her to even know where to start. Aside from sobbing right after his death, she hadn't cried. And the seam of her mouth had been a perpetual flat line.

Leanne spoke even less as the days went on. As much as she tried to force herself to talk to her friends, she didn't want to talk to anyone but Jay. And aside from those initial moments after he died, that wasn't happening. Leanne couldn't understand. And she could only say, "I can't believe this is real, that it actually happened," so many times. It grew monotonous and redundant even to Leanne. But those were the only words that came to her, and so she asked to be left alone. She told them not to worry, since she could hardly tell them she was fine.

And she would eat. "I'll gag something down every day no matter what," Leanne promised. And she would call if she needed anything. Reluctantly they agreed, knowing there was no point in arguing. Jay and Leanne had always been very private, and Leanne continued to be so.

She relaxed some once she had the house back to herself. And she slept more. It was almost as if she were sleeping to pass the time until she heard from Jay again. Leanne was on hold, waiting for him in her sleep.

Despite everything they had talked about, all the scenarios they had tried to imagine, the visceral absence of his presence was something she had not been prepared for. More precisely, she was not prepared for the way it felt. The idea of him not being there had been very different from the reality she was now living. She needed him and he wasn't there.

Leanne kept coming back to his words to her immediately after he died. They had proved to be a distraction in some ways. Instead of dealing with her grief over his death, she was feeling increasingly exasperated and confused by his subsequent silence and disappearance. "If we were so darn right, Jay, then where are you now?" She was beginning to demand an answer. Her numb, quiet sadness was morphing into vocalized anger.

After almost three weeks Leanne had had it. She felt as if she were going to explode. All her clear thoughts of how she was going to deal with Jay's inevitable death seemed like laughably inane memories to her now. Part of her wondered what they had possibly been thinking before.

And what was she thinking now? That she actually heard him? Leanne couldn't take it anymore, and finally she just let him have it, whether he was there to hear it or not.

"I hate this, Jay. Why aren't you here? You said, 'We were right'! I heard you! So why aren't you here? I keep waiting. Where the fuck are you, Jay? I am getting really pissed off here. If we were so damn right, you should be here!" Leanne screamed as she paced frantically around the attic. "I can't see you. I can't hear you. I can't feel you! Nothing. Goddamn nothing! Hell! I can't even have one moment of peace."

She flopped down on the bed in angry bewilderment. "Every time I try to think of something good we shared, some happy moment, just wanting one freakin' second of relief . . . every damn time, it changes and I'm right back there, losing you all over again. I told you I couldn't do this. I was right. I told you so. Fuck! Shit. I don't think I've sworn so much in my whole goddamn life."

With her legs now dangling over the edge of the bed like a desperate child straining to reach the ground, her head fell sharply downward. Her hands slammed into the back of her head and slowly slid down her neck. Leanne gradually looked up, and as she stared forward, her rant continued.

"But it's either I swear my fucking head off or I'm going to start punching walls. Hey, now there's an idea. Maybe if I get really lucky, I'll slam my head into a wall and that'll be that. Reunion here I come!" She fell backward onto the bed. "Yeah, that would work, except for one little detail, that damn promise I made—live my life. Whose dumb idea was that?"

Leanne was finally beginning to calm down. For the first time since her outburst began, she was speaking quietly. "Living," she almost whispered. "I do want to do that. Dammit." The odd silent tear began to fall. "Even without . . . you."

As another tear fell, she rolled onto her side, hugging his pillow to her chest. She wrapped her arms completely around it until her hands rested on her shoulders. Leanne closed her eyes for the first truly restful moment since Jay had died.

Also for the first time since that day, a hint of a smile came over her face. Her first good memory of a happy moment was at last being relived. Her smile grew broader and then turned into a gentle laugh. She let out a sigh as if she'd been holding her breath since his death, and only now, let it go.

And then it happened. Leanne finally sensed him, and she squeezed the pillow proxy as hard as she could. "Jay." Her voice shook in relief.

Then she heard him speak. "Yeah, Lee, I'm here. Finally. Thanks for that."

"What do you mean, thanks? What did I do?"

"You let go," he said. "You let go of your anger, your need for that anger, and even your need for me. That's been blocking me out. I hated it, Lee. Being separated from you ..."

"Why now?" she asked, still not understanding.

"Now you just want me. You don't need me."

"No," Leanne protested. "I'll always need you. I need you ... desperately. I can't do this alone. I know what I promised, but—"

"That promise was for both of us," Jay interrupted. "We both need—gotta love that word—but we both need you to go out and live. Do your life proud. It deserves it. You deserve it. And I'm not going anywhere. But your need now, it can't be that angry 'how dare the universe do this to me because I need you' need. That need is blinding, Lee. And that's what's finally gone, or at least gone enough."

His tone then softened. "And now that I've been so gloriously featured in a happy memory just moments ago, you're on your way."

Instead of being pleased by his explanation, Leanne surprised Jay by getting annoyed. "Oh, so it's OK I'll always need you, as long as it's a what, a happy need? I can be with you as long as I'm not mad at the universe? That's kinda backward isn't it? When I most needed you these last few weeks, I couldn't have you because I was angry and hurt and scared? Because I needed you, I couldn't have you? That's seriously fucked, Jay."

"Hey, I didn't set this thing up. It's pretty new to me too. But I'm finding out, you know, just how true it is there really are things we have to figure out on our own. We've got to muddle through, suffer through. Death's just like life in that way, I'm sorry to say. And before you go thinking you were the only one hurting, let me remind you, I was there. I was with you every step, every agonizing step. You couldn't see me, but I was there . . . for all your tears, all your screams, every second since I died. You don't know what that was like."

Trying to lighten things up, Jay emphasized his verb choice when he said, "It killed me to know what you were going through." But then his voice almost trembled. "And I couldn't do anything. You had to get there yourself. You had to be able to remember the good times too."

Leanne was trying to absorb what she was hearing. It really was Jay. He was right there with her. "It's good to see we can still argue."

"Vigorously debate," Jay countered.

"Argue." Leanne wouldn't let go. "Yes, it's good we're able to do that, what with one of us being dead and all."

"Yep. We always could, so why stop now?"

Without her consciously realizing it, Leanne's left hand was gently stroking her right shoulder. With the pillow still pressed between her chest and arms, her right hand moved to squeeze her left forearm. It was all her, but all she felt was Jay.

"I'm still me," Jay said as her right shoulder was given a squeeze. "And you are most definitely still you, my love."

"I've missed that—my love. And I've missed this." The hand on her shoulder moved to caress her neck.

"I know . . . believe me . . . I know, Lee. It's been hell in heaven without you, figuratively speaking, of course. Wherever and whatever I am, I'm here."

"You're you." Leanne paused before daring to add, "So we can, whenever I want—not need, at least not angry need—we can . . ."

"I think so. I know I hope so. What do you think? Still stuck with me?"

Remembering vows that seemed as if they were said both yesterday and yesteryear, Leanne sighed blissfully. "Man and woman not just until death. Yeah." She closed her eyes and spoke slowly, enjoying every word. "Most definitely yeah. Yeahhh." Wrapped up in her arms, she fell into a peaceful, long-awaited sleep.

CHAPTER FOURTEEN

"Mmm . . . Jay . . . mmmmm," Leanne purred as she woke up.

"Mmmmm is right, Lee."

Hands stoked and caressed gently as arms and legs entwined themselves, giving the feel of two loving bodies where there was only one.

After quietly savouring their reunion, Leanne was finally forced to break the silence. "I hate to move, but I'm dying of thirst."

Anyone looking at the bed would have sworn one set of arms actually released another set, enabling Leanne to lean over to the nightstand to reach her glass of water.

Off to the side of the glass was evidence of the loving night before. It wasn't latex or polyurethane anymore, but silicone. Retrieved from their memorabilia box, but now resting upright by the bed, was an anatomically correct silicone dildo whose actual identity went unnoticed, having served as a proxy for the one who was really there.

After propping pillows up against their headboard, Leanne resumed cuddling with Jay. She absentmindedly caressed her left hand with her right. "Amazing."

"Thank you," an immodest Jay replied, earning the pillow a nudge from Leanne's elbow. "And yes, it is amazing."

"But how, how are you . . . how is this possible? I don't know how . . ."

"Don't have to, Lee." With joined hands held up in the air, "I just know this, this connection's not broken, not yet. And I hope it never will be."

"Not ever. Please, not ever." Leanne closed her eyes. "But if . . . if it ever is, broken you know . . . I'll be OK. I know now. It won't be forever."

"Hey, I thought you believed in us, love forever and all that," Jay teased.

"Who me? I've only been stringing you along all this time as part of my master plan. I couldn't wait to have my dead partner here while I masturbated."

"And I thought I'd been actually making love with you."

"Oh, Jay. You were. Your body may not have been, but you were."

"Yes, and forever, Lee."

Her head tipped slightly to the left, and she nestled a little farther down the bed.

Jay continued to speak. "What a gloriously long time this forever thing is. It might even come close to being long enough."

Smiling, Leanne made another observation. But this one, Jay didn't like hearing. "Besides," she said, "just a blink until we don't have to worry about any of this. We'll both be dead."

"Hey, now, I thought we'd been through all that, Lee. No sneaking out early, not you," Jay said in a voice that both begged and demanded.

Leanne's reply was tinged with bitterness. "You did."

"That's not fair. And you know it. You know my reasons, our reasons for that. It wasn't as if I could have gone on much longer, not in any real capacity, anyway." Jay paused, unable to resist thinking of what might have been. "Oh, if only I'd gotten sick later. The way treatments keep improving, maybe almost normal lives will be lived soon, and for so much longer too."

"Time sure is a damn funny thing," Leanne said. "If we were able to shift our birth dates, then whammo, you could still be alive."

"If, if, if, huh? Yeah." He paused before saying, "Let's not do regrets, Lee. It doesn't do any good. Besides, it's bloody depressing."

Jay got up from the bed, pulling Leanne up as he did so. He really needed to walk around, to move, to feel the floor beneath his feet, even if only vicariously. "You know, I thought that once I died, I wouldn't have to deal with death anymore," he joked. "And now you're spoiling it for me."

"Sorry about that," Leanne half apologized. She was torn between being grateful for having him there as he now was and feeling devastated that that was all it would be. There were also thoughts of her own mortality floating around, toying with her mind. "But at least yours is over with. I still have my own death to worry about here."

Then left hand squeezed right hand and she closed her eyes, letting in what Jay was trying to share the only way he could. And she quietly amended, "No, not worry about, deal with, and experience one day."

"You'll be amazed. But not—"

"I know, not now," Leanne interrupted knowing where he was headed, no matter how much part of her wanted to disagree.

"And not now for a long time," Jay said emphatically. He knew that deep down Leanne had too strong a survival instinct and will to live to consider doing anything rash. She appreciated life too much, even now that he was dead, and perhaps actually more so in some poignant ways. But Jay's body hadn't been gone from him that long yet, and the corporeal need for reassurance had surfaced just then.

Their banter continued as easily as ever. In certain respects it was even freer. There was no longer any hint of a pall over their lives to try to ignore. Jay was no longer sick. They no longer had his death looming over them. And Leanne, well, Leanne was taking great comfort in knowing she could join him in death, not just life.

Although that wouldn't be for a whole bunch of "nows," Leanne still whispered to herself, "One day." But there was no such thing as an unheard whisper anymore. Yet Jay remained quiet, understanding her current need to at least partly wish away her life. They both needed to get used to the way things were now.

The headiness of all that had happened during the last day and night was catching up with Leanne. Her body had grown accustomed to extra sleep since Jay's death, born out of a mix of exhaustion and escapism. It had been easier not having so many waking hours to fill with uncontrollable thoughts, even though when she did wake up she felt as worn out as when she went to sleep.

Leanne's first rejuvenating sleep in weeks had ended only a few hours before, but those blissful moments in

Jay's arms were starting to feel like an ancient memory. She needed to make her burgeoning confusion stop. She needed to stop thinking so much.

Moving back to the bed, she burrowed under the covers and curled up into a protective ball. She felt only her own arms, but she was too tired to think about what that meant. Sleep was taking much needed control. And it kept control for most of the day.

But instead of waking up and being slapped in the face all over again with his being dead, Leanne woke with ease, emerging gently from sleep. Without even realizing it, she reached out her right hand. With equal ease, it was met by her outstretched left hand.

Shifting to lie on her side, she faced a grinning Jay.

"You slept so long," he said, "I thought you might be dead to the world."

"Maybe dead to the world, but never to you." Leanne reached up to stroke his cheek as she touched his pillow.

"So you're feeling better?"

"Yeah." But then her mind began whirling again. "I was getting all mixed up with what I want, with what is but can't possibly be, and with what's gonna happen if I let myself believe. What if it all goes away? I can't lose you again, so I better hurry up and join you, just in case. But what if I'm imagining you? And you're only here if I'm alive to do that. If I'm not alive, then I'd lose you that way." She was tying herself up in knots, caught between two worlds, feeling as if she didn't belong in either.

With her right shoulder being gently stroked, Leanne felt pulled into a hug, the large pillow pressing tightly against her. "Lee, you know all this. You know this world, and you know me. It's still me. I'm here because this is the only place I want to be, however we can. And I'm not going anywhere you don't want me to," Jay said.

Wanting to give Leanne some time to process what he'd had a head start on, Jay added a distraction. "I'm of course hoping you want me right here." He gave her an extra nudge that reminded them both of the night before.

A smile slowly appeared on Leanne's face, growing ever bigger as she breathed in the scent barely lingering on his pillow—a combination of soap and Jay, but mostly Jay. Closing her eyes, she gave the pillow another squeeze. "You've always known what to say," she said. "I guess I shouldn't be surprised you still do."

"Well, there may have been a time or two I didn't."

Leanne could feel his grin. Silliness had crept back in, and it was almost as if he had never died.

There was still the odd moment, though, when Leanne questioned her connection to both reality and this new world—which she could share with Jay—that seemed to be emerging.

Just as Jay had at times been afraid he'd infect Leanne, she too had her own recurring fears to revisit. What her mind told her was impossible, her heart told her was the most possible thing in the world. As had happened with Jay's transmission fears, the questioning moments waned, and her mind finally accepted what her heart already knew. Jay had said they were right, and the how of that, wasn't what was important. He was there with her.

There was a lilt and lightness to Leanne's voice now when she talked with Becky or Donovan. They attributed it to the passage of time and the whole healing-of-wounds business. But what they didn't know, both because they didn't ask and because she didn't offer, was that Leanne was quite simply no longer mourning Jay's death. She was finding workarounds to it. No, she and Jay were finding workarounds together.

Physically, their passion had found an outlet that first silicone-assisted night. Pillows helped as well, but what amazed Leanne the most was the feeling of shared limbs. The touch of her left side to her receiving right was Jay, always left for Jay and right for Leanne. In their attic they had almost morphed into one body.

It just sort of happened.

When they were together, Leanne's left arm no longer felt like her own. It really was Jay's somehow. The whole thing was no more odd than having a preferred side of the bed. The left and right division of limbs felt like another natural development, an automatic extension of how they had lived when both were alive.

While neither liked to focus on the pragmatics of their physical union now, they didn't want to completely shy away from it either. That might mean they weren't connected with reality and fully aware of what they were actually doing—and not doing.

"You know," Leanne said to Jay one day as they were lounging on their bed, "I find it rather ironic that I'm the right side when you're the one who said, 'We were right.' And that you're the left when I'm the one who got left, at least in some ways."

"Or you could say that through your left side, you get to feel what's left of me," he countered.

"OK, maybe I'll accept that. But you didn't address the 'right side' of all this." It felt so good to be mindlessly playing with their minds.

"Well, maybe . . . maybe it's because"—Jay was trying to come up with something—"it must be because . . . hey, I know, I've got it now, it's because you feel me right there, on your right. And because I'm right here with you," Jay said satisfactorily.

"You're good, and right. Or should I say left?" Leanne laughed.

"How about we make even better use of both sides?" Jay suggested.

Lips then gently touched. With eyes closed, a tender left forearm pressed into her kissing lips, while a left hand caressed the back of her neck. With increasing passion, her mouth opened farther. Tongue mixed with warm skin. Arms began to wander and a drawer was opened, revealing their silicone helper. In that nightstand drawer, next to the dildo, lay a collection of lonely condoms.

Leanne rolled onto her stomach and her hands disappeared under the covers with the dildo. For some reason she naturally gravitated to that position. The downward pressure meant less work she had to do herself, reinforcing the feeling she wasn't alone. Gravity, along with the bed itself, helped the dildo fulfil its role as loyal stand-in.

And it was always a silent dildo, not a noisy vibrator. There was nothing like battery buzz to spoil the organic feel of his presence. When Jay was alive he may have hummed, but he had never buzzed.

As Leanne moved, her eyes were mostly closed. But even when open, they didn't visually register that she was physically alone in the room. In their attic bedroom, under the skylights, Jay and Leanne continued to make love.

During the all-consuming drive for release, there was no room for rational thought, no time for any consideration that Jay's body was no longer actually in the mix. While Leanne no longer doubted his presence, there were still fleeting moments of unwelcome awareness of their changed circumstances. But that couldn't happen when they were having sex and the drive within her so singularly focused on orgasm, and the delicious buildup to it. Everything else was blissfully blocked out automatically. Whatever limitations there were the rest of the time, anything was possible right through to afterglow.

The post-orgasmic leftover bliss helped smooth the transition back to being aware she was kissing her own arm and hugging her own body. Otherwise, it would have been way too painful to go from experiencing complete togetherness to remembering that he was dead.

As Leanne lay there exhausted and sated, she couldn't help the little smiles and exhaled "ahhhhs." The familiar shivers of pleasure were always a surprise no matter how many times they'd surprised her before. And now they had a purpose beyond pure pleasure—easing her back to life with the formless Jay.

And from there it was an easier path back to their new everyday life, replete with their enduring closeness and absentminded touching, familiar talking, laughing, and living in their attic.

CHAPTER FIFTEEN

I N A WEIRD WAY, life rolled along more smoothly than it ever had before. Gone were the intervening worries and health scares that had tried so hard to interrupt their life. There was no longer the same need to try to lose track of the passage of time. Their timetable had now been expanded to be at least as long as one of those statistical life expectancies. As long as Leanne was alive, they felt confident that they could continue their rendezvous as they had been.

Time was no longer so poignant since, at the very least, neither would ever have to know life without the other.

Still, there were obvious limitations to deal with that were painful in their own right. Not going out in public together was probably one of the biggest, for obvious reasons. There could be no walks spent chatting or visibly holding hands, though under the cover of a draping coat, hands did occasionally clasp.

And there would be no more overnight campouts on Mount Bauldron. But that was because Leanne didn't feel entirely safe staying up there when she knew she was physically alone.

There could also be no talking of Jay in the present tense. That challenge was made a little easier since she had never talked a lot to others in the first place. But there were times Leanne wished she could speak to a face that had a shape when it looked back at her.

When she was around other people, she was reminded of how wrong it felt to go from talking about someone when they were alive to then, just not. Forget not speaking ill of the dead, some people stopped talking about them altogether after the initial mourning.

And while using "was" or "used to" would have been viable options when speaking of Jay, that approach posed another problem for Leanne. It felt like lying.

There could also certainly be no public use of plural pronouns when talking of any of their new conversations or activities.

Leanne valued her freedom, so she wasn't about to risk being committed by concerned—albeit well-meaning—friends who would worry about her sanity if she shared information about her current living arrangement. For that's what it was, a living arrangement, a simple continuation of their lives, just one with certain forced modifications.

She lived alone officially and where eyes could see, but upstairs it was another story. Always pretty private about private matters, she felt no need to change now. People hadn't really understood their togetherness when Jay was alive, so what chance was there with him being dead? Leanne conceded that perhaps others hadn't understood because they were never really given the chance, but it was all too ingrained to retroactively try to explain.

Besides, she still liked the feeling of it being just the two of them, in a way only they understood.

As time went on, Leanne did go out and enjoy many of the things they had enjoyed together, she just had to wait until she got upstairs to share them all with him.

It had definitely been a good move to buy the tallest house in the area. Attic windows could be free of coverings and still be private. They spoke some downstairs, but since Leanne was visibly using words, they usually only did so after she closed the blinds. And that felt too closed in, and too calculating, as if she were trying to hide something. Or, in this case, someone. It was better all around to be upstairs, where the sun or the stars openly illuminated according to the hour.

But being outdoors also had a powerful effect on her. While feeling more alone out there than in their attic, a deep sense of gratitude washed over her. She still got to be alive.

Leanne inhaled the air, littered as it was each spring with flower pollen, and in the summer by barbecues and park food. And the fresh damp breaths of autumn and the invigorating cold of winter filled her lungs after storms of rain and snow, as she sat on their porch glider, surrounded by aromatic wet wood.

The feel of everything she touched helped keep her in the moment—from their marble kitchen counters to the dirt under her fingernails after digging in their garden.

One thing that Leanne did not want to do, however, was work. While she still had her favourite bookkeeping clients, she was finding it more and more difficult to get excited about working with the numbers she used to love.

Leanne found herself getting antsy whenever she was sitting at her desk. She wanted to get up and move around and have some place to go once she did.

It felt as if there were too many other things she would rather be doing. And every second not doing those other things was killing her. "Well, not literally," she casually joked to Jay one day as she looked up from her files before muttering, "but killing time for sure."

She was ready for a change.

Leanne tried to think about the things that were most important to her, hoping to see some way to translate them into a job. She definitely appreciated her flexible hours and adored the people she had kept as clients, but Leanne wanted more. "I don't want my job to feel so separate from my life. It's as if it bears no connection to the rest of my day now. I know it's the same job I've always had, but I feel a real disconnect now that I have more hours to fill on my own."

"Well, you do like to talk," Jay said.

"And you don't?" Leanne laughed, curious about where he was headed.

"I'm just saying, maybe you could use that. Besides, you are a great listener who really cares. Hey, I know, why don't you become a talk-show host? Everybody's got a show these days from what you tell me," he joked.

"No, wait, I think you're on to something here."

"Lee, I wasn't serious."

"I know, but think about it. Where else could I use those two things? Specifically, how could I put all that together, along with what we've been through?"

"You mean—"

"Not sharing what we've been through directly or anything," Leanne said. "That would feel weird. And rather inappropriate too, since one half of us can't defend himself anymore. But using what we've experienced to be a better listener for—"

"What someone else is going through," Jay finished.

"Exactly." Leanne was beaming with excitement and relief after tossing around seemingly countless ideas over countless days.

"It'll mean going back to school."

"That might be fun. I could see if I do better the second time around." She continued thinking about the idea. "A counsellor, some sort of grief or, what would you call it, a death counsellor?"

"Oh, that sounds lovely. Really draw 'em in with that moniker. But I know what you mean—no euphemisms. However, maybe you should go with a more generic, not to mention gentler, plain *counsellor* name to start and let the location imply the rest."

"Like a hospice or something? Or maybe there's some place where the newly-termed terminally ill get referred?" Leanne put air quotes around the phrase they'd first deplored so long ago.

Instead of bringing back sad memories from the past when Jay was dying, they were both caught up in the moment of actively planning the future. Tossing out ideas and hashing out plans, just as they always had, made it easy to forget only Leanne really sat on their bed or could be heard talking out loud.

Going back to school meant Leanne had to allow for other ideas, sometimes ones very different from her own.

It was actually a bit of a relief to see that alternate paths could also work. Despite making for no pat answers, having no one right solution opened up more possibilities to help. It was more about listening, and within certain parameters, guiding each client to discover what was already felt somewhere inside.

"I must stop calling them clients," Leanne said to Jay midway through her studies. "They are not bookkeeping customers or something, they are patients."

"No," Jay said. "Don't even think of them that way. They're people, just people going through a tough time."

Working with those dealing with death and dying may have seemed like the last thing Leanne would want to do after all she and Jay had been through, but the idea was strangely comforting. Maybe it was because the subject had grown so familiar. The words were so well worn in her vocabulary that the devastation of their meaning had lessened.

Or maybe it was because of the left hand that now rubbed her right shoulder as she sat cross-legged on the bed studying, reminding her of possibilities. Her book was propped up on her lap, and as the reading glasses she now wore began to slide down her nose, she reached up and pushed them back. Her right hand then settled naturally on the left forearm that remained beneath her chin, left hand still gently working her shoulder.

As the months turned to years, Leanne felt more and more invigorated working toward something that was both intellectually challenging and had the potential to help ease fear and grief. And as bookkeeping had once felt, counselling was like puzzle solving sometimes, only in a different way, a more human one that she needed now. It also felt good precisely because it was different from what she'd done for so long. Impersonal numbers were replaced with very personal people.

At the end of each day out in the world, Leanne returned home, careful to publicly just call it home and not "our" anything. The protective semantics had long since become habit, but that didn't mean there couldn't be slip-ups on occasion.

"I nearly blew it today," Leanne blurted out as they were sitting on the bed one afternoon.

"At lunch?" Jay asked.

Becky had arranged a lunch gathering of old girl-friends while she and her family were in town to help her parents move as they downsized. Her father's health wasn't the greatest anymore and being closer to emergency care made everyone feel better.

However, Leanne wasn't so keen on the idea of leaving a well-loved home for a rather sterile apartment. But they didn't ask for her opinion. She hated it when people gave her unsolicited advice, so she kept quiet. Most importantly, she could tell it was what Becky's parents wanted, given their limited options. Besides, this lunch was supposed to be a lighthearted break for Becky, and a good gab session for scattered friends who rarely got to see each other.

But it did have it's awkward moments.

"Yeah," Leanne said, "they were all in their let's-help-Leanne-get-out-there mode, even more so than usual."

"I wonder when they'll stop doing that and just give up on you, Lee."

"Thanks a lot." Leanne jabbed at the pillow to her left as she sat propped up against the headboard. "Maybe when I'm a completely lost cause, and not a partially lost one."

"Well, you're on your way. Look who you're talking to— a dead guy."

"But a very adorable one."

Her right hand was given a squeeze, and then her left thumb gently began stroking the back of it.

"So, tell me what you did to nearly blow it. And blow just what, exactly?"

Raising an eyebrow, Leanne otherwise ignored his little double entendre. "Our life," she said, "our private time, being able to live all this without having to explain or justify it to anyone."

"It would be rather hard to explain."

"Exactly, Jay. And I know they only do it because they care and are worried, I really do, but all those 'shoulds,' you know? I should do this. I should do that." Leanne was growing a little agitated just from retelling the story. She shifted positions to sit cross-legged, facing him. "They don't know. It's not their life to live, and it's not theirs to know."

"The surest way to get someone not to do something— tell them they should. And that especially holds true if her name happens to be Leanne," Jay said, a smile emanating from him. "You'd think they'd have learned that by now."

"You would, wouldn't you?" She chuckled. "I guess it comes back to that we-love-and-care-about-you crap. I don't mean to be mean, but seriously, they were going too far this time. They even tried to get me to agree to this group-date thing"—Leanne rolled her eyes—"with some guy they knew who would be absolutely perfect."

"I hate him already," Jay kidded her. "But really, maybe you sh—"

Leanne smiled as he caught himself.

"Scratch that," he corrected. "But have you considered it might be time?"

Instead of getting angry or hurt at a suggestion that would have engendered such feeling coming from anyone else, Leanne calmly answered, "I have. Considered it. It's a no go. Not now, I can't, and I don't want to."

"Why?" Jay asked with equal calmness. Being dead, he found it easier to envision Leanne actually being with someone else. Perhaps it was because he knew he could never really lose her, even if she fell in love again. Their beings were bonded beyond bodies. Having no corporeal form created a different perspective on some things, including the whole physical-jealousy issue.

"Why?" Her surprise at the unexpected question was evident in her tone. "You're really asking me why?"

"I'm trying to play the devil's advocate here, Lee."

"The devil's?"

"Don't try to change the subject here. It was only a figure of speech—no great clue to the afterlife or anything," Jay said before refocusing the conversation. "So why don't you want to go on this date thing and see if there are other possibilities out there?"

"You're really gonna make me say?" Leanne couldn't believe he was asking her to spell it out. The reason should be so obvious, not to mention painful.

"We've never shied away from saying anything to each other. Don't start now."

"Fine." Leanne was a little annoyed but she knew she needed to verbalize it, probably for both their sakes. And leave it to Jay to not let her off the hook. "I know how it must seem. I'm not blind. All this time I've appeared to be on my own, looking to the outside world that I am all alone. But when I come home, to our room, to this attic, we share and do things I thought impossible."

Leanne continued looking in the direction of the space next to her. She never actually saw Jay—his old form or image—she just looked wherever in the room she knew he was. "I feel like we have this gift, this, whatever it is, this, being able to still be with you, to talk with you, to feel you. I mean, it's obviously not the way I wanted it, not the way I'd make it if I could, but it is what we have, and it's more than I ever thought I could have after you died, once your body was gone."

Jay felt it too. "So much more than 'we were right.'"

"So much more than I ever dreamed. And that's what I want—you," she said.

By this time, Leanne's arms were wrapped tightly around her body in a mutual embrace, reaching and stretching around her back, squeezing hard as her chin tipped downward into the crook of her left arm.

They stayed like that for a while, blissfully content for the simple contact. But like all moments, new ones kept coming. Jay and Leanne were brought out of their silent contemplation and back to their earlier conversation.

"So you never did finish about lunch and their date idea," Jay said.

"What?" Leanne was still momentarily in the previous moment. "Oh yeah, dating," she said dismissively. "I mean, the very idea of it, Jay, of anyone else. It just felt so wrong—repugnant, actually—that I blurted out without thinking—"

"Always a dangerous thing."

"And no exception this time. Before I knew it, I'd said, 'Oh, don't worry about me. I had the most amazing night last night.'"

"Oh, shit. How'd you get out of that?"

"I tried to cover by saying how I'd gotten this really wonderful night of sleep after a crazy week at work."

"Ooooh," Jay groaned. "Did they buy that? That hardly sounds like justification for the 'most amazing night.' Not the way I remember them anyway."

"Me either. But at least I caught myself before I described what you did and just how amazing that was."

The compliment barely registered on Jay. He was focusing on what was best for Leanne now—not last night. "Lee, you could try telling them the truth you know. They might understand."

"They might." Leanne thought of the people she was closer to as she focused on the one she was closest to. "Probably wouldn't, though, not really. But you know, even if they did, I like it this way. It's still just us."

"You don't have to convince me." Jay understood exactly. Right or wrong, short or long term, they'd never been very good with sharing themselves—or what they had together—with anyone but each other.

Even now, they seemed to almost always be touching one another in some way. As Leanne leaned against the headboard while they talked, hands entwined, gently moving all around. Fingers and thumbs caressed the skin beneath without any conscious awareness.

As her head tipped to rest on the nearby pillow, she felt Jay's shoulder.

"I love this," he said. "Hearing you say things, telling me about your day, all the normal everyday stuff—it's so much better than seeing it from a distance."

Leanne looked up. "OK, now that sounds creepy, Jay. The thought of you watching me all the time—"

"Don't worry. Nothing like that. Although that could be interesting." The pillow received a nudge. "It's hard to explain. It's being there but not like some voyeur or anything weird, just there somehow, aware but not watching."

"I think I see, but I know I don't, not really. I know I can't, but sometimes I think I feel a hint of it too when we aren't together like this and actively talking, or anything else," she said suggestively, "which, by the way, you are not getting out of later."

"Thank goodness for that, Lee."

Hands squeezed together a little tighter before resuming their wandering finger patterns.

"But even when I'm just going about my day," Leanne said, "whether I'm at work, with friends, vegging out in front of the TV, whatever, there are these moments when I sense you and wonder if you're there right then."

"I am."

"But you're not like, waiting on me to be aware of that, are you?" she asked.

As they had occasionally done before, they spoke the same words in unison, save an alteration in pronouns.

"I'd hate that," Leanne said.

"You'd hate that," Jay said.

While not able to paint a clear picture of the so-called afterlife—or afterdeath, as he preferred to think of it—Jay could offer another reassurance. "You know how we never liked to measure time? Well, good news, you won't always have to. This is different. Time's not . . . well, it won't be a problem. So don't worry, I'm not waiting around or anything like that. But at the same time, I am still there."

Leanne closed her eyes and breathed in and out slowly, luxuriating in the love that enveloped her. "You sure are. And you see that—all this—is why I don't want to meet anyone else. I'm already with someone."

"It'd be a lot easier, though, if I could make an appearance occasionally for all the world to see."

"It sure would, Jay. How about you arrange that for next time, OK?"

"You got it, love. Now, as I recall, someone was making rash promises earlier that I most certainly do not want to be 'getting out of.'"

"As if you ever have," Leanne teased. "Well, once I finally persuaded you that with our mix of precautions, I'd be OK."

"And I will be eternally grateful that it worked too, more than you can ever imagine." Jay felt as if he'd been saved from a killer punch to the gut.

"No need for condoms now," she said, squeezing her left hand. At first it was to comfort, but soon, to arouse.

"Hey, at last a perk to being dead," he joyfully pointed out before Leanne reminded him of a certain obvious disadvantage that came along with that plus.

"We'll have to forget about your loss of a certain body part for those condoms."

"Ouch, let's not mention that detail," Jay said. "Besides, don't they say the mind is the most important sex organ anyway?"

"Whether it is or not, sweetie, I'm afraid you don't have one of those either anymore. And just how much you had before—"

"Yeah, yeah, 'is up for debate too,' you were going to say. Funny."

"Sorry about that," Leanne said. "I couldn't resist. It was a beautiful setup, don't you think?"

"And such a turn of phrase too. Speaking of which, how about we both do some turning of our own and turn in."

"That was weak, Jay. But points for attempting the segue. And even bigger points for a brilliant idea."

There was no need to turn off the lights. They'd never been turned on in the first place. There was no need to see in the attic. And dusk had turned into the darkness of night. Only a sliver of the moon and the neighbouring stars were still awake in the sky. Below, two lovers moved beneath the covers.

CHAPTER SIXTEEN

EACH YEAR WHEN the anniversary of Jay's death rolled around, Leanne felt she was living a heightened version of their outward charade. The passage of time had made his death more a memory than a current grieving for their friends, so it was most often only on this death-marking day that Leanne would be pointedly asked the awkward question of how she was doing.

From everyone who knew what had happened those years before, she would receive the telltale looks of genuine sympathy. But their expressions couldn't help but be tinged with unconscious gratitude that it hadn't happened to them.

They all knew this must be the hardest day of the year for Leanne, and they understood why she always asked to be left alone. They all knew why, or at least they thought they did.

Time had such a different meaning before Jay died. Keeping time secret when he was alive by not keeping track of it had given them the gift of no ticking clock, not a loud one, anyway. While vague awareness of time had been inescapable, Leanne was incredibly grateful that she genuinely did not know many of the dates and time frames of events during those years.

Since his death, however, there had been no need for such avoidance of clocks and calendars. There was no sickness—with its own perverted timeline—to worry about anymore, so time wasn't the same enemy.

But memorializing dates—even the happy ones—had never been something Jay and Leanne wanted to do, and certainly not for the days they wished had never happened. To commemorate any day gone by felt especially pointless when its poignancy saddened a current day.

And since Jay was still right there holding Leanne's hand when she woke up and draping an arm around her when she fell asleep, there didn't seem to be anything to 'work through,' as she might have said to a patient who was struggling with a loss. She didn't feel she was struggling. Jay wasn't gone, not euphemistically or otherwise.

Many of her patients confided that they felt the presence of those who had died. Leanne was careful never to detail how much she agreed with them, or how very far beyond that her agreement really went. Counselling wasn't about getting others to see things her way, but about helping them to uncover their own ways.

And Leanne's way saw her shutting herself off more than usual on the anniversary—a date on the calendar she begrudgingly admitted she did know was the day he died.

But it was also the day of Jay's first words to her after his death—a gift known only to her—and those words removed some of the day's sad horror.

Each year on that date—one she still never wanted to name, either aloud or to herself—Leanne was grateful to be left alone. But not for the reason others thought. It was because most of all, she didn't want to have to justify being OK.

That's not to say there weren't moments of pain, but they could happen on any day of the year. There were random times when Leanne found herself on the verge of tears. She always tried to hold them back until she got to the attic. There, Leanne would find comfort, hugging a pillow and feeling a caressing hand on her back that would move to her face, wiping away the moisture when it came. Whatever variable trigger had made her re-feel the loss of Jay all over again was soon forgotten as she lay curled up securely in his arms.

"Dammit, I hate when I get like that, Jay. Why do I do that to myself? I haven't lost you. You're still here with me. I may not know exactly where you are beyond this room, but you are not lost, not gone, not any of those misnomered euphemisms. Dead, yes. Gone, no. I know that. So why do I—"

"Feel like it anyway?" Jay finished. "Well, I hate to state the obvious, but you have lost something, not me, but all that we had, in the way we had it, that is gone."

"But it's been over ten years now, longer than we got"— Leanne exhaled—"before you died. Why does it still feel so immediate sometimes, so recent, and so raw?"

"I don't know." Jay had nothing reassuring he could say.

For all the insights he had gained now that he was without a body, he still didn't know why the hurt had to continue for those who still had theirs. Or, for that matter, why he too still felt pain, when he knew he shouldn't anymore. He didn't think that was how things were supposed to work, but then again, since when had they followed the rules? Maybe the link with Leanne kept him in touch with that all-too-real pain.

But as together as they continued to be, it still felt a little as if one were visiting the other sometimes. And as a result, they weren't always able to share or see everything in the same way. One had graduated and moved beyond, while the other was still in school.

As she often did whenever things became too overwhelming, Leanne found respite in sleep. Curling up and shutting out the competing worlds—the one outside and the one in her head—allowed her to just stop. She was able to stop thinking and be aware of only her physical senses. She lay there protected by the warmth of their duvet, the sunshine bathing her face as it beamed through the skylights, and the smell of the fresh breeze that blew gently through the open windows, peacefully stirring the air of the attic.

As she quietly slipped into near unconsciousness after an unusually sad day, Leanne was barely aware she was still awake. She felt herself sinking more deeply into the bed. Her face pressed farther into the pillow as her head shifted back against another pillow tucked in behind her, settling into the crook of Jay's neck.

And then she was asleep. Whether there were answers or not, at least she could stop asking the questions for a little while.

Stretching and relishing the blissful sensations that welcomed her body when she woke up, Leanne felt as if the former torment in her gut were from almost too long ago to even remember. Sleep managed to speed up the distancing process.

Leanne lay quietly a while longer, soaking in the coziness and comfort that came from the simple pressing of her body against the pillows.

As she lay there, she slowly exhaled a deep breath that seemed to keep on coming—a never-ending, soothing release. Arms crossed in front of her body with hands resting on opposite sides. Her right shoulder was caressed by the left hand, and the left elbow was in turn held by her right hand.

As natural and easy as always, Leanne felt abundantly grateful for such touches. Her intermittent questioning and pain was all worth it if they could still have these moments. She hoped she would always feel that way, because the good moments felt so good.

Ordinarily she rarely felt apart from Jay, even when away from the house. Whether she was out with friends old or new, walking alone, or at work at the counselling centre, wherever Leanne was she could share a nearly invisible moment with Jay when something funny was said or seen.

The only reaction would be a knowing—though virtually motionless—nod of the head at a shared joke, apparent from the outside by a slight glimmer in her eye or an almost imperceptible curl of her mouth as she and Jay enjoyed the humour together.

She found herself communicating with him more and more without words, as though none were really necessary to say whatever they had to share. A touch or look had often held that power for them since their earliest days together, but words had been along for the ride too. Now their importance seemed to be waning.

Jay and Leanne still used them at home sometimes—especially in their attic—but it was more for their extended conversations as opposed to random thoughts and observations. Those smaller talks were happening more wordlessly. It was so smooth a transition, however, that Leanne didn't consciously take notice.

Instead, she was enjoying a certain enhanced connection now that Jay seemed less isolated to their attic and more integrated into her life everywhere. She wondered if it was kind of like a living, pre-death version of what he had once described as his always being there, even though he wasn't hanging around watching her. Now she was more there too, in that wordless world.

Of course, Leanne was also in the regular world, with not only lots of out-loud words from lots of different people, but lots of noise in general. She wondered if, when she died someday, there would be quiet forever. The thought was both appealing and frightening.

And just which of the two was usually determined by what kind of day it had been in the noise-addled world of the living. Still, no matter how much of the outside world assaulted her senses some days, it was hard to fathom total silence when that proposed silence was forever. That sounded way too quiet.

"But I guess if I don't have ears someday, maybe I won't mind not hearing anything," she mused out loud to Jay one day, not expecting any sort of confirmation. Leanne was simply pondering stuff as they always had together, even though such discussions were certainly more of a challenge now, and sometimes, one-sided. Leanne knew such insider details weren't his to give or hers to hear yet. But she could still wonder.

It started out like any other day. Leanne was enjoying a leisurely day off from work. She'd spent the morning puttering around in the garden, followed by a light lunch on the porch, relaxing with the paper. The combination of sun and movement back and forth on the old wooden glider made her especially dozy.

She was not so much tired as craving the cozy bed upstairs, a peaceful place to lie down and do nothing but enjoy her body's feeling of physical labour done well in the fresh outdoors. And if something else should happen to develop that was more sensual than snoozy, then so much the better.

It often seemed that some of their best sex occurred when Leanne was almost half asleep and could drift off completely after climaxing. Certainly there were times when she was very much awake and bouncing around with renewed vigour afterward. But generally, she was so supremely relaxed after orgasm, that curling up and going to sleep—wrapped up in Jay—was absolutely the best afterplay.

It also didn't hurt that it was easier to suspend any hints of disbelief that Jay was actually there when she was half out of it herself, more feeling than thinking.

Often they came together—in every way—after chatting about the day or vegging out in front of the TV. Sometimes it was when the day was just starting or ending. But whenever it was, the time before was peaceful and fairly quiet, assuming their conversations didn't get too animated or the TV commercials too obnoxious.

And occasionally there was almost no sound at all.

So this day, with the sun beaming through the sky-lights and the general soothing laziness of the afternoon, a carefree Leanne let her hands wander about as she lay on their bed.

"Mmmm, Jay," she murmured as her left hand came in-to play and covered her right, giving it a loving squeeze be-fore moving lower. As she rolled onto her stomach—dildo deftly positioned—the lovemaking movements continued, just as before, just as they had for nearly twenty years now. It had been even longer than that if the count began be-fore Jay died. But those were the years they didn't keep count of, even though they counted more than anything.

But this afternoon, something was different. Without warning, without any indication anything had changed, Leanne abruptly stopped moving, as if she were frozen in time while trying to take in what had just happened. She had this blank look on her face, a face that should have been wearing shock instead, that should have been dev-astated by what she suddenly felt, or rather, didn't feel. But it was blank. Leanne was staring into the void of the room, expressionless.

Yet behind her empty gaze, she was beginning to un-derstand. He wasn't there this time, not in the way he had been. She was alone.

For the first time since those three tortuous solitary weeks after he died, Leanne actually felt alone in their at-tic. The blankness stayed as her eyes grew moist. But there were no tears. Nothing fell out of those staring eyes.

Somehow Leanne knew, even through the numbness she couldn't help but feel, that things had changed. And not only for this one time, but for them all. It felt like one of those forever you-can't-go-back changes.

Surprisingly, she had more of an empty feeling, a feeling of nothingness, rather than one of supreme sadness. There was almost a resolute acceptance that yet another part of their relationship was over. It was as if at last, there really was nothing left of his body to be felt. Maybe she was finally ready to know him only as he was now.

"It finally happened," Leanne spoke to Jay, to herself, and to the air in their attic. "So it's today is it? The twenty-seventh of May, two thousand . . . oh, it doesn't matter. It doesn't matter when. It matters that it happened."

Leanne was still lying down, but now half on her stomach, half on her side. With the appeal of sex so completely gone and forgotten, she was actually surprised when she saw the dildo fall to the floor after she moved to sit up.

She looked all around, as if taking in her surroundings for the first time. They seemed to have changed so much in the last few minutes.

Leanne looked up through the skylights, out through the windows, and then at their bed—the place of so much talk, and action.

"You know, I wondered if it actually ever would. Could I be so lucky? Hmph, guess not," Leanne answered herself.

Leaning back against the headboard, she propped herself up on the pillows and folded both her hands behind her head. It felt oddly OK to feel only her own hands.

"I guess I should count myself lucky. I mean, day after day I've had all this"—she gestured around herself—"for how many years now? Almost twenty? Has it really been that long? Time sure adds up fast when you count it. Oh, that's great, Leanne, really makes wonderful numerical sense." She laughed at herself. "And you used to be a bookkeeper? Good grief. Guess it's a darn good thing you made a career change. And now what are you doing? Talking to yourself."

But the words kept coming. "Coming here, to our bed, my bed I guess, being with you, really being . . . with you, Jay, it's always been so real. Yet when each visit was over, that was strangely fine too. There wasn't a horrible sense of loss, no smack of harsh reality in the face, because I knew there would always be another time. Always more. No good-bye. You weren't gone. I mean, I knew you were dead. I knew that before your first touch. But every time, there you were, with me. And you actively were. It was not some memory relived or fantasy imagined. I know it. It was new. Always new. We got more new time together, every time."

By trying to talk out all her feelings, she was hoping things would be clearer when she did stop talking.

"After so long, I guess I sort of took it for granted. I assumed it would keep on." Leanne chuckled and shook her head. "How exactly like normal life is that? Taking things for granted. And it's probably what we'd have ended up doing if you'd never been sick, if you'd been alive as you ought to have been all these years," she said with a gentle smile, half shaking her head as she exhaled.

"But, Jay, even now, you're still here in some way. You are. I can feel it, otherwise I'd be freaking out. I'm still going to talk to you, you know, and still hear you back."

The room was completely silent. But as always, she heard him. "I know, Lee. I know. And I'm grinning, in case you can't tell."

"I can always tell." She laughed before explaining how. "When you're happy there's an extra something there, in the way it makes me feel. I can tell."

"You amaze me. You always have. And I can't believe how long it's been," Jay said.

"It sure doesn't feel like it."

"You know time. It never did make much sense. One moment it was flying by, and the next it couldn't move fast enough." Jay remembered his time-based life, ignoring the momentous change that had occurred for Leanne moments earlier. He wasn't disregarding it, but just as she had to let her patients discover some things in their own wayward time, so she had to discover these bumps along her road.

"Unwrap my own onion, I know, Jay," Leanne piped in unexpectedly.

"What?" he asked, surprised. "How'd you know what I was thinking?"

"I don't know. But it sounds like something you'd be thinking right now. And I get there's stuff I can't have certain answers for, but you know the funny thing? I've been wondering lately if the reason I can't know, and why you can't tell me, isn't just the obvious you're-dead-and-I'm-not thing, but because deep down, I really don't want to know. I'm still feasting on an outer layer of my onion. And the centre can wait," Leanne said as she went downstairs, surprising herself that she was still happy.

CHAPTER SEVENTEEN

LEANNE CONTINUED TO remain uninterested in sex after Jay's abrupt sexual disappearance. It was the longest Leanne had gone without an orgasm since her early teens—when she first got inventive, discovering how glorious she could make herself feel. She still fondly remembered that first makeshift dildo, and how very glad she had been to have found something so innocent in its intended purpose.

The confidence to proudly and openly buy an actual sex toy was a few years away at that point. And a whole other dimension was added later when she had sex with a partner for the first time. But solo sex had continued, interspersed with the small handful of people she had been with before meeting Jay.

Since Jay's death, Leanne had lost interest in sex for brief periods, but never for this long. She later credited those earlier abstentions—once her sex drive returned—to being too busy and focused on school, then on her new career, to simply being too tired or not thinking about it, to even conceding that her hormone levels had to be different from what they used to be. Or maybe she just wasn't getting enough zinc in her diet. So Leanne tried to remember to eat more pumpkin seeds.

But now that her body no longer felt like a conduit for Jay, all touches seemed different. She felt separated from herself. The left side wasn't ever Jay anymore, but it wasn't all her again either. Occasionally Leanne caught herself holding her right hand with her left. She wanted to feel him again, but instead felt empty and alone. Her left thumb stroking the back of her right hand elicited nothing. There were no special sensations. It almost felt unpleasant.

Even a casual brush of her left hand on her right arm felt wrong, as if a stranger were touching her. So allowing hormones to have a say had been out of the question. She'd preferred to remain indifferent to the whole idea of sex. But slowly that was changing. Her body was reuniting and starting to trigger familiar feelings.

But would those last? Leanne knew that Becky and Brian had started to consciously schedule sex so they didn't lose it altogether as a part of their lives. The idea had sounded strange to her at the time, but less so now. "Maybe that's something I should try too. If couples have to plan sometimes, why shouldn't I?"

Jay pointed out that couples had scheduling issues that Leanne couldn't lay similar claim to. He was met with an amused glare.

"That may be true, but since I'll have to do all the work, all the remembering, and all the doing—with both sides now—that should like double-count or something."

"Gosh, Lee, you weren't just remembering your teens, you've reverted to a younger you. Are you sure you're old enough to have sex? I mean, like, you know, like double-count, that's just gnarly," Jay said before Leanne swatted at the air, making them both laugh.

It felt incredibly good to still be able to kid around with him, all while sharing feelings and thoughts. She was still with Jay the way it counted most.

"When I've been sexually inactive before," Leanne said, "everything seemed fine, nothing felt as if it were missing. Life was full and good. But then, when I reminded myself and got active again, I was like, 'What the hell have I been thinking? This is so indescribably fantastic! Why have I not been doing this all the time?'"

She ignored her recent foreign-body issues. Both sides were definitely tingling now. There was no need for any scheduling—silicone was absolutely coming out of the drawer later.

"Preaching to the choir, my dear," Jay said. It was unclear whether he was speaking from current experience or memory.

"I know, love. Man, I wish you could. I mean, I hope you can still . . . I just don't know how that might work, but I'm sure hoping there's some kind of spiritual orgasm. Something."

All Jay said in reply was, "I love you, Lee."

"I love you too. So much, so beyond all."

"Always in all ways," he added.

"OK, I'm going to start feeling really maudlin here. I thought we were talking about sex. How'd we get on to love?" she joked, needing to redirect the conversation.

After his death, "I love you" were the only three words she couldn't bear to hear from Jay or say to him without breaking down. While underneath all the sadness and poignancy there was also a rush of warmth and good shivers, the pain dominated, and so those words were spoken less frequently.

"That's right, you were rubbing it in about how great sex feels. Thanks a lot," Jay said, acting hard done by, but there was a tinge of truth mixed in.

"I was rubbing it in, huh?"

"You are so not helping. God, I wish I could be there with you, even just the way we were when I borrowed your left side. I'd so happily take that again."

"I still don't fully understand why all that changed," Leanne said.

"Well, all I can say is"—Jay wished he could share more—"I'm glad you're ready to enjoy sex again. And I promise, I won't be some dead voyeur getting my kicks from watching you masturbate. But it can be fun to talk about, can't it?"

"Sort of like phone sex? We never did get to do that since we were pretty much always in the same place."

"Well, we're long distance now, so I say we go for it. But," he then acknowledged, "I have a feeling it's going to be more memory based now, isn't it?"

"For the same reason you're not on my left side now, yeah, I think you're right. It's as if we'd be . . . I'd be right back where I—" Leanne stopped herself. "I don't mean that was bad, I don't. It was wonderful, but now, it feels different—"

"It's OK, Lee. Maybe it's good that it's different."

Even though she had technically been masturbating since he died, because she hadn't felt as if she were alone,

Leanne didn't count those times. So it was a reawakening for her as she rediscovered solo sex again. The difference wasn't technical but emotional as she enjoyed herself while completely alone in her thoughts. It was almost like being sixteen again and exploring herself—what she was thinking, how she was feeling, and what she wanted to do—all on her own.

The knowing looks and chuckles continued whenever she shared something with Jay, both in public and in private. That hadn't changed. And she still had to remember to dial back her public reactions so no one could tell, or at least ensure her reaction was subtle enough that no one would have the nerve to ask what was going on.

Since Leanne's best non-Jay friend was Becky, and she was thousands of kilometres away in Europe, their conversations happened largely on the phone. They were more often concentrated catch-up sessions, and less likely to have lingering Jay moments. He was occasionally spoken of, but Leanne tried to steer such conversations in other directions to avoid having the one that she feared Becky would choose if she could.

When Jay was brought up at any length, that was all the encouragement Becky needed to lovingly—but also annoyingly—press Leanne where she didn't want to go. What was Leanne doing with her personal life? Why was she still single after so very long? Wasn't it time—more than past time, in fact—to move on? Wouldn't that be what Jay would have wanted?

It always came back to Jay. And that led to Leanne's awkward avoidance of explaining his enduring presence in her life. It was easier to avoid the whole conversation, at least with anyone but him.

In her quieter moments, safely tucked away in their attic, Leanne did entertain the possibility that the world at large might have a point. On one particularly reflective day, she sat cross-legged on the dormer bench seat listening to her favourite oldies radio station, thinking about the choices she'd made.

But then Bread's "If" came over the airwaves. David Gates' words had always resonated with her on so many levels. The music and words melded together perfectly in a way that was both soothing and haunting. Leanne closed her eyes. Her left hand was on her chin as her elbow pressed into the windowsill. It was all her now, every part. But Jay was still with her.

In an odd way, she felt his presence more sometimes. When he was alive Leanne obviously felt her whole body completely as her own, and she had that again. So in that sense it was like old times. Or maybe that was merely how she tried to spin the ongoing changes to their relationship, changes which she never had a say in.

What she wouldn't have given to be able to really hold his whole body, in both of her arms. But that option was not on the table—or in the attic.

"Who knows, Jay," Leanne said as she leaned forward to pick up her glass of wine—an indulgence that she had decided to enjoy again. "Maybe they are right, maybe not. But look, it's what happened. It's what was right each day. It's my life, my choice. This is what I want and I've found a way to have it. The years pass so quickly. You don't realize how fast all those daily choices are adding up. Suddenly you're here, suddenly aware a good chunk of your life has passed."

The conversation had morphed into more of a monologue, something that was happening more often now. "But so what if I'm here all these years later looking back, and a part of me is thinking, 'Yikes, what have I done?' I've been happy day to day. I've lived the choices I wanted, what made me happy that day, the day after that, and the one after that. And on it went. On it goes.

"One of things I learned from you, Jay, is if the day isn't what you want and doesn't make you happy, if you don't live it as you want, then forget it. There's no way all those unhappy days are somehow going to magically add up at the end of all this, and be some big happy life lived. There's no way a bunch of bad days are going to become good years. Retrospective happiness or something? It can't happen—the cumulative sum of parts and all that. Making decisions based only on the future sucks. Yeah, let's base our life on what we think might happen rather than what is happening. Time sure has us fucked up. Yet again. Let's measure time, begrudge its passing, count off the minutes until our time's up. Yay!"

The sarcasm was dripping from her wine-coated lips. "Who of us actually wants to know almost no one lives a million hours? A million bloody hours! When I think of all the ones I've wasted, getting a million of them sounds like nothing. So I should, what? Make choices today that make me unhappy because I think they'll make me happier some future day? How fucked is that?"

"Pretty fucked I'd say," Jay said once Leanne had gotten out what she needed.

Her questions were not the kind that demanded detailed replies. It was more of a venting, an opportunity to give voice to fears and doubts she felt, in spite of her long-standing confident words to the contrary.

"Why does saying things out loud feel so freeing, Jay?" Before he could answer, she offered her own reason. "It's as if I'm releasing them somehow, sending them off into the universe to fend for themselves or something, so they don't keep churning inside me."

"But you've been happy, living this way, with me this way," he said. "So what does it matter now if you have a few doubts?"

"What do you mean, doubts? I just finished saying how stupid it would have been to have done things any differently than I have!"

"Doth protesting a bit much?" Jay asked. "And before you get mad at me for that jab, would you really be this upset if there wasn't some part of you that did have doubts?"

Leanne said nothing.

She felt a mass of negativity filling her instead of the fresh attic air. But she wasn't upset with Jay. She was upset that what began as a simple reflection had turned into this mess of conflicting emotions.

But instead of retreating to sleep, Leanne worked at calming herself down while she kept talking with Jay. She wanted her normal life with normal conversations. And she reminded herself that no one had it all.

While not as much as it had once been, they continued to communicate some every day. There was still the sound-less sharing of little tidbits from Leanne's day. Knowing smiles and looks filled the air wherever she happened to be. And occasionally they found themselves talking about the people in their lives, although Jay's personal reference points were rather outdated. It was especially fun to speak of those they both knew like Becky and Brian, Lissa, who'd now graduated from university, and Donovan, who still lived nearby. Jay's old pal always seemed to be there if Leanne needed help with the house whenever anything fell into disrepair.

While Donovan had been more Jay's friend, he and Leanne had gotten closer over the years from the sheer passage of time and the increased familiarity. Even though they didn't speak of Jay often—for the same reasons she avoided that with Becky—it was comforting for Leanne to be around someone who had been around the man she loved.

When she and Donovan would hug hello or good-bye, she was being hugged by arms that had hugged Jay. When hands rested on her back, they were ones that had once slapped Jay's back in greeting. A little lingering cell transference was a nice thought, no matter how unrealistic.

From Leanne's perspective, he was just their good pal Donovan. He entered their lives that way and stayed that way. So Leanne was caught off guard when Becky asked if the reason Donovan had never married was because of his feelings for Leanne.

She'd genuinely never thought of him that way. And so, perhaps naively, she had never considered he might feel differently. But as Becky recounted all the things that could signify deeper feelings on his part, Leanne began to see that Becky could be right.

"If he did, or does have feelings for me, that'd be weird. I mean, it's Donovan. I've known him for almost as long as I've known Jay," Leanne said, not meaning to open the "Jay door" with Becky, whom she hoped hadn't caught the lack of a past tense. But before she could try to close that door preemptively, Leanne had to hold the phone away from her ear.

"Exactly!" Becky yelled into the phone. "It would be perfect. You know he's a good guy, and that Jay would approve of him, and you—"

"Becky, stop." Leanne quietly cut her off. "Whether he does or doesn't think of me in that way, I don't think of him that way. And besides, I should at least be attracted to the man, don't you think?" Leanne tried to get Becky to laugh.

"What do you mean? He's gorgeous. If anything were ever to happen to Brian—" Becky started to joke, but was interrupted.

"Don't say that Becky. Don't you ever say that." Leanne couldn't see the humour she knew was intended.

"I'm sorry, I didn't mean—"

"I know. And I didn't mean to snap," Leanne said. "But when I hear stuff like that, I mean, I know there's no such thing as a jinx—or there better not be—but you do not want to find out what it's like when something does happen, even when you know it's going to."

"Well, that certainly takes the fun out of our little gab session. You go throwing reality into the mix," Becky said in a playful tone to show she wasn't really upset with her friend for growing so serious.

"You know me. Life of the party."

"Oh yeah, you're a regular party animal," Becky kidded. "It's always a real wonder when I catch you at home. And Leanne, you do know, I didn't mean anything with that crack before. Things may not be perfect anymore, but I love Brian. I do. I just want you to have that. Not my Brian, of course, but your own version."

"I know you do, and I love you for it, I do. But, Becky, I really don't want you to bring up my finding someone new anymore. I'm happy, as happy as I can be. You don't need to worry. Now, as far as Donovan goes, maybe you can help me that. You don't actually think I'm why he's single, do you?"

But before Becky could answer, Leanne had another idea. "Hey, maybe he's gay. That would make things so much easier. Of course, why wouldn't I know, or Jay, for that matter? Have known, I mean. Shoot, that means he's probably straight."

"I hope so, otherwise it'll spoil my fantasies. Or maybe it'll give me different ones," Becky said.

"You're a big help." Leanne laughed. "But look, I think we're getting carried away with all this. He's probably simply being a good friend looking out for his old pal's widow. Oh, God, I don't think I've ever used that word for myself before. I don't like it. It feels strange to think in those terms." Leanne was careful not to expand on why she felt only corporeally a widow.

"I bet it does. I can't imagine losing Brian. Leanne, are you OK talking about this? I won't bring it up anymore if that's what you really want. But I haven't wanted to believe you all those times you've tried to tell me. I guess I saw how much you loved being with Jay, and I wanted you to find that again, but—" Becky caught herself. "Here I am still talking about it. I'm stopping now."

"Thanks, for the stopping part, and for trying to understand," Leanne said. "You know, as I'm replaying things in my head, I'm feeling a little guilty I didn't think of this possibility sooner."

Specifically, Leanne thought back to how maybe some of their hugs could have been misinterpreted if Donovan had been wanting to see them a certain way. There had been a few times when he'd looked at her more intently than other people did. And there had been hugs that had gone on a little longer than maybe they should have, but not by much, not enough to make her wonder at the time.

It was funny, though, how easy it was to pick up on little things when more was desired, sometimes seeing only what was wanted.

"But surely he would not have kept quiet for almost twenty years," Leanne said, glad that Becky was on the phone and not in the room to see her sarcastic eye roll. No, no one would ever keep anything quiet for two decades.

The two old friends continued to rehash what, if anything, Leanne should do regarding Donovan, becoming rather silly and overly dramatic at times. Although they were trying to find a helpful solution, the best part was being able to talk like girls talking about boys, happily unconcerned with the fact that they were both well past the half-century mark.

"So what are you going to do, Lee?" Jay asked later on.

"I don't know. But I'm afraid I'll feel awkward around Donovan now that I'm wondering what he's thinking, if anything. But talk about awkward if I bring it up, and it turns out to be nothing but a figment of some fertile imaginations from this afternoon."

"Do you want it to be a figment? Or maybe real instead?" There was an ease to his questions, a gentle naturalness.

Most of all, Jay wanted Leanne to be happy, however she chose. Having no body to be jealous with anymore made loving someone more absolute and infinite. Physical jealousy or possessiveness seemed rather pointless when all that remained was the inexplicable connection of souls.

Of course, it didn't hurt that Jay knew nothing could take away from what they were to each other.

"A figment would be a whole lot easier," Leanne replied. "Donovan's not for me. He's a dear friend, and I love him, but not that way. He just doesn't send me." She imitated the romantic twang of a bygone era.

Jay smiled and Leanne felt it.

"I'm thinking, though," she continued, "maybe I can be more careful with the hugs and, you know, try to subtly do the opposite of leading someone on. Jay, maybe I'm taking the chicken's way out, but no matter how he feels, I don't want to embarrass him, or me either. Is that terrible?"

"I'm trying to think how I'd react, and whether I'd prefer seeing what would no doubt be a noticeable change in behaviour—no matter how subtle you try to make it— or having all the cards blatantly out on the table. I guess I'm thinking if I really liked someone, unless the changes were really obvious, I'd probably still try to find a way to misinterpret actions in my favour," Jay said. "That's not the answer you probably wanted."

"No, it's not. But on the other hand, wouldn't it be easier to continue being friends if I don't make a big deal out of something that might be nothing? I don't want there to be any hurt feelings or awkwardness."

"That might not be something you can prevent, Lee, even if you go with your first instinct and pull back on the hugs. That could still hurt if he's hoping you'll instead, well, push forward with the hugs."

"Even so," she said, "I think that's better than the alternative. Besides, as far as he's concerned you've been gone for a rather long time now, so exactly how long was he planning to wait?"

"My guess is, it's been more of a possibility he's floated around in his head, rather than something he was prepared to act on," Jay suggested. "You're a nice thought, a romantic notion, a maybe-one-day kind of fallback plan."

"You really know how to flatter a person, Jay." Leanne laughed as she shut down the house for the night. "It's a good thing I know what you mean."

"That reminds me, you called yourself a widow earlier with Becky," he said as Leanne made sure the doors and windows were secure and the stove was off.

"Yeah, it was strange. I've always talked so much more to you, rather than about you, that I don't have cause to use words like that. I know technically I am a widow, but it doesn't feel like it." Leanne hesitated slightly. "Well, at least not most of the time."

"But that's just it, since we never married—officially anyway—can you actually be a widow? You never had a husband. And with no husband to be dead, there's no official widow status, right?"

"I think you're taking Webster's a little too literally. But I do like where you're going—playing with the semantics. I'm not a widow due to a technicality!" she exclaimed. "And if I'm not a widow, then I can't possibly have lost my partner."

"Never lost, Lee, only dead," Jay reminded. Sometimes the odd euphemism was hard to avoid. They were so ingrained that, even now, one could slip out.

"That's right, only dead." Leanne smiled as she shut off the last light and crawled into bed. "You know the other reason I'm not so keen on the *widow* word? It's kind of weird, but every time I hear it—" She interrupted herself to yawn. "What I first think of aren't dead spouses, but black widow spiders." Leanne scrunched up her face as her entire body shivered.

"At least they're wearing a respectful mourning black," Jay said.

She yawned again.

"You have a good night, Lee."

"Mmmmmm." Leanne stretched languidly. And with that, the conversation for another day was done, and she fell asleep with a peaceful smile—as soon as she forgot about those spiders.

CHAPTER EIGHTEEN

A<small>T WORK A FEW</small> months later, Leanne was asked to show the latest new hire—a therapist transitioning from private practice—all around the counselling centre. This welcoming task usually fell to Leanne as she had both the knowledge of the place and the enthusiasm that came from joining the field as a second career.

On their more stressful days, her colleagues joked that since she wasn't burnt out yet, she wouldn't scare away the new employees with any jaded pessimism that might slip out of their mouths.

Leanne finished the orientation with a coffee break in the staff lounge. It was a good opportunity for the new person—Ryan Michaelson in this case—to informally ask questions about the lay of the land, to kind of get a head start on fitting in. Leanne wasn't a boss or supervisor, so it was just two peers chatting.

However, this particular work chat was taking on a distinctly different feel for Leanne. But she was too busy enjoying herself to consciously take notice or be concerned.

"So yeah, it's a pretty nice place to work, and it certainly offers those reduced hours you're looking for," Leanne said as they finished their second cups of coffee. "I think you'll like it, Ryan. It's a good place to come to each day, good people, good friends."

"I think I may already have met one." Ryan flirted with her, much to his own surprise, since he prided himself on his restraint. He certainly hadn't intended to look at any of his new co-workers the way he knew he was looking at Leanne, and absolutely not on the first day.

Ryan had seen Leanne when he had been interviewed. He'd even been introduced to her briefly afterward, but he had been introduced to a lot of people that day. There was a blur of new faces and names swirling in his head. But Ryan had to admit that he was noticeably glad when Leanne turned out to be the one to show him around the centre. Maybe it was because she was a semi-familiar face rather than a completely brand-new one. And that face was smiling at him now.

"Oh, you do, do you?" Leanne laughed.

"Yeah. Why is that so funny?"

Her amused expression faded a bit. "It's a long story, a long old story." Leanne didn't volunteer more. Meeting people and making new friends could be a double-edged sword sometimes. When she did venture forth, it was easier not to share the past, at least not what still existed in the present.

Getting the hint, Ryan moved on. "OK, then. New subject. What are you doing after work?"

"I'm not sure that's an entirely new subject there, Ryan. But no big plans," Leanne found herself saying.

"Good. So, do you maybe want to continue this over dinner later?" Time and disappointment had taught Ryan not to put off what he wanted to do, and he wanted to keep this conversation going.

Leanne shook her head in quiet disbelief at what was happening, and at what she was about to say. "Sure, why not? That sound's nice actually."

They settled on Mexican.

As they were sharing a large platter of nachos, Ryan asked, "So tell me, how did you get into counselling?" It was another of the otherwise mundane, let's-get-to-know-each-other details that they had been enjoying all evening.

But this question caused Leanne to hesitate because it wasn't about current likes or dislikes. "Part of that long old story, Ryan. I don't really talk about it. Never have, actually."

"So, I'm guessing, you don't want to start now, then," Ryan said gently. There was something about this woman, a strength he didn't think he had ever seen, but a scared vulnerability too.

"Yeah, no. I don't know. That career question, meeting you, all this, it's bringing back a lot of memories, things we," she inadvertently said, "that I haven't shared."

Ryan ignored her slip of the tongue. She didn't act as if she was involved with anyone. But maybe there was someone in her past that she didn't want to talk about. He understood what that could be like. "And you're not sure you ever want to."

Leanne was surprised by his understanding comment. "How can you know that?"

"You're not the only one with secrets, with memories, perhaps," he said.

Ryan had a faraway longing look that she recognized all too well.

"Hmm." She nodded slowly. "Maybe that's why this feels the way it does. Somehow you get it. You know." Leanne paused before asking, "What was her name?"

After a pause of his own, Ryan quietly replied, "Terri."

"I'm sorry." Words so long unspoken were brief. There was so much to say, and no way to say it all.

"Me too."

"Jay, his name . . . Jay."

"I'm sorry too," Ryan said.

"Yeah."

"Well, gee, this is fun, Leanne. Talking, or not talking about—"

"Whatever it is we're saying, yeah."

Despite what they had shared, or maybe partially because of it, they were both smiling gently.

"But being here with you, it's nice. Oh, brother," Ryan said. "What kind of word is that? It's soooooo nice. I'm sorry for that too." He laughed self-consciously.

"Don't worry about it. And it is, nice," Leanne said. "I never thought I'd actually want to even consider, well, getting to know someone . . ."

"New?"

"Someone, else," she substituted.

New implied out with the old. Ryan might understand the death of a partner, but Jay's continuing presence in her life was another matter.

Changing the subject, Leanne asked, "So, do you have any children or, dare I say, grandchildren? Not that we're in any way nearly old enough for that, of course."

"Oh, certainly not. Old enough, that is," Ryan said before conspiratorially whispering, "even though we are. That said, however, no grandchildren, but we, well, I have a daughter, Abigail. She's fantastic, successful, and most of all, happy. And she's married to a great guy. They live nearby, close to her ol' man. You?"

"No, no kids," Leanne said. "It wasn't possible. Let's just say it didn't happen." Ryan was silent, which prompted Leanne to continue. "Hey, sometimes that's the way it works out. I could've adopted. I didn't."

"I'm not sure what to say. We've said 'I'm sorry' too much already."

"Thanks for not saying it then." She smiled. "Really, it is OK. It didn't happen. Time went on, and here we are."

"And you seem happy, Leanne."

"Life may not have turned out as I thought it would— or wanted it to—but it has happened. And it's definitely had its moments. It's been good too. And full of surprises," Leanne said, smiling. Her cheekbones were starting to hurt she'd been grinning so much.

"Tell me about it," Ryan said. "I thought I was just starting a new job today."

"Speaking of which, it is getting late. And we both do have work tomorrow. I suppose we should get going." It was one of those comments that was said more out of an assumed expectation that it was time to call it a day, rather than a genuine desire to actually end the evening. It was only later, when Leanne thought of that crazy holdover of propriety, that she realized there was only one person with whom she'd never felt any compunction to follow society's rules. But at the restaurant, caught up in the whirlwind of the unexpected day, such thoughts of Jay were not in the forefront of her mind.

"Yes, I do suppose it's getting late." He nodded slowly. "How time flies."

"Oh, don't get me started on my views on time," she said, a little too emphatically.

"For another day then." Ryan wasn't one to press. Perhaps it was a reaction to a lifetime of counselling others to talk and share, but in his personal life he preferred to let people divulge whatever they wanted, whenever they wanted. "Come on, I'll walk you to your car."

They stood up and were standing side by side. Ryan hesitantly reached out his hand but made no move to take hers. Hesitating as well, Leanne smiled, and then she reached for his.

It was her first actual physical contact of that nature with a man in over two decades. There had been hugs and friendly kisses on the cheek, but those hadn't made her heart beat faster.

Neither spoke during the short walk to her car. Leanne felt an almost imperceptible squeeze just before Ryan let go of her hand.

Then they fell back on normal pleasantries. "Thank you again for the tour of the centre," Ryan said as she got into her car.

Rolling down the window, Leanne replied equally politely, "It was my pleasure. I'll see you tomorrow."

She then drove home in her now ten-year-old car. "I'm sure glad I got lazy about walking everywhere and bought this thing," Leanne said out loud as she pulled into her driveway. "It sure made for an easier exit than if

I'd been walking home or taking the bus." It wasn't that she wanted to leave exactly, but she felt so out of practice that this seemed a lot simpler than other ways to say good night. Driving herself avoided any potential offer of a ride home with its delayed exit. She needed some time to try to absorb her surprising day.

"I'm happy for you, Lee," Jay said as Leanne came upstairs and flopped down on the bed.

"Hmm?"

"I'm happy for you," he repeated.

"What are you talking ab—" Leanne started to ask before realizing that, of course, he already knew. Exactly how he was able to know things she hadn't told him remained a mystery.

The list of questions was endless, and largely unanswered. What was his existence like now? What did he do with his day when he wasn't with her? He'd said she wouldn't always have to worry about measuring time. Did that mean it wasn't even split into days for him anymore? His death was the one area of their life they couldn't share.

Somehow, though, Jay knew she had met someone at work.

"You mean Ryan," she said quietly.

"Yeah, I mean Ryan. Or did you meet more than one somebody special at work today?"

"No, just the one," she replied before hurriedly adding, "I mean, no, not as special as—"

"Lee, stop," Jay interrupted. "It's OK. It's not a contest. I can tell from your face that he's special. I'm happy."

"But, Jay, how can you be? All these years it's been just us." There had been conversations about the dating possibility in the abstract before, but now it was becoming real and felt entirely different as a result.

"It still will be us, just not in the same way," Jay reassured. "Yet another change to get used to." He laughed, but with a hint of bitterness creeping in. Maybe he had to be dead even longer before he lost that lovely human frailty entirely. Why couldn't he have been with Leanne all this time in every way? And why did they have to keep going through these adjustments? But before all the inequities bubbled up and broke the surface, Jay was drawn back to how on the flip side, they had gotten uncountably lucky in the first and most important place—they met in a park one random day.

"Jay?" Leanne wondered where he'd gone for a moment.

"I'm here," he said. "Wishing, feeling a little nostalgic, I guess. I'm thinking of when we first met. We had so much ahead of us. And now, here you are feeling . . ."

She squeezed her right forearm and closed her eyes, trying to feel his touch as she used to so easily. It didn't work.

"But, Lee, I am still so happy for you. Most of me is thrilled you have the chance to love again. It's so wonderful." Hesitating then, he sought reassurance. "You'll still come here, though, right?" Apparently, insecurity was another one of those visiting frailties.

"You said it to me, remember?" Leanne quoted Jay's words to her in those early post-death days. "It's still me. I'm here because this is the only place I want to be, however we can. And I'm not going anywhere you don't want me to." It was then Leanne's turn to hesitate. "But I don't think I can talk about . . . I mean, I know the sex thing isn't there anymore, and all the everyday touching too—"

"Hey, I thought those were the same thing with us," Jay interrupted in a vain attempt to ease what was coming.

"Oh, Jay, even talking about these things now, it feels so close, so intimate. Too intimate. I can't explain it. Oh, God, I hate this, I want to touch you, but I can't." The last word seemed to hang painfully in the air. "And now, I'm getting this pitted-stomach mess of feelings for someone who isn't you."

It had been more than twenty-five years since Leanne's last first official date and all its delicious anticipation. As she waited for Ryan to pick her up for their clichéd dinner-and-a-movie date, she was divided on whether or not she was enjoying these new feelings. However, this time it wasn't about conflicting emotions but rambunctious butterflies.

Leanne was anxious to get the date going so she could distract her jittery insides. She knew that once she saw Ryan, she would relax and be caught up in simply enjoying his presence.

But as Leanne looked in the mirror again, the thought of actually eating food anytime soon was about more than her stomach could bear.

One advantage of her rather sequestered life was retaining an almost juvenile innocence and optimism in the romance department. She hadn't been hurt by failed relationships. There had been no infidelity or trust issues to make her cynical. And at the same time, she didn't feel naive to the way the world was. She had seen friends go through bad breakups and be left a little more hardened each time.

Leanne had certainly lived through her own share of tough stuff, but there had always been love along with it.

As she went to answer the door at the first knock, she decided that maybe she did kind of enjoy feeling turned upside down. It made it feel as if the intensity of the evening had been turned up as well. "I haven't felt this alive since— No, I am not going to do that," she said to herself as she opened the door.

Three and a half hours later the door opened again. Neither wanted the evening to end. Leanne was grateful for another dating cliché. "Would you like to come in for a cup of coffee?"

"I'd love to, Leanne," Ryan said as he closed the door behind him. Setting his coat down while Leanne moved toward the kitchen, Ryan continued their critique of the movie. "You know, I never knew that guy could do comedy, not intentionally anyway."

"You're not speaking of his fabulous dramatic performances that have been so phony they've made my skin crawl, are you? I'm surprised I haven't shed a few skins over the years."

"That would be a neat trick. I'd like to see that," Ryan said before realizing how that might have come across.

After a slight hesitation, Leanne resumed the safer movie talk. "You know, I've almost felt embarrassed for that guy when I've watched stuff I knew he intended to be serious, and I've found myself laughing instead."

"Good thing this movie was actually meant to be funny, so we were allowed to laugh," Ryan said. "I wouldn't want to get thrown out of the theatre for misbehaving, at least not on our first official date." He too had a certain amount of innocence and accompanying insecurity, and hoped the reference to a first date wasn't too obvious or pushy, or needy, for that matter.

Happily, Leanne carried on with his line of thinking. "We'll have to save getting thrown out of places for at least our third date, I'd say."

Although neither said anything, thoughts of what else was often associated with the third date passed through their minds, resulting in momentary silence.

After pouring the coffee, Leanne led the way back into the living room where the conversation resumed. But even the caffeine couldn't stave off their growing tiredness. Before long, they found themselves standing somewhat awkwardly at the front door.

Leanne was a little surprised when Ryan bent down and, instead of giving her the good-night kiss she'd been thinking of giving him, he kissed her cheek.

But before she could start questioning his interest, he asked her, "What are you doing Saturday? I cook a mean spaghetti."

"That sounds great." Leanne smiled, stifling a yawn.

"We can set a time tomorrow, when we're both more awake. I'll give you a call tomorrow night if we don't get a chance to chat at work." While there was no rule about co-workers dating, Leanne and Ryan didn't want to exactly advertise it either.

"I look forward to it," she said.

Then Ryan surprised her a second time by kissing her on the cheek again before he left. The look Leanne saw on his face made her think he had temporarily forgotten he'd already done that. There was a hint of awkwardness when he pulled back that time, as if he'd realized his repetition and was afraid he would appear overeager, or maybe not eager enough for a full-on kiss.

"Guess he's not the only one overthinking every action." Leanne smiled to herself as she watched Ryan drive away.

CHAPTER NINETEEN

A S THE WEEKS PASSED, Leanne and Ryan found themselves spending more and more time toge- ther. There were many laughs, a number of fasci- nating conversations, and a few awkward silences. There were more formal dates on the weekend, and impromptu get-togethers after work, grabbing a quick dinner or hang- ing out at one of their houses and ordering in.

Leanne was really enjoying having someone to reg- ularly do things with again. Whether it was seeing the latest movie or play—and dissecting it right after when everything was fresh—or curling up at home feeling the warmth radiated by another right next to her, there was an added something special when that person wasn't just a friend.

Warm weather and short sleeves were also helping. The brush of a bare but hairy forearm was having an amaz- ing effect on Leanne every time they sat on the couch watching TV.

There was something so innocent about it. But at the same time, Leanne started letting herself think about what else she wanted to touch, and have touched.

For all the masturbation she enjoyed, part of her could not wait to see and feel Ryan, to explore their bodies together. It wasn't that orgasms themselves differed entirely when with a partner as much as the lead up to them differed, and the sublime closeness after. "But then again, I may have to rethink my orgasm theory after I actually have duet sex again." Leanne smiled to herself.

For his part, Ryan was enjoying taking things slowly as well—really getting to know Leanne first. Although he did wish things had progressed faster at times, especially when, after an incredible good-night kiss, he went home alone to his shower.

But Leanne definitely didn't seem like the type of person who moved easily from one relationship to the next. He didn't want her to regret anything if they jumped in too soon and it didn't work out between them. So he tried to take his cues from her.

Fortunately, after his cheek-kissing fumble, Leanne had been sure to kiss him squarely on the lips after their second date. Slow clearly did not mean too slow, which suited Ryan just fine.

But sometimes the speed issue wasn't always so clear. It had been about five years since his wife, Terri, had died in a car accident. He didn't know if suddenly or slowly was the easier way to lose someone or, as Leanne preferred to put it, "to have someone die."

Talking about loss and death had made for some odd conversations. Such topics were probably not on the prescribed list of what to discuss on a date with someone new, but it felt important to at least share the basics of what had happened in their lives.

Ryan had never felt entirely comfortably sharing even that with the few people he had dated since becoming a widower. It had also felt like too much trouble with them. But he wanted Leanne to know.

While they were two newly met people sharing personal views, likes and dislikes, and stories about their lives, none of that had the feel of the obligatory exchanging of facts. There was none of that urge to hurry up and find out the basics about someone to see if there really was compatibility, that it wasn't only chemistry and attraction, but a genuine interest in the person inside.

Everything they had experienced since that first day at the counselling centre had only served to cement their initial feelings. But would those last and continue to grow? Was it going to be anything like what she had with Jay, or he with Terri? Having each found such profound love before, neither could escape those questions in their solitary moments.

That spurred a thoughtful conversation centred around the idea of second loves. Did one just naturally compare them? Should one consciously try not to? Was it fair to do? Was it disloyal? Did it somehow minimize the past?

While they both had an idea how Jay and Terri would have felt about hypothetical future loves, Leanne had the advantage of knowing what Jay actually felt, now that it was becoming real.

But as always, Leanne felt that certain details of her life with Jay were reserved for just the two of them. And one of those rather large details was their ongoing contact. Even though she and Jay spoke little now, his presence was still felt.

And she knew the reason he was currently less an active participant in her life was because that was what was best for her. As her years in their attic had been with Jay, this time with Ryan was becoming another bunch of days lived the way she wanted.

One of the things that Leanne most appreciated about Ryan was his comfort with the fact that they had both lived complicated lives before meeting each other. Short of rewinding some non-existent video decades long, they could never fully know what the other had experienced, let alone felt. While their pasts had made them who they each were now, detailing how that had happened seemed less important.

"I want to know anything and everything you want me to know, Leanne, but we weren't together for a big chunk of our lives, and I'd rather know about you now," Ryan said after dinner one night at Leanne's.

He had been over a number of times before, but had always just been in the living room, dining room, and kitchen. This time he had gotten the grand tour, both inside the house and out. All except for one place. As they passed the stairs, all Leanne said was, "The attic's up there," and she kept moving.

But Ryan had noticed a funny expression on her face. It looked like a cross between being somewhere else entirely and feeling guilty she hadn't shown him the upstairs. That had led to his comment about letting some things from the past stay private.

While he sensed there was more in Leanne's past than his, he still didn't feel like going into the ups and downs of his relationship with Terri. And when he did think of

Terri, he preferred to remember the positives and how good things were before the accident.

Ryan could only imagine what Leanne's life had been like. She had told him Jay died after living with AIDS for years, and that she hadn't jumped back into the dating pool until he came along.

And he thought five years was a long time to go before getting serious with someone new, let alone not even dating for over twenty. Ryan was amazed, and a little humbled, that they were getting this chance to be together.

He still wondered what was so special in the attic, but figured it was probably boxes of memorabilia and other remnants of her earlier life.

Leanne's initial surprise and euphoria over meeting Ryan was growing into what she was having to admit to herself was probably love. "It is love," she said quietly after Ryan drove home that night.

Climbing the stairs to go to bed, she continued to marvel at what was happening. "Who'd ever have thought?"

"Me," a voice said. A smiling voice.

Nodding, and giving a smile of her own, she changed into her nightgown and crawled into bed. Instead of lying there with a sea of thoughts keeping her awake for a while, she was fast asleep a minute after her head hit the pillow. Dreams of a certain fellow counsellor greeted her and kept her company throughout the night.

As Leanne thought about it, she really couldn't pinpoint when she first started sleeping downstairs in the home's original main bedroom. It had begun years before, but the process was so gradual that she hadn't consciously noticed.

She'd be downstairs curled up on the couch reading or watching television, and find she was too sleepy to bother climbing the stairs to go to bed. It seemed easier to wander into the then guest room and fall into bed there.

Next came the notion of not lugging laundry up and down the stairs.

After that, there was the big-screen TV she treated herself to, which only fit in the living room.

It seemed the universe and her laziness were conspiring to get her downstairs.

More and more the attic bedroom became the place Leanne only went to when she wanted to feel extra close to Jay. She could feel him anywhere, but the attic had been just theirs and brought all her senses alive in a different way.

But while their life kept growing there even after he died, as their relationship morphed away from the physical she felt increasingly like a visitor upstairs. She was a completely wanted visitor, but nonetheless not someone meant to stay there for too long anymore. Leanne had more living to do first.

So as clothes were washed, they were put away in the guest room. When the seasons changed, summer sandals were brought down from the attic, but winter boots did not go back up.

Leanne finally realized she had actually already moved out of the attic when she was putting away the groceries one day. It suddenly hit her that she hadn't had to replace the toilet paper in the upstairs bathroom for ages. It just hadn't been used.

The guest room had become her bedroom.

Now, as she was thinking about being with Ryan for the first time, she was very grateful that it would be in a different bed. While never one to attach a lot of significance to material things, Leanne knew there was no way she'd ever share their bed with anyone else.

Then she wondered if *theirs* would always first mean Jay's and hers. Would she ever be part of an automatic *they* with Ryan? But as she put fresh sheets on the downstairs bed, Leanne smiled. "Our bed, Ryan. Ours."

And while lying in that bed in each other's arms later that night, they were both holding on tightly.

Although Leanne and Ryan had spent plenty of time looking at each other before and during intercourse, they hadn't been eye to eye since coming down from their orgasmic highs.

When they finally pulled back from their embrace, through smiles, they were both crying a little.

"That was . . . something," Leanne said.

"Mostly good, though, right?" Ryan asked as he gently wiped the falling moisture from her cheeks before it dried.

Leanne hugged him tightly again. "Yeah, just not what I was expecting."

"That doesn't sound good." Ryan tried to laugh, but he wasn't sure what to think.

"No, not in that way," she assured him. "I don't mean that. It was absolutely wonderful. It's just . . . there were times when I . . ."

"Saw Jay, was with him?" Ryan guessed.

Leanne nodded. "But then there were these other moments when he . . . he was completely . . . gone from my thoughts."

"And both ways feel wrong," Ryan said.

"Yes, but . . . strangely right too. When I think about it now, how else could it realistically have been? I mean, did you feel Terri?"

"I did, and I didn't." Another tear rolled down his cheek. "It felt wrong and right and all mixed up and—"

"Real, very real . . . so wonderfully real." Leanne ran her hands along his bare back, hugging him closer to her. It was a comforting motion, but one that soon led to another round of lovemaking—with no one else there.

Aside from some initial hesitation, Becky was thrilled for her friend, once she heard the emotion and love in Leanne's voice when she spoke of Ryan. Becky had secretly given up all hope that Leanne would ever get together with someone else. They'd stopped talking about the possibility at Leanne's insistence, but gradually Becky had even stopped silently hoping it would happen. She'd also started seeing the good side of Leanne's choice to be on her own.

Becky's feelings were influenced by the fact that as the years had gone by and Lissa grew up and away, Becky's marriage to Brian had not turned out be everything either thought it would be. What started out with such promise was now littered with disappointments. Disillusionment without crushing, marriage-ending problems meant they stayed together, had some happy moments enjoying their family life, but were not that happy overall with each other anymore.

In fact, when Becky first learned about Ryan, she was not nearly as excited as Leanne had hoped. But Leanne understood why. And she tried not to be too singularly focused on talking about the new person in her life. But some of her giddiness and delight bubbled out.

Through her friend's eyes, Becky began to see how much things had really changed between her and Brian. They couldn't keep avoiding talking about their problems.

And Leanne, in keeping with her plan where Donovan was concerned, made sure to reference Ryan casually from the very beginning. She did so not in a hurtful or in-your-face kind of way, but just as she otherwise would have mentioned him to a good friend. She had been trying to be subtly obvious to Donovan that he shouldn't wait for her to develop romantic feelings for him, and that plan included using Ryan's name in normal conversation.

For his part, Donovan seemed almost more natural around her now. Not that he had been stilted before, but it seemed to be a relief to finally know. Some hints could not be missed no matter how much he tried.

His behaviour change only confirmed Leanne's suspicions. Part of her felt bad that she hadn't seen it sooner. She hoped he hadn't missed out on meeting someone. Deep down, however, she had to believe that people met when they were supposed to, as crazy and unpredictable as that timing often was.

Leanne was grateful that she hadn't been pining away for years. While others might disagree, in her own way, she'd gotten on with her life, irrespective of anyone else being a part of it.

Jay, though intricately connected to her all along, had not been there for the day-to-day problems and routines of life. Those had been hers and hers alone.

While Leanne had had someone to come home to and share things with, a sounding board for life's twists and turns, she was the one who had to act on them all, big and small. And she was the one responsible for all the chores like home and car maintenance. She was the one to do all the cleaning, cooking, and bill paying. She was the one to take care of the yard, mow the grass, and tend the garden.

Sure, Leanne could hire help if needed for things like gutter cleaning and oil changes, but the responsibility for it, all the decision making, all of that was hers.

Any resentment—stemming more from missing Jay's active presence than the workload itself—had, over time, grown into her trying to see the benefits.

All the paint-colour choices and furniture-placement decisions were hers too she'd remind herself, trying to ignore the fact that they'd almost always agreed on those things anyway.

Still, Leanne had come to enjoy her independence and responsibilities, and to need her own space perhaps more than most. But that didn't mean she didn't want to share some of her space too.

Part of the mystery of the attic was revealed to Ryan when the issue of their sleeping arrangements came up or, more precisely, sleeping-over arrangements.

They spent at least three or four nights a week together and now had the proverbial drawer and closet space at each other's houses.

There were no latent furniture or room issues at Ryan's since he had moved after Terri's death, wanting to avoid the guaranteed daily reminders of seeing everything they had once shared. Ryan preferred to carry his memories tucked away inside himself rather than having them staring him in the face. The few special mementos he'd held on to were stored away in boxes. No rooms were off limits.

But when it came to bedrooms, there was something puzzling at Leanne's.

The closet in the main-floor bedroom appeared to have all of her clothes and things, and now a few of Ryan's. But Leanne explained that she and Jay had converted the old attic into the main bedroom of the house.

"That's what's up there, Ryan. I didn't want you to wonder anymore. I still go up there sometimes, but . . . this is my bedroom now, down here. And this is a new bed." She tried to wink, but it came out as more of a double squint. But it did the trick and lightened the moment.

"Let's rechristen it then," he said as they tumbled onto the bed, "seeing that my clothes are here officially now."

Their passion was coupled with the gentle understanding of what they had each shared before with someone else, with no need for further explanation.

Over the years, more bits and pieces leaked out naturally, but certain life compartments were allowed their permanent space and peace.

The sleepover routine continued to suit her and, thankfully, Ryan as well. Neither had expressed any interest in formally moving in together, let alone getting married.

In fact, the opposite was true for marriage. Leanne had sighed a huge relief over that one, especially since she knew how important it had been to him with Terri.

"But I'd marry you if I had to," Ryan joked after telling her he didn't see himself marrying again. "But seeing as how getting pregnant is now biologically impossible—

not that I'm so sure that would be a good enough reason anyway—I guess I'm off the hook." Then he grew serious. "If, however, getting married were really important to you, I would be down on my proverbial knee in a second."

"Lucky for you then, and for your knees, that I think things are just great the way they are," Leanne said as she pulled him in for a kiss.

They found it difficult to keep their hands—and other body parts—off each other.

From the stories Becky told about her waning interest in sex, Leanne wondered if part of the reason she and Ryan felt like two teenagers was because their relationship was so young and new, even if they themselves were not anymore. If that was the case, Leanne sure hoped they'd feel this fresh forever.

Still, sometimes it was also nice to close the door on the nights Ryan went home and have her house all to herself again. Over the years she had grown accustomed to the stillness, to the quietness of her home, save whatever noise she chose to make. Ryan was absolutely wonderful to be around, but she needed her alone time too.

Of course, lying in bed alone, she sometimes doubted the wisdom of living apart, but usually she fell quickly into a deep and contented sleep.

They would always see each other the next day. And in addition to being together some of the time, there would also be time spent doing their own things, enjoying the simple comfort of knowing there was another person nearby, no farther than the next room.

And occasionally there were times when it was nice to have even more people around.

"So when are they getting here?" Leanne asked.

Ryan's daughter Abigail and her husband Robert were stopping by for a late-summer picnic in Leanne's backyard. Having a garden full of people—at least fuller than her usual one or two—was a novelty for Leanne, and one she found she enjoyed, just so long as the familiar quiet resumed after.

But it was kind of fun preparing food and setting out different dishes for the small group. A simple afternoon took on a festive air when the conversation came from multiple directions.

"They should be here in about an hour or so," Ryan replied. "They're running a little behind, something about Rob's work. He got one of those non-emergency calls that require emergency attention. You know, like running low on coffee or that gross non-dairy creamer."

"Ryan, you know full well those responsibilities were taken away from him after he ordered wooden stir sticks instead of those awful plastic ones that the bosses wanted," Leanne said. Robert actually ran the local office of a big courier company, but sometimes it felt as if the head office were after him about details not actually very far removed from their hyperbolic jokes.

Work crisis averted, the foursome were soon enjoying a lazy afternoon snacking and drinking under the low-lying sun. As the evening air began hinting more at fall, the chill drove them inside.

"I sure love the changing of the seasons," Leanne said. "It's part one thing, part another, endings and beginnings all sharing the same time. It's pretty cool."

"Quite literally." Abby shivered, not fully warmed up.

Leanne handed Abigail a small blanket from the back of the couch to throw over her bare shoulders before she suggested, "How about some coffee to warm us all up? Cappuccinos, maybe?"

"That sounds great," Abby said. "Let me help, Leanne."

The two women had actually taken a little while to get to know each other. Abigail had the usual reservations about anyone showing interest in her father who wasn't her mother, even though she wasn't alive anymore. Abby had just gotten used to the idea of him dating casually when he up and met Leanne. And he talked very differently about this woman. Abigail felt herself go on high alert, ready to be critical of everything that remotely irked her about the new woman in her father's life.

But Ryan refused to listen to it, telling Abby what she already knew on some level. "Leanne makes me happy." While he was sorry Abigail was upset, it really wasn't her business. She could think whatever she wanted, but he didn't want to hear about it or listen to her unfounded criticisms. "Now, if you find out Leanne's an axe murderer or something, you can tell me that, but nothing else," he had joked, trying to end their talk on a lighter note.

Abby had always been close to her dad, and though intellectually she knew that he was right, emotionally she wasn't quite ready for the changes she saw happening.

After her mother died so tragically, she and her father had grown even closer, hanging on to what was left of their small biological family. And then this interloper had to appear and disrupt their new balance. But as she got to know Leanne better, little begrudging bits at a time, she starting feeling guilty that she wasn't more accepting of her dad's girlfriend. Abby felt like a walking cliché, which furthered her guilt even more.

Leanne, on the other hand, had her own issues to overcome, mostly centred around her dormant feelings about having missed out on motherhood. As with many things lurking beneath the surface of awareness, seeing what she could have had if things had gone a different way made her want to spend as little time with the reminder—Abigail in this case—as possible.

But Leanne didn't like how that made her feel. It was as if that level of avoidance were some kind of cosmic step backward and inconsistent with how forthright she tried to be, facing problems head-on. She didn't feel funny being around other people who were the approximate age of her would-be children. Only Abigail. But then this particular young woman was connected to one particular man.

When her feelings hadn't subsided fast enough to suit her, Leanne invited the problem over. In the same garden as their picnic just now, Leanne and Abigail had had a no-holds-barred conversation about why each thought they hadn't been getting along very well. While Abigail was more reserved than Leanne with regards to the so-called tough subjects—like death and its aftermath—she was more comfortable than her father.

Bittersweet for Leanne was acknowledging that, in many ways, Abigail was a combination of her and Ryan. She could have been the child they might have had. Abby was the visceral embodiment of a different path of decisions. "But she's not who Jay and I would have brought into all this," Leanne thought to herself. "That person sure would have been a real doozy."

The more Leanne heard Abigail speak, including re-counting wonderful stories about her mother and the life all three Michaelsons had shared, the more Leanne sur-prisingly felt better. She was coming to see Ryan's daugh-ter as simply another woman with her own life, separate and apart from her own. Abigail was Ryan and Terri's daughter. She was also someone Leanne hoped to gain as a new friend in her own right.

It was a tricky situation explaining her feelings about not having had children without talking a lot about Jay, and that wasn't likely to help matters. Leanne could tell Abigail was already conflicted about Leanne's interest in her father. Bringing another man into the mix—albeit it a dead man—might only confuse things further.

And Jay was the part of her that Leanne shared com-pletely with no one else. But enough details to explain her present reaction to Abigail were disclosed. They had to be. Ryan was important. And giving voice now to the closest thing that Leanne had regrets about—being childless—actually felt freeing.

Abigail left that day feeling that if this very private woman was willing to share herself this way—in fact, taking the initiative to talk—all in the hope of improving a relationship with her boyfriend's daughter, then maybe this woman really was everything her father said.

And now in the kitchen, Leanne and Abigail worked seamlessly together grinding beans and steaming milk, chatting easily the whole time. They weren't some vari-ation of mother and daughter, just two women who now understood a lot more about each other.

CHAPTER TWENTY

ALTHOUGH FORMALLY STILL living apart, Leanne's partner in life was now Ryan. Jay remained a presence, but was off in the distance. She almost never spoke out loud to him anymore. They still communicated, but it was almost exclusively a thought here or a silent word there, a smile, a deep breath, or occasionally a glance off into the distance.

The attic remained the one part of Leanne's house that Ryan never went into. It wasn't that she said it was off limits or even voiced a preference he not go up there, but Ryan felt it would be intruding. Leanne had expanded some on how special the attic had always been for her and Jay, and that it was also where Jay had died.

Ryan remembered that especially during the early days of dating Leanne, when he'd call and the phone would ring for a while, Leanne would pick up explaining that she had been upstairs. She always sounded different then, as if part of her were somewhere else. Since there was no grave to visit or urn of ashes on the mantle, Ryan figured she went upstairs to be extra close to Jay. He understood. He still went to the cemetery to visit Terri.

However, Leanne and Ryan's respective feelings on death went largely unspoken. Just as he sensed there were some aspects of her relationship with Jay that she didn't want to talk about with anyone, Leanne sensed the same was true for Ryan with regard to talking about death, dying, and all that went with it.

They were open about what they weren't open about. Everything else was fair conversational game.

But there was one area of the death topic that Leanne felt she couldn't totally avoid with Ryan. It had pragmatic consequences for both of them. She'd make it as short and painless as possible, but she knew he wouldn't enjoy it. Not that she particularly would either, but dealing with it now would surely make it easier later. She hoped so, anyway.

By the sheer bulk of circumstances that Leanne had faced with Jay, living from the very beginning with death as a virtual third person in their relationship, that topic of conversation came to feel very natural. It could almost be comforting because talking about death meant it was being dealt with in some way. At least some of the tough stuff was being taken care of instead of pretending the whole dying thing was permanently avoidable.

But possibly that was just a delusion she was operating under.

Maybe Ryan had the right idea and talking about something sad or scary ahead of time only meant there was that much longer to be miserable. Maybe ostriches had the right idea. There sure had been moments when a bunch of ignorance-giving sand sounded rather appealing. The problem was the relief was temporary. And

Leanne preferred to get the icky stuff out of the way more permanently if she could, even if it hurt at the time. But that wasn't Ryan's way.

Despite knowing their differences, Leanne had specific reasons for wanting to bring up what she hoped was her decades-away funeral. Since it was about her decisions, it felt wrong not to tell Ryan herself, as opposed to him finding out secondhand after she was dead. He also needed to know why she wanted things the way she did, so he didn't try to organize a big ceremony for her as he had for Terri. Not that she'd have to be in attendance, but grand and formal wasn't the way she preferred to be remembered.

"Gosh that sounds arrogant and controlling," Leanne said to herself. "'Remember me this way, not that way.' And maybe while I'm at it, I should leave lists of what I want people to remember about me, and what I'd like them to forget." She laughed inwardly. "I just want the thing to be small, and quiet, and gentle."

Leanne definitely needed to tell Ryan about the plans she'd made so long ago, on a crazy day she, Jay, and a certain shocked funeral director would likely never forget.

A few days later, Leanne and Ryan were sitting in her vegetable garden pulling weeds, removing clever plants invading those that they actually wanted to grow. Leanne decided she couldn't put it off any longer.

The irony struck her that while weeding was such a mindless and mundane task, it was all about making decisions about what lives or dies. "And what to do with the remains—throw away or compost," Leanne thought with amusement. "But I should probably leave out that part. 'Yeah, Ryan, while you're at it, please compost my body along with the weeds.' I do kind of like that idea, though. But I guess I better stick with my other arrangements. There's probably some kind of regulation against self-composting, anyway."

As Leanne dug out a particularly stubborn dandelion, she plunged in. "Ryan, I know you don't like talking about this stuff, and I'm really sorry I have to bring it up, but I don't see any way of avoiding this since there's a fifty-fifty chance you'll need this information."

Ryan was silent at first, both not wanting to hear what Leanne was ominously building up to and wishing she'd hurry up and get it over with. He knew that she was trying to make it easier by starting gently, but it was having the reverse effect. "Just say what you need to say, Leanne."

"I want you to know about the funeral arrangements I made for myself a long time ago," Leanne quickly said. "You won't have to worry about any of it—"

"I won't have to what?" Ryan interrupted. "Oh yeah, I'll be great, not a care in the world." His voice was loaded with sarcasm, masking his fear of losing Leanne. Living without her felt like more than he could take. First it was Terri. Now came the unwanted reminder that Leanne could go before him too. He selfishly hoped she'd be the one left to make his arrangements.

"That's not what I meant, Ryan, and you know it. This is why I haven't brought it up sooner," Leanne said frustratedly. Clearly there was never a right time for certain subjects, but she hoped this could be said and then let go of, or at least put away wherever Ryan stored such things.

As she looked at his stricken face as he was forced to think about something that scared him so much, Leanne wished she could understand his way better. Maybe then she'd be able to handle this differently for his sake.

As she reached for Ryan's hands, a memory flashed through her of all the times Jay had been the one to comfort her about his dying. Now it was the other way around. Why did that task seem to fall on the one going through the process instead of the one remaining alive?

"Ryan, please don't worry. It's all going to be fine. Trust me." She looked into his frightened eyes. They were eyes she recognized. Although they were surrounded by his aging, wrinkled face, they could just as easily have been her own so many years before, when every night a scared little girl begged her parents not to die. Maybe Leanne couldn't completely understand how Ryan dealt with certain things, but through his eyes she was remembering old feelings she'd forgotten.

"I'm not going to die for a long, long time." She tried to soothe him. "Neither of us is sick or anything. We're both fine. This is just me wanting you to know what my wishes are for way far off in the future."

"I'm overreacting and getting carried away. I know that. And I know you can't promise to never . . . need a funeral. How's that for denial and avoidance?" He tried to joke about how he avoided using the word *die*, but there was an undertone that said he was quite happy to stay in denial until the last possible moment.

But he also wanted to be there for Leanne, both now and later. As hard as it was for him to hear, he knew Leanne needed to share this with him just as much. "So, what's this funeral of yours going to be like?" He tried to be upbeat. Maybe if he did that enough he'd even want to plan his own service someday or be able to entertain the possibility at least.

Still sitting in the dirt of the garden, Leanne began to tell Ryan how she hoped her funeral would go. "I have this wish, and I know it's probably crazy and unrealistic, but I want everyone to be happy, or at least not sad whenever they think of me. And that goes for when they're sitting there at the service too. That's why I want things a certain way, so I can know I've done everything I can to make it as OK as possible. So no smelly lilies or anything that'll be forever ruined as a thing of joy, forever associated with funerals and death."

Leanne ran her hands through the dirt, feeling the bits of earth sift between her fingers.

Ryan sat motionless, concentrating on every word, remembering each detail so he wouldn't have to think about them again for years. "And not ever," he thought to himself, "if I'm lucky and go first."

"Not that death is as bad as I used to think," Leanne said, "but I sure wish I'd never smelled funeral flowers myself." The scent was forever entangled with her parents' deaths. "Now there's always that association for me. Lilies aren't so sweet smelling once they've surrounded a coffin." Leanne was so present in her own thoughts she lost sight of Ryan's less macabre sense of humour. Fortunately, he was so focused on the sentiment of what she was saying, her coffin reference slipped past him.

"You see, Ryan, I haven't even always been sure I want a funeral or ceremony of any kind. What Jay chose has an absolute appeal. It was so simple, so nothing except the world continuing on, and me on the water's edge looking out upon the ever-present waves." She paused for a moment.

"But I do want something I think, some kind of gathering, a last 'hey there' before I, well, I guess it'll technically come after I die, but at least the plans will have been made before. That's what I see it as, a way for me to say 'hey,' and then leave you to your own thoughts, to remember, to laugh, and admittedly to cry because I'm so darn fabulous," Leanne said with a grin, eliciting a small smile from Ryan and a large tug on her hand.

"But no depressing funeral dirges," she said. "I do really want music, though. Well, two songs in particular. And while I see—or maybe I should say hear—the same risk of causing lingering funeral taint, I really want these two songs to be heard. I need them to be there."

She was feeling torn between her emotional wants and her desire not to spoil the songs for anyone else. And she hadn't even said what they were yet. Leanne rarely beat around the bush.

"They will be there, Leanne. I'll make sure," Ryan said strongly. For some reason, this seemed to be the part of her plans that Leanne was most concerned about. If need be, he vowed to make things happen her way. "What will be played?"

Speaking with renewed tranquillity, Leanne described what she heard happening. "After people say or do whatever they want at this little gathering, I want Bread's 'If.' That will be for me." Inaudibly, she added, "And for Jay." There were so many *ifs* in her life with him.

Leanne inhaled and exhaled slowly as she delighted in silently paraphrasing the words of the song. She was filled with an almost overpowering surge of emotion. She and Jay really had poured themselves over the other whenever love for life was on the dry side. They couldn't paint the other, and the words would never come close to showing everything, but they were beside each other all the way. And the idea of spending the end together, of simply flying away after the stars went out, well, that was almost too perfect a way to end.

"That song," Leanne finally said, "gets right to the heart of everything for me. It's this perfect mix of hope and love and death and awe. It's life, beautiful life, and how I want to go out." She hummed the last few notes of the song, but not all of them made it out of her mouth. They were all there inside her, though, as she travelled along with the journeying words, eyes closed.

And then she was back, smiling.

"After 'If,' I want smiles, and joy and wonder, more of a living hope for you, Ryan, and for everyone else. 'What a Wonderful World' will be my wish, and my last words to you. It is a wonderful world. I want that 'Oh yeah' to ring through and bring you a smile, even if it comes through tears. And then, for you to get on with your life, in whatever way works."

Leanne and Ryan were quite the sight—two barefoot retirement-age characters sitting cross-legged in the dirt, facing each other, holding hands. They almost looked like two kids who might start playing patty-cake at any second. The image was all the more jarring given what they were discussing.

But seeing Leanne's funeral through her eyes was giving Ryan strength he hadn't expected. He was catching a glimpse of how Leanne saw death differently from the way he did.

"When I made these plans, when Jay and I both made arrangements, I wondered if I was overthinking and trying to plan out future emotions. It's funny, but those two songs are the only details of the gathering—or funeral thing—that I have ever been too particular about, aside from having no smelly flowers, of course. Flowers should be happy and smell like it." Leanne picked a cheery dandelion and inhaled its subtle but distinctive sweet scent. "I don't know why the music matters so much to me, and the smells too. But it feels as if through those senses, the memories of that day are gonna be made."

"I like that idea," Ryan said when it was evident that Leanne wasn't going to say more, her thoughts left hanging in the air acting as some strange form of comfort.

"I don't want to see anything," he explained. "You there like that, and all the sad, wet faces. I don't think I'd even want to hear people talk about you then. It'd hurt too much." His voice shook but remained strong. "But those songs for you, from you, with no smell, I think I might be able to handle that. And you know, I can almost picture the time during those songs as long moments of silence to be alone with my thoughts. Not silence in the actual sense obviously, but internal quiet while the music plays."

Leanne understood.

She remembered the funerals for her parents all too well. While some wanted other people around and found comfort from their presence, she wanted the services to be over quickly so she could go home and sleep and temporarily escape, and gradually heal. "Yeah, the music can be sort of a guaranteed time-out from talking because you know nobody's going to say anything to you right then," she said.

"It felt like I didn't get that." Ryan drifted into the past tense. "All the well-intentioned words of sympathy made me feel as if I were on display and expected to perform a certain way. All I wanted to do was be by myself and cry, and hug Terri's pillow." Tears were now silently pouring down his face.

The air was silent too. Leanne said nothing and, in her own way, tried to give him the quiet he had been denied before.

The sight of her dear Ryan crying quickly brought Leanne to tears as well. Feeling his loss seemed to bring back her own, and she soon found herself crying for two loves.

Leanne and Ryan then held on to each other, both squeezing hard, caught up in emotions old and new.

Gradually the streaming tears slowed. When only a few isolated tears remained stuck to their faces, they began to actually feel the arms around them, instead of the desolation their tears had released.

"I love you, Ryan," Leanne said as she pulled back to look into his eyes before tucking in again for another tight hug.

As her head was moving past his, she heard a muffled, "I love you too, Leanne."

Spitting out a few strands of her free-flying hair, he said, "Or maybe I just love your hair." Reaching up to remove one particularly stubborn strand, he pretended to use it as dental floss. "It tastes good too, nice and lemony."

And as easy as that, the earlier turmoil was gone.

It wasn't forgotten, though.

Ryan remembered all the details. He had placed them safely into storage. But it felt much better to be nibbling on Leanne's grey locks and, for now, having that lump gone from his gut.

CHAPTER TWENTY-ONE

THE PHONE RANG and Leanne jumped. The phone was not supposed to ring in the middle of the night. Only seconds out of a deep sleep, she was automatically alert. Her heart raced as she picked up the receiver. Words came rushing out, almost frantically. "Hello? What is it?"

"Leanne, it's me."

Hearing Ryan's voice on the other end of the phone caused her panic to go down a notch. Any worst case scenario had just been averted. Ryan was OK.

Of all the nights not to be spending together, they had to choose this one. It had made sense the night before. They'd been nearly inseparable for their days off and figured they could use some alone time. Besides, Leanne had an early meeting the next morning anyway.

Now, however, she sure wished Ryan were there beside her. But after the long split second her imagination had been in scary overdrive, having him there on the phone seemed like a dream come true.

But he had still called her in the middle of the night.

"Ryan, what's wrong?" She continued speaking quickly.

"Nothing's wrong. Quite the opposite, actually." Ryan could hear her breathing heavily. "Leanne, it's OK. Relax. Everything's fine. I'm sorry. I shouldn't have called you this late, or is it early? I don't know. I just couldn't wait. I'm so exited."

As her breathing slowed and she was able to think, it was finally registering on her that this was a good-news phone call, just one coming at a bad hour. "What is it?" she asked again, but with happy curiosity this time.

But before he could answer, Leanne put the pieces together and guessed. "Wait, did Abigail go into—" She stopped mid-sentence. "No, it's too early. She's not due until next month."

Ryan was enjoying hearing the excitement in Leanne's voice as she was realizing what had happened.

"But she did, Ryan, didn't she? And everyone's OK," Leanne said without needing confirmation. She already had that from his tone.

"It all happened so fast. You know how Abigail's husband is out of town? Well, she and I were having dinner last night, and suddenly she got this funny look and said, 'We've got to go. Now!' It was such a whirlwind from there. I couldn't even get a second to call you. It was as if everything were on fast forward. I'll tell you all about it later. But, man, Leanne, I saw a side of my daughter no father should ever see. I mean, I literally saw it." He laughed, beaming the whole time, still in a state of blissful shock.

"I'm getting dressed," Leanne said.

"Are you sure? What about your early meeting?"

"Are you kidding? I'll postpone it. I need to be with my family."

Ryan beamed even brighter hearing her say that.

"So keep talking," she said, throwing on the first thing she saw.

"Well, with Robert away, I became Abby's impromptu birthing coach. I wish you could have seen it." Ryan's excitement and joy was palpable. "But I feel bad he missed seeing his son being born. It's a boy, by the way. I missed Abby's birth myself. I couldn't get to the hospital fast enough. Seems the women in our family are big on the express side of delivery."

"They sure must be." Leanne was amazed that the labour was so quick. "But that's fantastic, Ryan. You're a grandfather! I'm so happy for all of you. I'm sorry Robert missed it, but that's amazing you got to be there right at the beginning of little— Wait, what's his name?"

"Oh yeah. It's Joseph Cameron Michaelson-McCoy." Ryan grinned broadly thinking of his newborn grandson.

"I can't wait to meet him—and hug his granddaddy. I'm heading out the door so I've got to hang up. See you soon."

"Drive carefully. It's still dark out," Ryan said.

"Yeah, that's because it's nighttime when people are supposed to be sleeping."

"At least you have been asleep. Some of us were busy delivering babies."

Laughing, right before she hung up the phone, Leanne added, "Oh, and Ryan? I'm still mad at you for scaring me. It's a darn good thing you're OK."

About fifteen minutes later she was sitting next to Ryan in the family waiting area. Robert had recently arrived from the airport and they wanted to give the new threesome some private time together.

"It still seems like a strange time to go to the hospital, though," Leanne thought out loud. "Unless there's some problem or big risk, in which case I can see it, but otherwise, isn't it kind of like going skiing in a hospital or something?"

Ryan spit out his stale coffee when she said that. "OK, what? Skiing in a hospital?"

"Yeah." Leanne calmly explained her thinking. "If you go to the hospital to have a baby when nothing's wrong— I mean, the baby is supposed to come out after all, that is not an unexpected outcome—then the reason people do so is preemptive. They go to the hospital just in case there's a problem. It's nice to already be where the sophisticated medical help is, right?"

Ryan nodded, beginning to see where this was likely headed.

"So," she continued, "wouldn't it be equally wise to go skiing right there in a hospital where all that immediate help is, just in case something goes wrong for a skier? In fact, it would be interesting to compare the percentage of skiers who get injured to the percentage of births that have problems."

"Well, Leanne, aside from the fact that there are no ski mountains in any hospital I know of, I'd say you're on to something." Ryan had to agree with at least part of her logic. "Still, I definitely felt better driving Abby to the hospital, even one without ski facilities."

"Well, all I can say is, if it had ever been me, I'd sure have preferred giving birth at home. Not that that should come as any kind of great surprise considering what a homebody I am," Leanne said, laughing.

It felt really good to be able to laugh and talk of having hypothetical babies without the twinges that once brought her. And although she and Ryan weren't married, or even living together, she still felt like a newly minted grandmother.

Wherever Joseph was born, he was here now, and it felt amazing.

But it proved almost too amazing when she first held him in her arms. She had to wonder one more time what motherhood would have felt like. "Don't go there," she told herself. "Love what you have, not what you don't."

As the years passed, Leanne and Ryan continued loving each other and sharing their lives, spending most of their time together. But they still lived apart in their respective houses, and each appreciated having a place to go that was separate from the other. In a way, it represented the lives lived before they met.

The two had not been young things just starting out and building a life together, beginning an adventure full of firsts, such as a first house or a first mortgage. They had both already done that.

Instead, they were two rather planted people continuing a strange mix of single and coupled life, a blend that had evolved naturally over time.

However, if he'd had his druthers, Ryan would have preferred to live together. He needed less alone time than Leanne did.

She had also been living alone in her house for a lot longer than he had in his—and his wasn't a first house with memories. So he would rather happily have moved into hers. But while there were no ghosts driving him away, he felt as if it were more her house than it would ever be theirs.

Ryan also knew that Leanne would never leave her home, not unless the attic could come with her. She seldom went up there anymore, but every once in a while he'd notice the hand prints in the dust on the worn wooden railing. Sometimes she would make reference to it or talk about some little memory of Jay, but usually she was quiet. That was often the biggest clue that she'd been up there—the quietness after.

But it never lasted, and soon she was again chatting up a happy storm.

Lately, however, he was feeling a little quieter himself, but for a very different reason.

While Ryan had started working at the counselling centre as a way to gently ease into retirement, after about ten years there, he was ready to stop easing. He wanted all of each day for himself and to be around only the people he chose.

And he was tired.

He knew it was really time to go when for the first time in his life, he was starting to resent his patients or, more particularly, the problems of his patients. No matter how many people could be helped, there would always be more waiting in the wings.

While Ryan had obviously known that to be true as a young man, years of actually seeing it play out before him had worn him down, and made him increasingly sad and angry that people had to suffer like that in the first place. He didn't want all that to harden him. And he knew it would if he kept on working. Cutting back was no longer enough. He wondered if maybe counselling was a young person's game. It was easier then to be optimistic and believe the world really could change. Maybe he had already hardened if he believed that.

Leanne thought he was as soft as always, except when hardness took on an altogether different meaning, and purpose. But she had started to see little changes that she hoped would disappear with the disappearance of work.

Ryan had always been an early riser, eager to start the day. But lately he'd grumbled more when the alarm clock went off, and whenever he got the opportunity to sleep in, he stayed in bed longer each time.

She did not want to concede that his tiredness could have anything to do with advancing age. Besides, wasn't seventy the new thirty these days? And quite honestly, his lethargy seemed more like a pattern she recognized very well—sleeping to escape so there would be fewer waking hours to deal with something troubling. Even a nagging frustration could weigh someone down if it persisted long enough.

Despite Ryan's growing personal issues with the job, there was the issue of his patients and what effect his leaving might have. Not so arrogant as to think he was essential, Ryan still didn't want to do anything that could possibly add to their challenges if they felt he was abandoning them somehow.

But as he weighed the pros and cons more objectively, he saw that that risk was radically reduced since as a part-timer, he was more the fill-in who saw many different patients, most of whom all had a primary counsellor.

The remaining few tended to be people who needed an understanding ear for an hour or two, rather than any kind of ongoing treatment. And he realized he had to look after himself, and that he could be comfortable knowing that many such ears were still there to listen.

Fortunately, after his first week of full-blown retirement, Ryan's sleeping patterns returned to normal—aside from the odd late rising thanks to Leanne and their still-active hormones.

Ryan was grateful for his step-down approach from work. It had almost completely prevented any antsy feelings of wanting someplace to go during the day. For years he'd already found ways to fill a number of days each week, now he could do the same for them all. He was loving it.

There was more time with Leanne when she was off work, more visits with his daughter and her family, and more opportunity to get into mischief playing around with different hobbies, which often involved his grandson's enthusiastic help.

Since Ryan had worked part-time in recent years, a lot of his shifts had fallen on weekends and holidays. Without that impediment now, he could see friends and family more often, and with less advance planning and coordinating of schedules.

Before long, Leanne started to feel a little hard done by. While she was already feeling the hints of being ready to retire too, what tipped her over the edge was more pure carnal comfort.

Whether it was at her place or Ryan's, she was the only one who had to crawl out of their cozy warm bed, get washed and dressed, and then face the outside world. He got to dig in the dirt in the backyard all day if he wanted, while Leanne dug around people's minds in an office.

Coming home to a fresh hot meal was certainly a perk, but she'd rather have been home fixing it with him, or ordering a pizza from Dufferin's Diner if they lost track of time and wanted reliably good food in a lazy half hour.

"You sure started something with this retirement business, Ryan," Leanne said as she kissed him good-bye before heading to the centre one morning.

"So you've decided?"

"Yep, you're too irresistible." She kissed him again. "Besides, it's not as if I still see that many patients. It's funny how that happened. I mysteriously fell into more of the administrative stuff after a certain someone"—she playfully glared at him—"bragged to the wrong person that, 'Leanne could sure get this centre's books in better order.'"

"Well, I was right, wasn't I?" Ryan proudly said. "And just why are you looking so surprised by that?"

Leanne was rolling her eyes and tipping her head as if she were considering some outlandish possibility. "Was I?" she kidded. "I have to admit, though, you actually were right. In fact, it's been kind of a perfect blend of my first and second careers."

"Not to mention it makes leaving now a whole lot easier I bet, with less of the patient issue," he pointed out.

"Absolutely. I know I haven't been considering this for long, but you know me, if it feels right, why wait?"

"You won't get any argument from me," Ryan said as he opened his front door for her. "I can't wait to be able to come over to your place pretty much whenever I want and not have to think what day of the week it is."

Leanne laughed as she walked down the path to her car. Going to work this day there was an added bounce in her step. Yet another change had begun. Smiling, Leanne glanced up and all around her. He knew.

For Leanne and Ryan's fifteenth anniversary—marking the coffee-filled day they met at work—she surprised him with a wooden double lounger in her back garden. The wide contraption could be positioned into more of a bench seat, or made much deeper and longer, with the lower part pulled up and extended out front. There was a storage box attached to one side, and a bunch of supposedly waterproof cushions and other padding on the seat itself. And over the top was a roof-like panel, just in case the waterproof claim proved an exaggeration.

"It's a bed outside among the flower beds," she joked before saying, "and what better place to be, since you truly do make me feel alive and growing myself." But she was unable to resist poking fun at her saccharine-sounding words. "Not to mention you've got me blooming."

"And ready to be plucked?" Ryan asked, quite pleased with himself.

"Well, it is our anniversary, so I can only hope." She tried to keep a straight face.

"Oh, you think so, do you? Tell me, Leanne, when have we ever needed an excuse?" He feigned insult.

Leanne laughed and nodded her head. "Let's hope we are still saying that in another fifteen years."

She began unbuttoning his collared shirt. Even in retirement, he still usually dressed semi-formally. She, on the other hand, rarely even wore shoes at home.

"We will be saying that, Leanne, one way or another—and doing this. It's too much fun not to."

They shared a grin before she raised her arms and he removed her T-shirt.

"And it's comforting," he added, "to know that science is there if we need it, and all the different things I read about in those books you have on alternative medicine."

"Mm-hmm." As more clothes came off, Leanne cast her eyes around their outdoor surroundings. "How very thoughtful of the trees and everything else back here to grow so well too. It means only the birds or a low-flying helicopter can get a little peep show."

Later, as they used their discarded clothes as a makeshift blanket, a jet flew overhead. "That's perfect timing." Ryan spoke his own anniversary thought out loud.

"What do you mean?" Leanne murmured, still partially in the awe of afterglow.

"I know how you feel about staying close to home, but we've both been retired some time now and have no real schedule and, well, I was thinking how much I'd like to go away with you—have an adventure together someplace neither of us has been. Maybe we could even go to Europe. You could visit Becky and see their new place outside the city. When was she last here? It had to have been before we met. I know you two talk, but the phone's not the same as being in the same room." Ryan kept on talking, trying to throw everything out there he could think of. At the very least, it would delay her rejection of the idea.

But when he finally paused—more from needing to take a breath than running out of ideas—she surprised him by saying nothing at first.

Leanne was actually considering travelling.

Then she shifted onto her side to face him. "And that would mean flying."

"It would. But I was thinking, given how you like being near the ocean, what if we took a cruise over? Then we'd only have to fly one way."

"Hmm." Leanne had to admit the idea was really starting to intrigue her. She wasn't even sure why the idea of traversing more of the world was appealing to her now. But the thought of travelling and seeing new places—and for some reason, being on a cruise ship most of all—really sounded exciting.

Maybe it was because of all those early episodes of *The Love Boat* she watched when she was in college the first time around. Or maybe it had more to do with spending a big part of her life near the water. She knew the Pacific, but now she could know the Atlantic Ocean too. And she'd never really thought about what it would be like to be out there in the middle of all that water, actually feeling the motion of the waves. And now that she was, the idea sounded almost irresistible. "Let's do it."

"Really?" Ryan asked. "You really want to, for yourself, not just for me?"

"I really want to. But even if I didn't, which I do, but even if I didn't, I can see how much you do, and for that reason alone, I'd still want to. I know I can't give you everything you want, living together in particular. But, hey, this way we will be living together, at least temporarily."

"So we're doing this," Ryan said with a wide-eyed grin.

"I guess we are." Leanne laughed in amazement. "But do you think we could fly over and cruise back instead? I understand floating, and all that water-displacement stuff, a whole lot more than tin cans staying up there in the sky."

"And you'd like to get the tin-can part out of the way first, right?"

She nodded, smiling.

As with talk of death, dying, and funerals, Leanne tried to get the hard or scary stuff over with as soon as possible. But Ryan rather liked the idea of putting such things out of his mind, and living as if they simply didn't exist.

While neither approach always worked, as a confident flyer, Ryan had no problem with either travelling order. "We'll fly first then. It'll actually be kind of nice that way. Even under the best of circumstances, cruising certainly sounds more relaxing than flying."

"It sure does. And while I may be no travel expert—don't laugh—even I know how amazing it would be to come home and not need another vacation."

"Of course, I don't know how much rest we'll get on board ship," Ryan said. "Between all the food and entertainment we'll be kept pretty busy. Mind you, when it comes to cruising I think there's some overlap between those two activities, so that'll be a good time saver."

"And don't forget the views. They do the moving so you don't have to. Hey, that should be a slogan if it's not already." Leanne was starting to get silly from the excitement, and they hadn't even gotten their tickets yet.

They kept talking about their plans and researching different options on the Internet. Leanne found it hard to believe that there was once a time she shunned computers. Now she couldn't imagine not having her laptop. Maybe some people just took longer to accept changes to the status quo. "I bet I would have been one of the holdouts during the shift from horse-drawn carriages to the horsepower of automobiles too," Leanne thought to herself. It made her wonder what her great-grandparents must have thought living through that transition.

"Leanne? Shall we pick this one?" Ryan interrupted her ancestral thoughts.

"Hmm? Yeah, sorry, my brain got sidetracked there." Leanne looked at the computer screen. "That ship looks especially amazing, and I like how it's not as big as some of those newer floating-city ones. Some of them are so big I might start questioning my acceptance of the entire water-displacement thing."

Ryan's sharp intake of breath reflected his mock anxiety that she could actually have such doubts. After they shared a laugh, Ryan turned back to their plans. "So I guess the last thing to do is to decide when."

"Yeah, other than actually booking everything and paying for it all," Leanne, the former bookkeeper, said. "I'll call Becky later, when it's not in the middle of the night there." She grinned at him thinking of a certain nocturnal phone call he'd once made. "And then we can see what works best for them."

"Speaking of the time, let's go to bed ourselves. Then it'll be one less sleep before our big trip." Ryan waved his arms up and down like a little kid, his fists clenched in excitement.

"You've been spending too much time with Joseph. You sound just like him before Christmas," Leanne said, smiling. "But let's go to bed anyway."

CHAPTER TWENTY-TWO

PLANS WERE FINALIZED and before they knew it, there was only one more sleep to go before Leanne and Ryan set sail. In the excitement department this time, they were both giving his grandson a run for his allowance money.

Sleep was sporadic at best, and they were both grateful when it was finally time to stop trying to keep their eyes closed.

Donovan picked them up and drove them to the airport. After that, he was going to drive up the coast to visit a friend he had been talking more about lately. Leanne hoped this person, if not already more than a friend to him, soon would be.

Donovan rarely spoke much about his personal life to Leanne. But recently, his excitement had grown so much that he felt he would burst if he didn't release at least some of the details to his longtime friend. The hug they had shared afterward felt more genuine and free than any ever had in all the years they'd known each other.

A similar hug was shared all around when he saw Leanne and Ryan off at the airport.

Despite her brain telling her everything that could go wrong, Leanne wanted to enjoy the trip, the whole of it. She didn't like feeling at the mercy of any fear, including that of airplanes.

Leanne set her mind to trying to approach the flight the way she tried to live life in general, aiming to feel every moment. In this case, the hours in the air could be like a mini life of aerial sensations, hopefully with as little thinking as possible about the potential consequences. "Besides, I've had a pretty long life already, so maybe anything more will simply be bonus time," she thought dryly before telling herself, "OK, that's not helping."

Letting herself go had the bonus of making the flight feel like one big amusement-park ride, particularly the takeoff. The roaring power of the engines as they helped catapult the massive plane upward was intoxicating. Part of her wished it had gone on for longer. "Ryan, next time, jet me all the way to the moon."

The smoothness of the flight once at altitude almost got boring, but was interrupted with just enough pockets of turbulence to keep things interesting for Leanne. As with her approach to life and death, she was trying to simply be along for the ride. "As long as life and death don't meet today," she macabrely thought to herself.

The landing was smooth, although Leanne thought the little bounce immediately after touching down was a little too substantial to be called smooth. But all in all, the flight was much better than she'd expected. Most of it had actually been fun.

Becky picked them up and, after a round of hugs, they were on their way to the hotel.

When they were first talking about the trip, Becky had objected to their desire to stay there instead of with her and Brian. But Leanne had pointed out how they would all likely need their own space after visiting so intensely. "I don't want to get on your nerves, or you on mine," Leanne said bluntly to her friend of more than half a century.

"Oh, I can't believe you're here, Leanne. And it's so great to meet you Ryan," Becky said. "I never thought this woman would actually leave Clementine, let alone come all the way over here. Ryan, I bet you had something to do with this, and I'm ever so grateful. Brian and I don't seem to travel that much anymore now. And when we do, it's never that far." Becky's parents had both died a number of years earlier, and with that went her regular visits across the pond.

"So it's still working out with you two?" Leanne asked. Their marriage, though improved from what it had been for a while, always seemed to be very tenuous whenever Becky and Leanne talked.

"Yeah, overall, yeah," Becky said. "I have to say, part of it is, it's just easier than splitting up. But sometimes there's more of us actually wanting to be together too. Whenever I think I can't take it anymore, I imagine not seeing his face in the morning, and the decision seems so easy. I still love him. But other times, I get so frustrated because he seems to shrink from any little confrontation. He shuts right down. But I'll save all the gory details for later when we're not boring poor Ryan here."

"You're not boring me," a groggy male voice said. "I'm sleeping." Ryan was leaning back in a reclining chair that was tucked into the corner of the large room.

Just then, Leanne yawned and started to eye the bed with sleep lust.

"I'm not thinking. Of course, you're both exhausted," Becky said. "OK, I'm going to go now. But how about you call me when you've had a chance to get some rest? I'll come get you and bring you to the house. And Lissa can't wait to see you either, and for you to meet her family. But I'm getting ahead of myself. I'm going now. I really am."

"We'll call you later, Becky," Leanne said as she moved toward the door. "But right now"—she yawned again—"I've gotta go curl up with that man and sleep."

Over the next couple of weeks, in various combinations, the group spent time chatting as well as playing tourist. Lissa's children, in particular, got a kick out of going to all the attractions that locals only seemed to see when company visited.

Lissa's partner, Kelsey, was a delight, and Leanne was grateful that the relationship issues of Lissa's parents hadn't appeared to transfer to their daughter. Whether it was at home or out it public, Lissa and Kelsey were just naturally in contact with each other—a brush of a hand here or an arm around the shoulders there. Becky and Brian kept their arms to themselves.

Leanne and Ryan took a few train trips to neighbouring countries. "It still utterly amazes me," she said after they crossed back into England for the last time before their cruise home. "I can't believe we were in France a couple of hours ago." Back at Becky and Brian's, Leanne continued to marvel. "It's remarkable to be in another country in practically the same amount of time some people spend commuting to work every day."

"But if I lived here," Ryan said, "I don't know how often I'd end up taking advantage of that incredible opportunity. The countryside right here is so spectacular."

"We do get our share of rain here, though," Brian said. "Many an overcast day when that lovely countryside is all but obscured."

"Remember where they're from, Brian," Becky snapped harshly. "They're used to rain."

"Oh, that's right. Clementine is pretty similar to this I suppose. Sorry," Brian replied quietly, as if he was, sadly, used to being spoken to that way. It just wasn't worth the fuss anymore to do anything but apologize, and then ignore it. He didn't care enough to defend himself.

And the cumulative annoyances Becky felt over time had given her a shorter fuse that was now too easily set off.

There was an awkward silence in the room as each person tried to think of what to say to avoid that precise awkwardness.

Finally, Leanne couldn't take it any longer. "Moving on," she said with authority. "Brian, didn't you say earlier that you were going to tell us all about the community centre you volunteer at now?"

"You mean since I've packed it in and need a way to fill my days?" Brian half joked. While Leanne was the oldest of the group by a few years, Brian was the youngest and had only recently retired. But it had just seemed to help his relationship with Becky in the very beginning. Once the blissful holiday feel had worn off, his greater presence at home further accentuated their differences.

"It's a really cracking place, Leanne, quite a diverse group of people go there, a really eclectic lot," Brian said.

"But all together, they feel like this big extended family that's always there for each other. And the staff and volunteers get to be part of that. If there's time, would you two fancy a visit there to see it for yourselves?"

"That'd be nice, Brian. Thanks," Ryan replied.

Becky was silent. It wasn't a stony silence but more of a contemplative one. Although she would never admit it, she knew she'd overreacted earlier.

After a few more days, it was time to go. Leanne and Ryan's Atlantic cruise awaited.

Becky and Leanne felt as if they were finally completely caught up, even with the minutiae of their lives, in a way that happened only when they could hang out together in the same place for a while.

"It feels as if you just got here and I was picking you up at the airport, and now I'm leaving you at the dock. What happened?" Becky tried to laugh, but she nearly choked because she was also trying not to cry. Brian wasn't there as he had said his good-byes earlier before going to the community centre to call some bingo games.

"I don't know, Becky," Leanne fought back her own tears. "But we'll both be fine as soon as we're all on our way, and this awful good-bye part is done," she said, trying to comfort them both.

Seeing Becky in person again, hugging her instead of calling her, had made the regular distance between them feel greater. Although neither said so that day, given the strains of travel and their advancing ages, they both new it was entirely possible they would never see each other again. This was possibly not just a temporary good-bye.

A gentle hand on her arm reminded Leanne that it was time to go. Placing a hand over his and squeezing briefly, she let go and gave Becky a final hug. They murmured reassurances to each other that before they knew it, they'd be happily back into their phone routine.

Since there were a number of steps to go through before actually boarding the ship and getting out on deck, they had agreed Becky shouldn't wait around to wave them off. It was better for everyone not to drag things out. Becky could get back to a normal day rather than waiting at the terminal building feeling lonely. She had more to think about after seeing a fresh reminder of a happy couple. She wanted that.

By the time Leanne and Ryan finally set foot on the ship her tears had been rubbed away, and the excitement of the journey ahead had taken over. Going immediately to the top passenger deck for the best view, they were amazed by their surroundings. "This is better than any episode ever of *The Love Boat*," Leanne remarked.

"I love how your references are so current," Ryan said with chuckle.

"Well, can you name me another show in the last fifty years that centred around cruise ships? If so, I'd be happy to update myself."

Ryan put his arm around Leanne's waist and hugged her closer.

As the ship got under way, the two were grinning from car to ear, and couldn't resist waving along with the rest of the passengers. "I know it's silly, Ryan, but I can't help it."

"I know. I feel a little ridiculous waving when I don't know anyone down there. But I'll feel like an idiot if I just stand here while everyone else is waving," he said, loving every moment of the crazy display.

"And there must be something to it, because whether we're talking about the *Titanic*, *The Love Boat*, or this modern ship, waving on departure seems like some kind of requirement."

"Now why did you have to go and say that, Leanne?" Ryan cringed as he rolled his eyes. "I mean, do you really want to tempt fate and make a reference to the *Titanic* now? Here? What are you trying to do to me, put me in an early grave?"

"No, wait, Ryan, you did not just make a death joke." Leanne almost squealed in surprise.

"Well, it appears this whole adventure is a bunch of firsts for us," Ryan said rather proudly. "But don't go getting the idea I want to talk more about that funeral of yours, which I don't, despite the fact that I just brought it up. Damn, look what you've done to me, Leanne."

"And swearing now too, on top of everything else." She shook her head as she smiled at him.

As the ship pulled farther away from land, the crowd of waving passengers dispersed, intent on settling into their floating home.

Aside from the odd crew member, Leanne and Ryan were soon the only two people on the forward deck. They felt beautifully dwarfed by the massive ocean, enjoying being mere specks in the universe. "All this, and we get to be here." She smiled peacefully.

Ryan placed his hand over Leanne's, which rested on the smooth wooden railing. "It's getting a little chilly," he said a few minutes later. "Do you want to head inside?"

Leanne inhaled deeply, bringing a wave of salt-scented air into her lungs. "In a minute," she nearly crooned as she closed her eyes. "Oh, smell that, Ryan. It's even more powerful than I realized. I've always thought the ocean air at the shoreline was something else, but out here surrounding us like this, it has a regular scent monopoly."

Just then, Leanne screwed up her face, cringing when a competing scent assaulted her nose. Smokestack exhaust. "Eww, now I'm wishing we had gone in. I did not need to smell that."

"Come here." Ryan tugged her close, and she buried her face in his chest.

"Oh, that's better. Thanks," Leanne said as sweater wool and Ryan's natural scent soothed her nostrils.

"I know you and your smells," Ryan said with a smile. "But you're right. That really did stink."

Moving inside, they found their way to their stateroom for the first time. One of the many perks of cruising was not having to mess with certain regular travelling chores like handling their luggage. Their mismatched collection of bags was already happily waiting for them. But as the day was beginning to catch up to them both, instead of unpacking, they crawled into bed for a nap. The gently rolling waves quickly lulled them to sleep.

They woke up feeling rejuvenated and ready to spend more time in bed—not sleeping. Dinner could wait.

Choosing to travel across the Atlantic Ocean, instead of cruising an area dotted with different ports, meant uninterrupted sea days and plenty of time to enjoy the ship itself and all its amenities. They felt no sense of urgency to explore everything in between stops, for once the voyage got underway in the open ocean, there were no stops, just water everywhere as far as the eye could see.

Floating around in all that wetness for days on end had an almost embryonic feel. They were safely cocooned in the strong vessel. Despite the technical advancement of the ship, the principle keeping it afloat was primitive. Liquid could support and carry everything from floating fetuses to floating ships.

One morning as Ryan was taking pictures of the vast expanse of water, Leanne leaned over the railing into the wind and closed her eyes. She could almost believe she was on some early sailing ship making its way to the New World for the first time.

The two continued looking out over the ocean for a while, and then took another trip around the deck. The view from the ship didn't change much except at sunrise and sunset, but there were other sensory benefits. Ryan enjoyed the people-watching opportunities, and Leanne, the commingling scents of salt air and grilled cheese wafting from the outdoor grill.

"I'm going back to the cabin. I forgot my book," Ryan said as Leanne, reclining on a wooden deck chair, got fixed under her blanket. When she didn't say anything, he asked, "Leanne, did you hear me?"

"Uh, yeah, I'm sorry, cabin, book, yeah. I'll be here."

As Ryan disappeared from view, she had the strangest feeling. Something just clicked when he said the word *cabin*. They'd talked about their stateroom, but never had they called it their cabin before. Suddenly Leanne was back in her thirties, and in another cabin. She was not on the ocean, but on a mountain. With her eyes closed, one word passed her lips, and it was barely audible. "Jay."

For the first time in more than fifteen years, Leanne's left hand successfully squeezed her right in that familiar way she thought she'd never feel again. Soon her left thumb was caressing the back of her right hand, moving gently back and forth, in sync with the gentle rise and fall of the waves. Her mouth dropped open slightly, absorbing every sensation, oblivious to all else around her. Only when she opened her eyes did she realize that more than a few moments had passed. Ryan was back, and sitting there reading in the chair beside her.

"Hey." Ryan looked up when he heard her shift positions. "Did you have a good rest?"

"Was I asleep?" Leanne asked, trying to process what had just happened, and for how long.

"Mm-hmm, I think so, anyway. You sure had this really peaceful look on your face."

"I was . . . someplace else." Her voice still sounded far away. As Leanne readjusted to her surroundings her tone changed. "But I'm back now." Smiling, she reached out for Ryan's welcoming hand. He continued reading his book, and Leanne closed her eyes again. But this time she really did sleep.

Leanne spent part of the following day browsing the ship's vast array of shops. While she wasn't interested in buying souvenirs or other knick-knacks that would just sit on a shelf being ornamental, it was kind of fun looking around and seeing all the stuff people somewhere had thought up.

The requisite souvenir T-shirts, with scratchy decals that looked as if they'd come off in the first wash, hung limply on racks. Miniature plastic models of monuments from both sides of the Atlantic decorated many of the glass shelves. There were, of course, other shops on board catering to more expensive tastes, but this trinket store was like a contemporary social-commentary museum, a plastic and synthetic-fibre mecca.

"Is this really how some people want to remember their cruise?" Leanne thought to herself as she wandered out of the shop.

She liked to remember—or *se souvenir* if she recalled her high-school French correctly—just by thinking of the experiences, not looking at objects that harboured those memories. Because it was all internal, she felt more as if she were re-experiencing them that way, and not just rec-ollecting. But maybe not everyone felt that way. Maybe for some, it was even the other way around, and those shops were helping make memories.

When Leanne joined Ryan for coffee on the aft deck later, he asked, "Have you checked out all the stores? Or should I be asking, 'Did you leave of your own accord or were you asked to leave?'"

"I wasn't that bad—only because you weren't there en-couraging me, mind you—but I behaved myself." Leanne remembered the expression of the patient clerk looking on, who must have wondered if Leanne was ever going to actually buy anything. "If you'd been there, though, I wouldn't have been able to keep my mouth shut, or at the very least, you'd now have a sore side from my jabbing elbow. You wouldn't believe some of the stuff. Did you know they still make those pens with the little ship inside that slides back and forth?"

"I did not know that, Leanne. But good to know some things never change. I suppose they also still have those plastic, collapsible travel cups?"

"Actually, no, not that I saw. Maybe I should go back there and see if they can do a special order and mail some to us. I think I broke the last one we had last month."

"Uh-huh. As if you've used or eaten off of anything plastic in all the years I've known you," Ryan said.

"Well, if you're sure you don't need any . . ." Leanne put her tired feet up on the neighbouring chair. "But I did get you something." Ryan raised an eyebrow in mock fear. "Don't worry, that wasn't the only store I explored."

"Phew." Ryan wiped his forehead. "So what did you get me?" His eyes were big and bright with anticipation. Whether it was Christmas, birthday, or, best of all, "just because" gifts, his inner child always made an appearance, just as it had when he was counting down sleeps until their trip.

"It's back in the room." She was getting used to hearing it called a cabin, but the word didn't flow naturally from her lips. A cabin was somewhere else, with someone else, and that's not where she was. "Do you really want me to tell you what I got? It's just a little thing, Ryan, something you can use back home, not anything grand enough to warrant all this excitement."

"But better than a floating-ship pen, right?" he asked eagerly.

"Yes, better than that, I certainly hope." Leanne loved seeing him so silly.

"Then tell me what it is. I can enjoy hearing about it now and enjoy it all over again when I see it. And thank you."

"You know how your feet are always cold in the bathroom?" Ryan wasn't a fan of slippers, preferring to feel the floor more immediately beneath his feet, before he dressed for the day. But that posed a problem on the cold stone floor of Leanne's bathroom, and the tile in his wasn't much better. "Well," Leanne said, "they had this incredibly thick, cotton bath mat that's really more of a rug. It makes you want to walk on it barefoot, rather than using it as more of a sponge for sopping up water."

"How about while sitting down? It sounds absolutely perfect for resting my bare feet on," Ryan said, thinking of it's more likely use when he read the paper and got his morning going.

"Definitely. Your little toes can wiggle around, and be all nice and toasty the whole time. And as an added bonus, it has a tasteful version of this ship's logo woven right into the mat itself. There's no flimsy decal to peel off." She alluded to the souvenir T-shirts.

"What a neat way to be reminded of this trip." Ryan beamed broadly. "Thank you again." It was a little thing, but not for Leanne who just didn't think in terms of collecting souvenirs. This was going to be one special bath mat, and one he would keep forever.

In between seemingly endless eating opportunities both inside and out on deck, Leanne and Ryan also enjoyed the ship's entertainment. They didn't catch all of the evening extravaganzas, but being able to see a quasi-Broadway show mere steps from where they went to bed heightened the appeal of staying up late.

They also enjoyed checking out the various lounges and nightclubs—though Ryan wasn't so sure that's what they were still called. Since this was their version of an adventure, they wanted to be sure to at least see everything on the ship.

And that caused some heads to turn in the retro disco club when they took a turn on the dance floor. Grey hair flew about as bellies and other body parts jiggled, but all seemed to be forgotten once the younger crowd realized how completely comfortable Leanne and Ryan were themselves. They didn't look out of place because they didn't feel out of place inside.

But after a couple of songs, and feeling a little winded, they chose to have a drink somewhere quieter. Their favourite spot on the ship was the lounge on the top deck at the front of the ship. Surrounded by floor-to-ceiling windows and big comfortable chairs, it was the perfect spot to wind down another day.

Even though it felt as if every crew member remembered them wherever they went, Ryan and Leanne felt extra special in the quiet lounge. The table nearest the bow always seemed to be waiting for them. They chose to ignore the fact that they were usually there at less popular times when most passengers were watching late-night shows or enjoying the midnight buffet.

Their first night in the lounge, Leanne had raved about some biscotti-shaped onion-cheese bread that she'd eaten at lunch, and how she couldn't get enough of it. Normally only served at lunch, a basket of that bread now magically appeared every evening when they arrived. "See, Ryan? We are special," Leanne said with a big grin.

"They've probably just never seen anyone devour onion-cheese bread while drinking twenty-year-old scotch. And they need to keep seeing it to believe it."

"Whatever gets me the bread." Leanne munched happily on another bite of the half-gooey, half-crispy crust.

The next day was the last full day of the cruise. They would be docking the next morning. Leanne and Ryan were determined not to focus on the ending of their trip. They wanted to treat the last day the same as the first—with wide-eyed enthusiasm.

"I'm sure I've done my share of stupid things before, but, Ryan, if I ever get into an elevator to get to the other side of it, please have me carted off."

"What are you talking about?" he asked.

"I was upstairs by the elevators near the lotto booth, you know, the one with that nice lady who gives out more information than tickets—"

"The one we're always bothering with questions ourselves?" Ryan interjected.

"That's the one. And there was this other woman up there who was looking for directions to the Lido Café, the same place where everyone's already been having breakfast all week. Well, kind lotto lady—I wish I could remember her name—explained that the café was on the other side of the elevators, and she motioned behind and around her booth. But guess where the woman headed?"

"No, she didn't." Ryan's jaw dropped open slightly.

"She did," Leanne confirmed. "Went straight into the elevator to get to the café on the other side. Lotto lady and I just looked at each other. No one else was around and she quietly said things like that happen all the time. Apparently, it's some sort of a running joke among the crew that people seem to leave their brains at home when they go on vacation."

"Maybe since everything gets done for us here, we don't have to think, so we don't," Ryan said. "But that's everybody else. Not us, certainly."

"Oh, of course not, we would never do that." Leanne grinned at him. "You know, she told me that once, after the captain announced the ship would soon be passing its sister ship, a passenger asked her if she could see it from either side."

"And I take it the other ship wasn't sailing around them in a circle at the time?"

"Nope. But, in a way, Ryan, I can almost see how you might say something that sounds ridiculous after you say it or think about it, but as you're speaking, it pops out without getting thought through first. Mind you, apparently another passenger explained that her friend was going to be on that other ship the following week, and she wanted to know if she could wave to her."

Ryan shook his head. Maybe the brain was an optional travel accessory after all. "And lotto lady wasn't making this up?"

"She said she'd heard it all with her own ears, and that she'd heard stories of far crazier stuff, but not firsthand, so she didn't share the details. She probably shouldn't have told me what she did, but after we shared that elevator-to-café moment, I think she needed to let out some of her frustration. I mean, how many times must she have seen things like that and not been able to say anything?"

"I hate to think," Ryan said. "Lucky for her you were there, and the captain wasn't, for her job's sake."

The next day, as they were walking back to their cabin after breakfast, they passed a man asking one of the stewards, "Do these stairs go up or down?" Leanne and Ryan looked at each other and grinned. To anyone watching, it would have looked as if they were simply enjoying each other's company—which of course they were—but they were also enjoying the inadvertent humour.

"Maybe we'll have to go out more at home." Leanne reached for Ryan's hand. "Even if everyone's not on vacation there, I'm sure we can find some good people-watching opportunities in Clementine."

"And maybe even some bread and scotch too," Ryan said as the first announcement to disembark came over the loudspeakers.

Chapter Twenty-Three

COMPLETING THEIR AIRPLANE-FREE return trip, Leanne and Ryan rolled along the rails the rest of the way home. Travelling by another train—this one for days instead of hours—was the perfect way to transition from the indulgent vacation mindset to their more balanced life at home. The scenery seemed to move around them as it had on the ship, but nearer and faster. With little to do but gaze out the panoramic windows, their fast-moving surroundings were almost hypnotic.

The world outside moved by in a blur from the combination of the train's constant speed and the progressive relaxation of those riding inside.

In contrast to the train's power and pace, Leanne and Ryan felt their minds slowing down completely from the excitement of the last few weeks. While the water had supported the "baby" ship almost embryonically, now the train rocked its passengers to sleep.

As they had hoped, Ryan and Leanne arrived back in Clementine feeling refreshed, and in no need of another vacation for recovery purposes. They had seen and done everything they most wanted, but not at the expense of sufficient rest and the ability to really enjoy what they did do. There was certainly much more they had not seen, especially while overseas, but they'd seen a little corner of it. And best of all, they'd seen it together.

But Leanne was definitely ready to be home. "Do you want me to say it?" she asked him as they walked through her front door.

Ryan knew what was coming next. Leanne even said it after spending only a few nights in a row at his place. "Go ahead and say it." He grinned before adding, "At least in this case, I won't have to take it personally."

"East or west, home is best," Leanne stated as if she'd made the most profound and original pronouncement of all time.

Leaving the unpacking for later, they kicked off their now more worldly shoes and flaked out on the couch.

"Clichéd proverb or not, I've got to agree with you," Ryan said. "This is best."

They'd spent so much more time around other people than they were used to, that they sat there relishing the silence for a few minutes. Leanne rested her head on Ryan's shoulder as he leaned to rest his cheek on her head. They were tucked in together, but alone in their thoughts. Then hands started to wander, and the same thought came to them both.

"After getting used to the ship's steward making up our bed every day," Leanne said, "I must say, I'm glad I put fresh sheets on our bed here before we left. Now it's waiting for us just like on the ship."

"Did you happen to put any chocolates on the pillows, by any chance?"

"No, but good idea, and with such multipurpose possibilities too." She flirtatiously tipped her head in the direction of the bedroom.

"Oh, Leanne, what am I going to do with you?"

"I hope you mean, do again." A little fun edible variation now and then didn't hurt.

"Absolutely. Why do you think I asked about them in the first place?" Ryan laughed when Leanne went to the kitchen to get some chocolate.

They didn't have sex as often, or as rambunctiously, as they once had. But it was still an important part of their life. What changing hormones had reduced, they compensated for in other ways. But as during some of Leanne's solo years, a reminder that it had been a while was sometimes necessary.

Crazy as that would have sounded to them when they were younger, the older they grew, the easier it was to get busy enjoying other things in life and simply lose track of sex.

But between the two of them, their odds were pretty good that one of them would think of it before too much time had passed. And that led to being physically reminded of just how amazing sex felt.

As Leanne and Ryan lay basking in after-chocolate and afterglow, they felt as young as ever, or at least as young as they ever felt now. They were a bit slower and less athletic than in earlier days, but once reached, orgasm was orgasm.

The animalistic nature of sex, and the singular driving force for release once they got going, made them feel as if they were active participants in the very vibrancy of the universe. Rather than observing the wonder and power of nature, in those intimate moments, they were creating some of that wonder and power themselves.

The years moved on and added up. And one warm summer day they were sitting outside on Leanne's backyard patio after enjoying an early dinner.

Leanne looked around the garden she only puttered around in now. She'd hired out the heavy-duty work for the last number of years. But she still dug in the ground some, refusing to accept that she wouldn't be able to get herself back up. "It might take a little creative engineering and patience," she had recently explained to the concerned tree pruner who thought she'd fallen down, "but it's worth it to sit right in the dirt."

Time had been an interesting player in Leanne's life. It could be so limited and hated for its briefness, but loved for its limitless ability to keep going on. But instead of feeling as she always had—young and energetic—Leanne increasingly felt the tangible signs of the persistent movement of time.

Setting two glasses down on the outdoor table, she asked, "Do you feel old, Ryan?"

"Older than this scotch certainly," he said after taking a sip.

"I would hope so," she said with a laugh, "otherwise I could be put in jail for having sex with a minor. But, seriously, do you?" Leanne asked her question again.

Rather than considering what prompted her to bring up the subject, Ryan sat quietly for a moment as he tried to think how to properly answer. Did he feel old? If so, in what way, physically, mentally, emotionally? And was it all the time or only some of it?

"Don't think about it so hard," Leanne encouraged him when she saw his wheels turning. "What's your knee-jerk reaction? What do you feel?"

"Yes," Ryan said immediately, before his thoughts really started flowing out. "I feel old when I need a veritable microscope to read my medicine bottles, or I try to pick something up off the floor, or when I have to take a break after mowing my lawn for only a few minutes, that kind of thing. But . . . not when I remember how old I felt after Terri died, thinking I'd spend the rest of my life alone. Even though I tried dating again, I felt like I was only going through the motions. I was doing what everybody said I should do instead of what I wanted, which at that time was not much. I felt like I was just passing time until I died. I was already a widower, facing the rest of my life unexpectedly alone. And work wasn't an escape from the lonely house, but another daily hurdle to get through. I was slowing down in every way."

Leanne already knew most of what he was telling her, but it had trickled out of him in bits and pieces over the years. Ryan was linking it all together now.

"It never ceases to amaze me how things can change," he said. "And even though I knew that then, when I was in the thick of it, feeling good again seemed perfectly impossible. Until, of course, I did feel good again. And then I was left wondering how I ever felt so lost. Or, in that case, so old too. Funny how all that led me to you a few years later. If I hadn't semi-retired by starting at that centre . . ."

"I can't imagine my life without you being a part of it, Ryan. And for a very long time that was something that felt perfectly impossible too. Part of me feels younger and freer today than I have for nearly fifty years," Leanne said, before finishing in her head, "when Jay was alive."

Her scotch this evening sat untouched.

"I feel more peaceful, more the way I used to when every sense felt intensely alive, fully aware of each moment with every breath, every touch, every thought. Back then, it was spurred on because Jay's time was so limited. Now, it's because mine's getting that way."

Ryan sat quietly, sipping his drink. He closed his eyes as he listened to Leanne speak of what he so feared—one living without the other. Feeling his stomach twist into a mass of knots, he tried hard to focus instead on the lightness in her voice, and the hope and joy that was somehow emanating from her.

"It seems no matter how much we try not to let them," she said, "as the moments remaining get fewer, they inevitably feel dearer. Why do they have to become dearer? Aside from the laws of supply and demand, that is."

Ryan tried to smile.

"I've always tried to savour them all equally instead of fearing their disappearance. But these days, Ryan, it feels different sometimes. Maybe that's some sick benefit of getting older, like it or not, you get a deeper appreciation of what's coming closer to ending, or maybe just changing."

Leanne wondered in a new way now if this was how Jay had once felt. There was only so much that could be described. Some things had to be lived.

"How about I get us some of that onion-cheese bread you baked today," Ryan appeared to say randomly. It was his way of saying he needed a break before he could say anything else.

Leanne understood. Her need to share and his need not to be overloaded were still at occasional odds.

But both had tempered some over time, with Leanne needing to release less, and Ryan wanting to share more. It was just sometimes easier for him to do that when he first gave himself a chance to think privately, or at least let an idea sit inside him for a bit.

His time-outs also gave Leanne a chance to breathe and think more slowly herself. Her mind could unwind and relax if it started going into overdrive.

And while Leanne still did a good amount of thinking, for the most part, Ryan was glad she did. Thanks to her need to figure things out and process them verbally, he knew he had dealt with some of his own issues that would otherwise have gone untouched. And difficult as the thinking and talking was for him, if done in moderation, he felt clearer and more relaxed later.

After Ryan returned with their bread intermission, the conversation turned easily to gently mundane subjects. There was the silly exchange of words about inconsequential things that only mattered because they were shared with someone special.

What did it really matter that the price of gas was up or down a penny, or if a person walking down the street had an unusual swagger, or what dinner could be imagined from observing the random contents of a stranger's grocery cart?

But observing those little details together helped create the feeling of being less alone in the curious ol' world, and it served as a nice counterbalance to dealing with the issues that really did matter.

"So," Ryan said a few slices later, "this whole getting-older thing, there's no way out of it, huh?" He tried to joke, but would have been more than willing to hear about some magical way to just keep on keeping on.

"Not without going through another step that I know you really don't like talking about." Leanne didn't want to open the death can of worms sooner than it had to be, so she chose to focus on what they'd been talking about earlier, and what seemed to be permeating more of her thoughts lately. She was starting to feel old.

"I've seen the gradual changes for years, but I've always felt like the same old me," Leanne said, "except whenever some wrinkly old face would stare back at me in the mirror." She tugged at her sagging cheeks and laughed with a shrug.

"There have actually been times when it startles me. For a split second, I think someone must have hung a portrait of an aged great-grandmother above my bathroom sink. And then the face's eyes blink, and I'm jarred back to reality. People may have seen a family resemblance to deceased relatives before, but that's nothing in comparison to the one that develops once you catch up to those ancestral pictures.

"And, Ryan, just when did my hands get so spotted and thin-skinned? They're so frail looking."

Leanne didn't normally focus on things she couldn't change. She was the one who forged ahead regardless of external influences, whether they were the outside opinions of other people or the gradual changes to her physical outside.

Ryan tried to rouse her back to her more regular disposition. "Oh, I don't know about frail, Leanne. You've still got a pretty good grip there, if you ask me."

Leanne let out a good laugh. And while it was genuine, she immediately resumed her train of thought. "But always when I'd look anywhere else, away from mirrors or my own flesh, I'd still see myself as a young woman, you know? I felt that way inside and that was what mattered.

"Lately, though, it's starting to feel as if the outside and inside are matching up better. It's not that I feel bad exactly, just not the way I'm used to. It's new to me. I don't care to do so much now, as if it's no longer the time for big-scale wants."

She picked off a bit of cheese from the bread on her plate. "And contrary to how you think that might feel, it feels perfectly fine." As she chewed the savoury morsel, Leanne laughed gently this time. "Things are precisely as they should be at this particular moment. I guess my perspective's different now, but what I keep coming back to"—she took a fresh breath—"is maybe whether it's at the end of a day, or the end of a life, you get tired, and you just want to be comfortable. Happy, easy, simple comfort . . ." Her voice drifted off.

"I don't know what to say to that, Leanne. I don't think I feel that way, at least not yet. And I'm not sure I ever want to," Ryan said. "I'd like to think I'll always want to have plans and goals, and do more than simply exist. I mean, is that what you're talking about? Just existing while you're waiting to die?" He cringed at the word and where this conversation was going.

"No, it's not that, not exactly," Leanne replied. "I'm not waiting for anything. I want to enjoy this life a while longer, but watching more from the wings now rather than centre stage. And I like that new place most of the time. But then"—she slightly gripped the armrests of her chair—"there are moments when I'm this scared young thing who can't believe she got here so fast. When did I go from being a kid to being next in line to die?"

Greeted by silence, she looked at Ryan and said, "You don't need to say anything. What's there to say, really? Talking's just always helped me. It makes it easier to sort things out in my mind if I let the words loose first. And for the record, I'm thrilled you want to want stuff forever. Maybe you will. I'll be rooting for it."

Ryan leaned over and kissed Leanne, saying what he couldn't with words. His lips pressed into hers and held still, almost as if suspending time.

But regular life resumed pretty much as before. The biggest remnant of their conversation was the small but noticeable increase in the time Leanne and Ryan spent apart in the following years, respectfully doing, or not doing, their own things.

Ryan started working on a reference guide for people struggling to find information in plain language about various mental-health issues. And in addition to increasing the time he spent with Abigail and her husband, he also did more things with his grandson, Joseph, and his new family.

Joseph had married very young and helped create the next generation, giving Ryan a great-grandson and great-granddaughter. Both little kids thought it was terrific fun to build stuff with their great-grandpa in his garage workshop.

They made all sort of things using old scraps that on any other day would have been recycled or tossed into the garbage. Instead, the transformed remnants now sat proudly on shelves in the homes of their adoring family. "I have my own personal objet d'art makers who happen to be infused with inventive genius," Ryan often bragged.

Leanne spent more time puttering quietly in her garden, reading a lot both indoors and out, and of all the seemingly oxymoronic things, working on LSAT problems. Although she professed to want to do less, to take it easy while being cozy and comfortable, one of the things that gave her that relaxed feeling ended up being sample Law School Admission Tests. Doing them only for fun gave her the freedom to ignore the questions she didn't want to bother with—namely, the reading comprehension problems that seemed too much like tedious work to Leanne.

But she got a real kick out of the analytical and logical-reasoning ones. Playing around with the mental puzzles created by the different questions kept her mind moving at a comfortable speed, but without any sense of urgency. And like any other sort of puzzle or game, the LSAT problems were always there, ready and waiting whenever she felt like whiling away a few hours.

And the rest of the time? Leanne and Ryan continued to spend it happily together.

Coming through Leanne's front door one evening, Ryan called out, "So how's Becky?"

"Oh," Leanne said, laughing. "You've been trying to call, haven't you?"

Ryan grinned.

She and Becky had been having one of their old gab sessions and had only just hung up, afraid their ears would fall off if they didn't. As it was, Leanne felt as if she'd never have full feeling on that side of her head again.

"Yeah," Ryan replied. "I wanted to know if you needed anything from the store before I came over. And I kind of figured if your line was busy for that long, it had to be Becky. So how are things over there?"

"Good. Her daughter surprised her with a freezer full of homemade favourites. You know how much Becky hates to cook since she's been living on her own." After too many years of living with mixed feelings, Becky and Brian's emotional limbo land had ended. They had both moved into a condominium, just not the same one.

"How thoughtful of Lissa to do that for her mom, but I bet there wasn't any pizza in the mix. How Becky can deny her taste buds that way is beyond me. That's gotta be bordering on masochism." Ryan licked his lips as he started making himself hungry.

"Now I remember a time when you weren't so far from her level of anti-pizza sentiment," Leanne reminded him, grinning.

"Ah, but that was before I tried yours, and all those little hole-in-the-wall pizza places you seem to find. I'm forever converted."

"Good thing, or else this would have never worked out."

CHAPTER TWENTY-FOUR

"WHERE IS SHE? Leanne Porter. Take me to her!" Ryan yelled as he came running through the main entrance of the emergency room. She may have been slower the last few years, and maybe a little more tired recently, but Leanne did not get sick. So why had he just gotten a call saying that, as her next-of-kin contact, he needed to come to the hospital right away?

"If you'll come this way," a nurse said as she motioned for him to follow her. They were headed in the direction of those dreaded little rooms where people were given the news that a loved one had died.

"Oh, God." Ryan nearly collapsed. "Leanne can't be—"

Realizing what he'd mistakenly inferred, she immediately interrupted him. "No. Oh, no, sir, she's not, she's right over here waiting to see you." The nurse quickly showed a shaking but relieved Ryan past those rooms, and into a curtained-off area beyond them.

As Ryan entered the makeshift cubicle, a doctor was on his way out. A different nurse was removing wires and tubes from Leanne's chest and arms. Her face looked a little pale and drawn, but otherwise she looked like herself.

Ryan didn't know exactly what he'd been expecting to see, but considering his panic-stricken earlier moments, he was just thrilled to be in her presence, with her still present. He hadn't gotten to the hospital in time for that after Terri's accident. The fear that history had repeated itself left his legs still feeling a little shaky.

Leanne seemed OK now, but she had called 911 instead of him, which meant it had to be a real emergency. His relief that he wasn't in one of those bad-news privacy rooms was starting to turn back into panic.

"Leanne, what's going on? Are you all right?" Ryan clasped her now tube-free arm.

Before she could answer, the doctor said, "Ms. Porter, I'll send someone back with that AMA form for you to sign. However, I do strongly urge you to reconsider."

"Thank you, Doctor, for getting the form," Leanne said rather calmly, with no reference to the second part of his statement. Whatever was going on, it was clear her mind was made up.

"Leanne, what did he mean by that? Are you all right?" Ryan asked again.

But instead of giving her a chance to speak, his whirling mind kept him spewing out questions while also trying to answer them. "Are you OK? No, of course you're not OK, or you wouldn't be here, and that doctor would not be asking you to reconsider anything. Wait, what does he want you to reconsider?"

Understanding his present behaviour, Leanne covered his trembling hand with hers, physically reassuring him that she was there. Laughing warmly, she said, "Well, if you'd actually like me to answer any of those questions . . ."

Ryan let out a breath, but he couldn't respond to her attempt at humour. "Leanne, please. What's wrong?"

"That's not important, Ryan."

"The hell it isn't, Leanne!"

"Let me finish. I know this is important, but as for what's wrong? What's medically, physically wrong? No. It doesn't matter. The result's the same."

"What are you saying?" Ryan asked, bewildered. "They don't know what's wrong?"

"They know, love. I know. We'll talk about it. But there is nothing they can do. Bodies wear out. It's OK." Leanne was so calm.

"OK? Are you crazy? There's got to be something they can do." His mind was spinning, trying to find acceptable answers, and a way to make everything go back to how it had been only this morning. The world was perfectly fine at breakfast. How was this happening? "There has to be something to at least"—Ryan couldn't believe what he was about to say next—"give you more . . . time." His voice nearly squeaked on the last word.

"Maybe, Ryan, they think so, if I stay here. But not much, not enough to make it worth it. And not so that I could ever get out," Leanne said, hoping her intentions were clear.

"But it would still be more time, more—"

"I am not staying here!" she shouted. "That is not up for debate, and you know it." Then her voice eased. "I wasn't born in a hospital, and I don't want to die in one. I won't be recovering. I'm just dying. Home birth, home death."

"I know what you've always said, but if it can help, if staying here—"

"Will what, Ryan?" Leanne gently interrupted. "Let me live a little longer hooked up and monitored every second, with machines checking on my every breath, commenting every time my heart beats? Until I die, that is. Because that's what's gonna happen wherever I am, whether it's here or where I'm going, and that is," she almost sang, "home."

Ryan was making the connection with what the doctor had said before. "Against medical advice ... he said AMA."

"Wouldn't be the first time I, or someone ... did that." Leanne paused as she couldn't help but vividly remember another time long ago when medical advice wasn't completely followed. "It's their job, I respect that, and for some people maybe it is best to stay, but, I can't. I can't be here. I will not have my last breath here. I can't."

"I know," Ryan said. Tears that he could no longer contain slipped out. "I don't like it, but I know. I'm not ready, Leanne."

"I know, but I am. It's been over fifty years," she said, more to herself than to Ryan. Then squeezing his hands as hard as she was able, she looked into his eyes. "And you and I have had almost thirty years together. Such wonderful years."

Ryan leaned down and their arms snaked around each other reflexively. They held on tightly, needing the other's solid presence. Then he gave her hand another squeeze. "I'll go see what's taking them so long with that form."

The days and weeks that followed were spent in constant contact. Ryan stayed at Leanne's the entire time. Either Donovan or his now live-in coastal friend brought over groceries and anything else that was needed. Ryan could not face missing any possible moment with Leanne. And being away for one particular moment was simply out of the question. Not again.

When Terri was killed so suddenly, Ryan obviously had no warning. There were no last pleadings to somehow keep living, no chance to say good-bye, no anything except for countless replays of their last ordinary exchange from earlier in the day. But he hadn't had to think about any of it ahead of time. While that had left him with certain regrets of things not said, he was spared the waiting time he now found himself experiencing with Leanne.

Having for some time hidden her declining health from everyone—including herself in some ways probably—Leanne had continued living in the moment, not really considering how her moment-to-moment choices might affect her actually having future moments.

There were loving phone calls from those far away and visits from those nearby, but Leanne tried to keep them brief. Her closest friends—Becky, Donovan, and Abigail—all understood. They could hear the need for quietness in her voice. And what words she spoke were all the more special for their brevity, and for the precious energy they knew she used to say them.

But as much as Leanne loved those in her life, her focus couldn't be on them now. She needed to save her strength for taking in every living moment in every way she could, not dwelling on the sadness of others.

The changes were becoming much more evident, and Leanne seemed almost content to let things wind completely down. But that didn't stop her from loving every second. Pain was thankfully not an issue, allowing her to be intimately aware of every sensation. It was almost as if she was trying to really enjoy every single aspect of a process that came but once in a lifetime—dying.

"What choice have I got?" Leanne laughed weakly.

"Well, you could have gone for help sooner." Ryan was still trying to let go of his bitterness that she wasn't fighting this the way he wanted her to.

Leanne was glad he was still challenging her and not treating her differently. "But then we'd have had more of this dragged-out so-called good-bye time that you love so much. We'd have been waiting even longer at the proverbial airport for my flight to leave."

"Or the ship to set sail." Ryan remembered the last time Leanne had seen Becky. While he was conflicted about some of Leanne's medical choices, he looked at the woman with whom he'd shared nearly three decades, and he knew. She needed this her way. And hard as it was to hear her speak of her death and to see her weakening every day, he wanted to be there for her more than ease his own hurt.

"I sure have never known anyone else who talked of death so easily." Ryan was stroking the back of her hand, tenderly tracing the aged, bulging veins.

"I've had to. It's been too much a part of my life not to talk about it. It gets easier," she said. "Besides, I like the continuity of it all. Focus on that, not the missing someone or lonely part, but on what continues. Death, being dead, it's just another state of being. It's not nothing."

Suddenly a wave of emotion seemed to almost paralyze Leanne for a moment, as if a floodgate of fears and doubts long ago set aside had suddenly opened. "God, I hope I'm right." She had a faraway look in her eyes. "I mean, I know I am. I have to be, but still, what if? I mean, what if . . . is it possible I've been fooling myself all these years?"

"I've never heard you doubt it before. Why now?" Ryan asked as his hand stilled, and the only hint of movement was the transfer of warmth between them.

"Last-ditch paranoia, perhaps?" Leanne blurted out.

"No, no," Ryan reassured her. "Basic human fear maybe, yeah. But wrong? No, no way. Not you. Not after every-thing . . ." He grew quieter. "Maybe it's my fear talking too, willing you to be right for all our sakes—dead and alive—because there's just gotta be . . ."

"Yeah? You really believe?" she asked, but it came out as more of a statement.

"I feel someone too, you know. I mean, I can't always control when I sense her, but I know I do, as sure as I know we loved, we love." Ryan shared thoughts he'd long kept inside for fear of losing them if he openly acknowl-edged them. They'd felt that fragile to him. Until now. "I wish I could call her up whenever I want, darling-on-demand, hell, I'd gladly take pay-per-view." Their quiet laughter poignantly filled the air.

"I used to," Leanne then murmured.

Ryan didn't question what she meant. There was no need as more pieces of the attic puzzle fell into place.

During the moments of silent understanding, Leanne remembered all the times she'd spent together with Jay those first twenty years after his death, and all that she'd never spoken of, but kept safe and close inside. Saying

"I used to" was the closest she had ever come to telling anyone else.

Her feelings for Jay and Ryan were starting to coalesce. Leanne wanted to share more about Jay with the man she was leaving. "But he's more of just a presence now, there, most definitely always there, but not reachable anymore. It's almost as if we've been in the same room but couldn't talk to each other, or see each other, or touch, or smell, or taste. But we knew the other was there, waiting, knowing that one day . . ." Leanne let out an exhausted sigh, not sure where the strength had came from to say all that, but knowing she needed to for Ryan's sake, and maybe also for her own.

"And, Ryan, someday"—she looked into his eyes—"it will be more than you just sensing her."

One day after Ryan helped her get settled on the couch, Leanne said, "I can't thank you enough for bringing me home, for making sure that happened, and for being here."

Through the big picture window, she could look out at the lush back garden. Looking up through the living room skylight—the one Jay had envisioned when they first looked at the house—Leanne could see the world above. And though unseen from her vantage point, their attic was there too, while down the hall was the bedroom that was Ryan's and hers alone. She smiled. Soon, someone else would have a turn loving the old Montrose Avenue house.

Opening the window to let in some fresh air, Ryan tried to joke, "You did look rather out of place in that hospital gown. Jeans and T-shirts are far more you."

"Stretch jeans these days." Leanne chuckled softly.

"Of course, I'd secretly hoped I'd be the one to go first. What am I supposed to do now?" He laughed to try to keep from crying.

"Ryan, I am sorry, but I can't honestly say I wish it were the other way around, you know?"

"Yeah, I know," he replied, resigned to the inevitable. "One of us was bound to go first."

"But I'm second, second after Jay."

"And I'll be second after Terri . . . guess third now, after you."

"I feel so lucky to be going this way, knowing I'll be in your arms, here with you, and you connecting me to this world. I'll never be able to thank you enough for that."

"Then let me go with you now, Leanne," he said, only half kidding.

"Nah, can't do that. It's not up to me. But if I could . . ."

"Yeahhh." Ryan closed his eyes and sighed. "And then there would be this great big double date heaven style."

"But please, no harp music," Leanne said.

"Deal. And don't you worry, I haven't forgotten about your 'If' and 'What a Wonderful World' requests. They will be there." Ryan surprised himself that he was able to talk about her funeral gathering without breaking down. Even though Leanne's physical strength was waning, her resolve and peace seemed to be empowering him. "Can I get you anything now, Leanne? What can I do for you?"

"It's such a beautiful evening. I don't want to sleep inside." On warm summer nights they had occasionally slept outside on their fifteenth-anniversary lounger. They even kept a comforter in its attached storage box. And Leanne wanted to be outside now.

"Are you sure?" Ryan asked, concerned. He didn't want to throw a stumbling block in the way of her wish, but it wasn't even fall anymore. It was early winter, and though warmer than some years, it was hardly warm out. "Even under a bunch of covers, you still might get too chilly in the night."

"What's the worst that could happen?" She laughed in anticipation of her own joke. "I could catch my death?"

Ryan flinched, but he laughed a little as well. "You are wicked."

Leanne tried to get up from the couch but had to sit back down after she started to stumble, partly from not having moved around much, but mostly from weakness.

Ryan wished he could scoop her up in his arms and carry her out to the backyard, kind of an odd reverse of the carrying-over-the-threshold thing they'd never had.

But working together, they slowly made their way outside, with Leanne leaning heavily on Ryan, and his arms wrapped securely around her helping to hold her up.

Once she was on the lounger, Ryan tucked her in with the cold comforter from the box. He then made several trips back and forth to the house for more blankets, some water, and a little food.

By dusk, they were both settled comfortably side by side on their makeshift bed. Leanne didn't eat much, but the few bites she tried tasted good. But she was more interested in the smells. As she had on the ship, Leanne nuzzled into Ryan's chest. But this time there was no exhaust to avoid, just the irrepressible need to inhale Ryan.

Tipping her head forward when she needed more air, Leanne was greeted by the glorious smell of the night, and she was aware of the cool breeze brushing gently across her face. The fragrant smell of warm, wet wood filled her nostrils. Rain earlier in the day had dampened the nearby cedar planter boxes that lay in wait for spring blooms.

The last leaf holdouts of autumn rested on the grass, damp and matted together. They were just at the point before rot set in, giving off a sweet earthy smell on their own brink of decomposition.

"I'm so glad it's night time," Leanne said. "I'd hate to miss a new day. It's better to die when everything else is winding down too." She paused and, with her mouth barely open, just breathed in and out. Her cheekbones raised slightly as did the corners of her mouth. "I like this, being here in the dark, quiet, mysterious night. It's almost as if it's making a bridge between life and death, guiding me along the way that I can't see." Another inhale and exhale.

Ryan held on tightly to her hand, watching her.

The late-evening air was indeed chilly, but with the comforter and all the blankets Ryan had assembled on and around them, Leanne actually had to uncover her arms when she grew too warm. She then pushed up his sweater sleeve so that she could feel his bare skin. Her fingers tingled as they touched the soft hairs of his forearm. She felt the heat radiating from his skin. Every nerve ending seemed to be extra sensitive and aware. And very little was said.

As the quiet night continued, Leanne slept off and on. But each time she woke up, Ryan was always awake, and his hands were gently moving somewhere on her body.

Sometimes he would be stroking her face. Other times he'd be focusing on her arms, or hands, or fingers, or even her fingernails. And once he knew she was awake, her body would get a little squeeze.

In the still-dark early hours of the morning, Leanne stirred again and shifted positions. She was then lying almost crosswise on the lounger with her head resting on Ryan's lap.

He ran his fingers through her hair, grateful she was in no pain and just seemed to be slowly shutting down. He wondered how she knew that day at the hospital. She had changed after that. Aside from a few bursts of words, she had been quiet, absorbing everything around her.

It had been a surprisingly peaceful time, and not filled with the horror of impending loss that he'd expected. But he supposed that was mostly due to him trying to experience every single moment with her, and not letting himself think beyond that. He couldn't go there now, not if he wanted to help make this time what she needed it to be. "Grieve later, not while she's here," he tried to tell himself whenever he felt his sadness getting the upper hand.

"Mmmmmmm," Leanne murmured in her sleep as she pressed back into him automatically.

Struggling to control his own breathing, Ryan whispered, "I don't know how I'm ever going to do this without you."

Startling him, there was an ever so quiet, "You will." Leanne had not been sleeping so much as drifting in and out.

"I love you, Leanne."

"And I love you. Not good-bye," she added.

"I always did hate that—some movie deathbed scene and they won't say 'I love you' because that would make it too final, as if it were some synonym for good-bye. What is up with that, Leanne? Why not say 'I love you?' Hear it one last . . ." Ryan was unable to finish the thought.

"Guess that's why," she said, "the *last* part. Thinking of it that way is too painful."

"Yeah, but I'm still glad I got to hear it again, and say it again."

Leanne worked hard, even with Ryan's help, to shift around so she could look up and see his face. Smiling, she looked at him as long as her tired eyes would allow, and then she tried to open them again and look some more."

"It's OK," Ryan said. "You just rest. I'm right here."

Leanne blinked, looking up again before closing her eyes. But a short while later, she surprised him by her request. "I want to go for a walk."

He hesitated briefly, knowing it was absolutely impossible in her condition now, but then he had an idea. "Yeah, let's go."

Ryan took her hand that was closest to the edge and held it slightly down and away from the lounger. Then he swung their joined hands gently back and forth. "It's such a beautiful night for a walk."

"Mm-hmm. So nice."

"Shall we go around the block or do you want to wander a bit?" Ryan asked.

"Don't know. Just keep moving."

He clasped her hand tighter as they continued their stationary stroll. His other hand gently stroked her face as her eyes remained closed.

"Quite a place," Leanne said after a while.

Thinking she was fading and crossing over, Ryan asked, "Heaven?"

"No. Earth."

There was more quietness, more breathing in and out. Then Leanne almost imperceptibly gasped. Her breathing paused, and her body completely relaxed into a gentle, final exhale. "Jay." Her mouth froze in a smile.

Ryan felt frozen himself. He was motionless except for the silent tears running freely down his face. It was over not only her death, but what her last word meant for her, and for him. "Son of a gun," he said, looking straight ahead with wonder. "You were right."

He then kissed her still-warm forehead and held her body close. But as he tried to squeeze her tightly once more, he felt what he already knew. The body he held no longer held Leanne.

She was somewhere else now. And maybe he was too—with Terri, enjoying a flash of the future Leanne had just given him.

Meanwhile, still in words, at least for the moment, came a voice that was absolute music to someone's figurative ears. "Here I am."

"Yes. Yes you are. Oh, Lee."

"Hey," Leanne said in a way that sounded like the biggest smile ever.

"Hey," Jay said back, his voice almost cracking. He had not lived with time as Leanne had, but it still felt like forever since they'd shared the same state of being.

"So what happens now?"

"Anything we want." Jay radiated utter joy.

"Anything?" Leanne laughed. "Just what did you have in mind?"

"Well, you know, Lee, it has been a while." He kidded her as if no time at all had passed.

"It sure has been a while, Jay. So we can still, even with no lips, not to mention no—"

"Ever pragmatic." He chuckled. It felt so good to laugh with her again. "But seriously, though, all the feelings, the love . . . it's still you and me."

"Just us," Leanne said.

"I feel you right now, don't you?"

"Oh yeahhh. I do, my love." She exhaled in a richer way than she'd ever known, feeling it everywhere.

As they had on occasion so many years before, Jay and Leanne spoke in unison. "Aaaaaaahhh," they almost purred. It was the release of all they were feeling, blissfully oozing forth as they both absorbed being completely together again.

Moments passed, but for the first time, it was truly irrelevant. They were both dead. And in life's attic, there was no such thing as time.

At some point, Leanne used words once more, "So this, this is what it is. What you've let me glimpse, but now . . ."

"Now," Jay said, "you live."